THEORIES *OF* FLIGHT

SIMON MORDEN

www.orbitbooks.net

Copyright © 2011 by Simon Morden
Excerpt from *Degrees of Freedom* copyright © 2011 by Simon Morden
All rights reserved. Except as permitted under the U.S. Copyright Act of 1976, no part of this publication may be reproduced, distributed, or transmitted in any form or by any means, or stored in a database or retrieval system, without the prior written permission of the publisher.

Orbit
Hachette Book Group
237 Park Avenue
New York, NY 10017
Visit our Web site at www.orbitbooks.net

Orbit is an imprint of Hachette Book Group. The Orbit name and logo are trademarks of Little, Brown Book Group Limited.

The publisher is not responsible for websites (or their content) that are not owned by the publisher.

Printed in the United States of America

First United States edition, May 2011

10 9 8 7 6 5 4 3 2 1

ATTENTION CORPORATIONS AND ORGANIZATIONS:
Most HACHETTE BOOK GROUP books are available at quantity discounts with bulk purchase for educational, business, or sales promotional use. For information, please call or write:
Special Markets Department, Hachette Book Group
237 Park Avenue, New York, NY 10017
Telephone: 1-800-222-6747 Fax: 1-800-477-5925

FOREWORD

*W*hen I was a very new writer, I—for reasons explained in the dedication for *Equations of Life*—fell in with a bunch of horror writers. It was more by accident than design, but one of those happy accidents I've never regretted. It started in the early days of what became "the web," when things were beginning to move off the newsnets and list servers. Message boards were becoming popular, and I ended up at the place where most of the UK's young horror writers hung out. That site was Masters of Terrors.

Now, to think of the bunch of us—and most of us still meet up every year at the British Fantasy Society's FantasyCon—as young...well, we were once. Honest. Now we're pretty much all in our forties, bald or balding, with a preponderance of black T-shirts and silly beards. There's been some fall out: some people we don't see anymore, some have gone on to do other things and live different lives. But the number of us from Masters of Terror, from that first pub meeting in London (at the Dead Nurse, I think), who are still active in writing is quite startling.

We write fantasy and crime and horror and SF: short

stories, novellas, novels, screenplays and script and tie-ins. All sorts, whatever pays the bills and keeps us interested. Some have become publishers, even. What hasn't changed is that we still like to tell each other tall tales and we still try to scare our friends and our readers. Learning how to terrify someone through the medium of prose—mere words—ought to be a weapon in every writer's armory. And I learned how at Masters of Terror.

So this one's for Masters of Terror's webmaster, Andy. Thanks, mate.

THEORIES OF FLIGHT

I

Petrovitch stared at the sphere in his hands, turning it slowly to reveal different parts of its intricately patterned surface. Shining silver lines of metal in curves and whorls shone against the black resin matrix, the seeming chaos replicated throughout the hidden depths of the globe; a single strand of wire that swam up and down, around and around, its path determined precisely by equations he himself had discovered.

It was a work of art; dense, cold, beautiful, a miracle of manufacture. A kilometer of fine alloy wound up into a ball the size of a double fist.

But it was supposed to be more than that. He let it fall heavily onto his desk and flicked his glasses off his face. His eyes, always so blue, were surrounded with red veins. He scrubbed at them again.

The *yebani* thing didn't, wouldn't work, no matter how much he yelled and hit it. The first practical test of the Ekanobi-Petrovitch laws, and it just sat there, dumb, blind, motionless.

Stanford—Stanford! Those *raspizdyay kolhoznii*

amerikanskij—were breathing down his neck, and he knew that if he didn't crack it soon, they'd either beat him to his own discovery or debunk the whole effort. He was damned if he was going to face them across a lecture hall having lost the race. And Pif would string him up by his *yajtza,* which was a more immediate problem.

So, the sphere didn't work. It should. Every test he'd conducted on it showed that it'd been made with micrometer precision, exactly in the configuration he'd calculated. He'd run it with the right voltage.

Everything was perfect, and still, and still...

He picked up his glasses from where he'd thrown them. The same old room snapped into focus: the remnants of Pif's time with him scattered across her old desk, the same pot plants existing on a diet of cold coffee, the light outside leaking in around the yellowed slats of the Venetian blinds.

Sound leaked in, too: sirens that howled toward the crack of distant gunfire, carried on cold, still winter air. Banging and clattering, hammers and drills, the reverberations of scaffolding. A tank slapping its caterpillar tracks down on the tarmac.

None of it loud enough to distract him from the hum of the fluorescent tube overhead.

He opened a drawer and pulled out a sheet of printed paper, which he placed squarely in front of him. He stared at the symbols on it, knowing the answer was there somewhere, if only he knew where to look. He turned his wedding ring in precise quarter circles, still finding it a cold and alien presence on his body.

Time passed. Voices in the corridor outside grew closer, louder, then faded.

Petrovitch looked up suddenly. His eyes narrowed and he pushed his glasses back up his nose. His heart spun faster, producing a surge of blood that pricked his skin with sweat.

Now everything was slow, deliberate, as he held on to his idea. He reached for a pencil and turned the sheet of paper over, blank side to him. He started to scratch out a diagram, and when he'd finished, some numbers to go with it.

Petrovitch put down the pencil and checked his answer. *Dubiina,* he whispered to himself, *durak, balvan.*

The ornate sphere had taunted him from across the desk for the last time. He was going to be its master now. He reached over and fastened his hand around it, then threw it in the air with such casual defiance that it would have had his head of department leaping to save it.

He caught it deftly on its way down, and knew that it would never have to touch the floor again.

He carried it to the door, flung it open, and stepped through. The two paycops lolling beside the lift caught a flavor of his mood. One nudged the other, who turned to see the white blond hair and tight-lipped smile of Petrovitch advancing toward them at a steady gait.

"Doctor Petrovitch?" asked one. "Is there a problem?"

Petrovitch held the sphere up in front of him. "Out of the way," he said. "Science coming through."

He ran down the stairs; two stories, sliding his hand over the banister and only taking a firm hold to let his momentum carry him through the air for the broad landings. Now was not the time to wait, foot-tapping, for a crawling lift car that gave him the creeps anyway. Everything was urgent, imminent, immanent.

Second floor: his professor had given him two graduate students, and he had had little idea what to do with them. The least he could do to compensate for several months of make-work was to include them in this. He needed witnesses, anyway. And their test rig. Which may or may not be completed: Petrovitch hadn't seen either student for a week, or it might have been two.

Either way, he was certain he could recognize them again.

He kicked the door to their lab space open. They were there, sitting in front of an open cube of wood, a cat's cradle of thin wires stretched inside. An oscilloscope—old school cathode tube—made a pulsing green line across its gridded screen.

The woman—blonde, skin as pale as parchment, eyes gray like a ghost's...McNeil: yes, that was her name— glanced over her shoulder. She jumped up when she saw Petrovitch's expression and what he was carrying.

"You've finished it."

"This? Yeah, about a week ago. Should have mentioned it, but that's not what's important now." He advanced on a steel trolley. In time-honored fashion, new equipment was built in the center of the lab. The old was pushed to the wall to be cannibalized for parts or left to fossilize.

He inspected the collection of fat transformers on the trolley's top shelf. When he squatted down to inspect the lower deck, he found some moving coil meters and something that might have been the heavy-duty switching gear from a power station. "Do either of you need any of this?"

He waited all of half a second for a reply before seizing the trolley in his free hand and trying to tip it over. Some of the transformers were big ferrite ones, and he couldn't manage it one-handed. McNeil and the man—Petrovitch's mind was too full to remember his name—looked at each other.

"You," he said to the man, "catch."

He threw the sphere and, without waiting to see if it had a safe arrival, wedged his foot under one of the trolley's castors and heaved. The contents slid and fell, collecting in a blocky heap on the fifties lino.

He righted the trolley and looked around for what he needed. "Power supply there," he pointed, and McNeil scurried to get it. "That bundle of leads there. Multimeter, any, doesn't matter. And the Mukhanov book."

The other student was frozen in place, holding the sphere like it was made of crystal. Hugo Dominguez, that was it. Had problems pronouncing his sibilants.

"You all right with that?"

Dominguez nodded dumbly.

The quantum gravity textbook was the last thing slapped on the trolley, and Petrovitch took the handle again.

"Right. Follow me."

McNeil trotted by his side. "Doctor Petrovitch," she said.

And that was almost as strange as being married. Doctor. What else could the university have done, but confer him with the title as soon as was practically possible?

"Yeah?"

"Where are we going?"

"Basement. And pray to whatever god you believe in that we're not over a tube line."

"Can I ask why?"

"Sure." They'd reached the lift. He leaned over the trolley and punched the button to go down.

"Okay," she said, twisting a strand of hair around her finger. "Why?"

"Because what I was doing before wasn't working. This will." The lift pinged and the door slid aside. Petrovitch took a good long look at the empty space before gritting his teeth and launching the trolley inside. He ushered the two students in, then after another moment's hesitation on the threshold, he stepped in.

He reached behind him and thumbed the stud marked B for basement.

As the lift descended, they waited for him to continue. "What's the mass of the Earth?" he said. When neither replied, he rolled his eyes. "Six times ten to the twenty-four kilos. All that mass produces a pathetic nine point eight one meters per second squared acceleration at the surface. An upright ape like me can outpull the entire planet just by getting out of a chair."

"Which is why you had us build the mass balance," she said.

"Yeah. You're going to have to take it apart and bring it down here." The door slid back to reveal a long corridor with dim overhead lighting. "Not here here. This is just to show that it works. We'll get another lab set up. Find a kettle. Stuff like that."

He pushed the trolley out before the lift was summoned to a higher floor.

"Doctor," said Dominguez, finally finding his voice, "that still does not explain why we are now underground."

"Doesn't it?" Petrovitch blinked. "I guess not. Find a socket for the power supply while I wire up the rest of it." He took the sphere from Dominguez and turned it around until he found the two holes. His hand chased out a couple of leads from the bird's nest of wires, spilling some of them to the floor. The lift disappeared upstairs, making a grinding noise as it went.

They worked together. McNeil joined cables together until she'd made two half-meter lengths. Dominguez set up the multimeter and twisted the dial to read current. Petrovitch plugged two jacks into the sphere, and finally placed Mukhanov and Winitzki's tome on the floor. He set the sphere on top of it.

"Either of you two worked it out yet?" he asked. "No? Don't worry: I'm supposed to be a genius, and it took me a week. Hugo, dial up four point eight volts. Watch the current. If it looks like it's going to melt something, turn it off."

The student had barely put his hand on the control when the lift returned. A dozen people spilled out, all talking at once.

"Yobany stos!" He glared out over the top of his glasses. "I'm trying to conduct an epoch-making experiment which will turn this place into a shrine for future generations. So shut the *huy* up."

One of the crowd held up his camera phone, and Petrovitch thought that wasn't such a bad idea.

"You. Yes, you. Come here. I don't bite. Much. Stand there." He propelled the young man front and center. "Is it recording? Good."

All the time, more people were arriving, but it didn't matter. The time was now.

"Yeah, okay. Hugo? Hit it."

Nothing happened.

"You are hitting it, right?"

"Yes, Doctor Petrovitch."

"Then why isn't the little red light on?" He sat back on his heels. *"Chyort.* There's no *yebani* power in the ring main."

There was an audible groan.

Petrovitch looked up again at all the expectant faces. "Unless someone wants to stick their fingers in a light socket, I suggest you go and find a very long extension lead."

Some figures at the back raced away, their feet slapping against the concrete stairs. When they came back, it wasn't with an extension lead proper, but one they'd cobbled together out of the cable from several janitorial devices and gaffer tape. The bare ends of the wire were live, and it was passed over the heads of the watching masses gingerly.

It took a few moments more to desleeve the plug from the boxy power supply and connect everything together. The little red light glimmered on.

Petrovitch looked up at the cameraman. "Take two?"

"We're on."

Petrovitch got down on his hands and knees, and took one last look at the inert black sphere chased with silver lines. In a moment, it would be transformed, and with it, the world. No longer a thing of beauty, it would become just another tool.

"Hugo?" He was aware of McNeil crouched beside him. She was holding her breath, just like he was.

Dominguez flicked the on switch and slowly turned the dial. The digital figures on the multimeter started to flicker.

Then, without fuss, without sound, the sphere leaped off the book and into the air. It fell back a little, rose, fell, rose, fell, each subsequent oscillation smaller than the previous one until it was still again: only it was resting at shin-height with no visible means of support.

Someone started clapping. Another joined in, and another, until the sound of applause echoed, magnified, off the walls.

His heart was racing again, the tiny turbine in his chest

having tasted the amount of adrenaline flooding into his blood. He felt dizzy, euphoric, ecstatic even. Here was science elevated to a religious experience. Dominguez was transfixed, motionless like his supervisor. It was McNeil who was the first of the three to move. She reached forward and tapped the floating sphere with her fingernail. It slipped sideways, pulling the cables with it until it lost momentum and stopped. She waved her hand under it, over it.

She turned to Petrovitch and grinned. He staggered to his feet and faced the crowd. *"Da! Da! Da!"* He punched the air each time, and found he couldn't stop. Soon he had all of them, young and old, men and women, fists in the air, chanting *"Da!"* at the tops of their voices.

He reached over and hauled Dominguez up. He held his other hand out to McNeil, who crawled up his arm and clung on to him in a desperate embrace. Thus encumbered, he turned to the camera phone and extended his middle finger—not his exactly, but he was at least its owner. *"Yob materi vashi,* Stanford."

2

At first, Petrovitch thought the buzzing coming from his leg was the first sign that his circulation was failing like it used to do, and his heart needed charging up again.

Then he realized it was his phone, the one that Maddy made him carry on pain of death—his, naturally. He unVelcroed his pocket even as staff and students swirled around him, slapping his back, shaking his hand, kissing him. Some of them were crying, wetting his cheeks with their tears of joy.

It was party time, and he'd brought the best present of all.

He palmed the phone and glanced at the screen. He was clearly lucky to get a signal at all down in the depths. He checked the caller ID, and frowned. It wasn't his wife, and he wasn't aware of anyone else who would know his carefully guarded number. He ducked clear of the crowd, which seemed to be growing by the minute, and walked further down the corridor to answer the call.

"Yeah?"

"Doctor Samuil Petrovitch? Husband of Sergeant Madeleine Petrovitch?"

It definitely wasn't her. And with all the noise around him, it was almost impossible to hear the man at the other end of the connection.

"What's wrong?"

The reply was lost, and Petrovitch growled in frustration. He jammed his finger in his ear and tried to cup his hand around the phone.

"Say again?"

"Sergeant Petrovitch has been injured. She's been taken to..." and that was all he could make out.

Petrovitch lowered the phone and yelled at the top of his voice: "*Past' zabej!* I'm trying to talk to someone here." When the sound level had dropped below cacophony, he tried again. "Where is she?"

"St. Bart's. She's—"

"She's what?" he interrupted. He had no control over the speed of his heart. It had no beats to miss, but it felt like it had momentarily stalled. "Do I actually have time to get there?"

"Walking wounded. Three rounds to the chest, but the armor held up. But that's..."

"*Yebani v'rot,*" said Petrovitch, exasperated, "shut up and listen. Who are you?"

"Casualty clearing orderly."

"Is she going to die?"

"No."

"Has she asked for me?"

"Yes."

"Then why the *chyort* didn't you say any of that in the first place? I'm on my way." He cut the call and plunged back into the mass of people, heading purposefully for the lift.

McNeil caught his arm. "Who was it? Press?"

"The militia. I have to go." He tried to advance, but she held him back with surprising strength.

She leaned in close. "You have to talk to the press. Get the news out about what's happened here today," she said.

"They're going to find out soon enough, with or without my help." He pried her fingers away. "Why don't you and Hugo talk to the cameras. You'll do just fine."

Petrovitch pushed through to the stairs to find she was still on his heels.

"We can't do that!" she complained. "We don't even know what you did!"

"The field attenuates to the seventh power. Upstairs, it had nothing to push against: down here, it does. Can you handle it now, because I really need to go?"

"Doctor, the head of department is here," she called after him. "He wants to congratulate you."

Petrovitch was already starting to climb. "You know what? *Do pizdy.*"

She tried one last time. "But Doctor Petrovitch: science!"

He stopped and brought his knuckle up to his mouth. He bit hard into it to stiffen his resolve.

"This…this is going to be with us forever," he said. "Now we've discovered how to do it, everybody will be copying us. Good luck to them. My life is more than this now. Someone else needs me, and that won't wait. Give my apologies to the head. Tell him…I don't know—tell him my wife's been shot. He'll understand."

He left her, her mouth forming a perfect O, and ran up one flight of stairs to the ground floor. He was passed on the way by more people, some of whom turned their heads as they recognized him, and some, like the ninja reporter with a broadcast camera and an armful of studio lights, so intent on getting to the site of the miracle that they failed to spot the prophet.

He skipped past the ground floor and kept on going: he wasn't dressed for outside, and he'd need money, travel-card and identification if he was going to get across the central Metrozone and not get stranded, arrested or worse en route. It had never been the easiest of journeys: now it took wits as well as patience.

Back on the fourth floor, he took everything he needed out of his top drawer and threw on the scorched leather coat that had become his prized possession. In his pocket were clip-on lenses in a slim case. He slid them over the bridge of his own glasses, and the world became info-rich.

He knew the temperature, the wind speed, the likeli-hood of rain. He knew that the tube was still completely out, shallow tunnels crushed, deep tunnels flooded, but that there was a limited bus service along the Embankment as far as London Bridge. He knew that there was Outie activ-ity around Hampstead Heath—firefights all along the A5/M1 corridor as well—but that was too far out to affect him. A bomb in Finsbury Park earlier, with twenty dead and a legion of whackos ready to claim it for their own.

As wedding presents went, the clip-ons were pretty cool. Even cooler when he'd hacked the controller and got it to display lots of things the manufacturers hadn't meant it to.

Back down four floors to the foyer: a mere ten minutes after he'd discovered artificial gravity. There was still a steady drift of people heading for the basement, enough that it had started to become congested and the paycops didn't quite know what to do with everyone.

Petrovitch was ignored, and in turn, he ignored them.

He headed for the street, passing through the foyer doors and experiencing one of the flashbulb flashbacks he sometimes had. The present blinked into the past, and he was striding out into the night, Madeleine behind him. A packet of hand-written equations burned in his pocket.

The scene vanished as abruptly as it had arrived. He was back with weak daylight, the sound of people, the swoosh of automatic doors.

It had been quiet and cold when he'd trekked in from Clapham A and through the *govno*-smeared realms of Battersea—even the Outies had to sleep sometime. Now it was even colder, and there was an electric tension in the air, not helped by the battle tank parked on the corner of Exhibition Road, gun muzzle trained across Hyde Park. There'd always been direction to Metrozone pedestrians—a purpose for being on the streets, A to B, going to work, to school, to the shops—now there wasn't. There were gaps between people, and they spilled aimlessly along the pavements.

The city was broken, and he hated the thought that something he'd spilled good, honest blood over was losing its way. He hated it, and still he stayed.

He headed south toward Chelsea, where he had to pass through an impromptu checkpoint thrown hastily across the road. Even though it was nothing more than a few waist-high barriers, a white van with MEA stencilled on the side and two paycops with Authority armbands, he took them seriously because of their guns. He affected a calm, cool exterior as he approached the screen. The cops were edgy, looking for those who might dodge through the unscreened, northbound stream in an attempt to avoid the scanner. They were edgy in a way that suggested they might shoot without warning.

It was his turn. He walked smartly through the arch and kept going. No contraband, no weapons: he was clean. There was nothing for the computer to latch on to, and no human operator to spot anything out of the ordinary.

Petrovitch's hand went to the back of his neck, where his hair had grown uncharacteristically long. His fingers touched surgical metal.

The buildings around him bore scars, too. The visible tidemark on their street-side faces rose higher the closer he got to the river, and such was the pressure of population, some people found themselves forced to live in the stinking lower floors, amidst walls and floors and ceilings still damp and contaminated with gods-knew-what.

He came to the Thames, brown and sluggish, shining wetly. A barge, once embedded in a riverfront property, lay broken and sad on the mudslick that had been a line of trees. Across the Albert Bridge, he could almost see home.

The Embankment road had been scraped with a bull-dozer, washed down by pumps. The white line was visible again down its center, and off to one side beside the Regency town houses swathed in scaffolding was the temporary bus stop. The virtual arrow above it was almost unnecessary, but finding he only had a five-minute wait was welcome news.

There was a queue. There always was. He took the opportunity to view the chasm carved through the London skyline, right through the heart of Brompton and out onto the Chelsea embankment. Across the river, the clear-cutting of buildings continued along the shoreline before petering out.

He was one of the few who knew it was the route of the Shinjuku line, mark two, terminating at the Oshicora Tower. Almost everyone else saw it as a random wound, born of chaos like everything else that night.

The bus, windows glazed with grime and protected by close-meshed grilles, strained along toward him. It sagged at the curbside and folded its tired doors aside. Inside, it was literally standing room only. The vehicle had no seats apart from the driver's: they'd been stripped out and thrown away. Passengers grabbed at a pole or a hang-strap, or each other. Cattle-class for all: egalitarian transport for the twenty-first century.

Petrovitch slid his pass across the sensor and elbowed his way toward the back, where the crush would be less and the air a little clearer.

The journey along the north bank of the Thames was dreary and dull. The filth on the windows was sufficiently thick to render the view outside nothing more than variations in dark and light. With his info shades on, he was provided with a virtual map of his journey. Most of his fellow passengers had to rely on the driver's announcements over the tannoy to give them clues as to where they were.

But no matter their status, they were all stuck together on the same bus, rocking this way and that, jerked by the inconstant acceleration and braking, clinging on to handles welded to the roof.

Chelsea Bridge, Claverton Street, Vauxhall Bridge, Lambeth Bridge—where the putative Keiyo line was driven through, narrowly missing Westminster Abbey—and Westminster Bridge. At each stop, people got on or off in an exchange that was interminably slow. No one would move out of the way from simple courtesy, choosing instead to shuffle sullenly aside. Fights were common, but there were no paycops on the buses. MEA, always on the verge of bankruptcy, couldn't afford them.

He used his pocket controller to catch a news wire. The Metrozone's litany of disasters was usually relegated to the third or fourth item on any given day, unless someone pulled off a spectacular. Top of the cycle was rioting in Paris—*l'anglais* causing problems as Metrozone refugees filled up French parks. Second was a late-season hurricane bearing down on Florida. Third, was him, managing to push the Outies' latest incursion into fourth.

Antigravity demonstrated in London Metrozone lab.

That it wasn't actually antigravity didn't bother Petrovitch. It behaved like it—or like the popular perception of it—so why get cross? Instead, he nodded with satisfaction. At least they were reporting a science story. Stanford would be reading the wire at the same time as he was. MIT and CalTech, too, Pasadena and Houston; all those scientists, all that money, beaten by a once-great but now impoverished institution hemorrhaging talent like it had contracted academic Ebola.

After Charing Cross was Waterloo Bridge, where boats had lost their moorings in the Long Night and plowed into the spans, rendering it useless for motorized traffic. On to Temple, and as that stop was announced, Petrovitch started to move forward, easing himself through the mass of gray passengers until he could move no more.

The bus shuddered to a halt. The doors opened. The first few people waiting tried to get on before those already on could get off. There was some pushing and shoving. Someone outside fell back after gaining a foothold in the entrance, and the disturbance rippled out from there, inside and out.

It died away after a few moments, as most of those involved were just too tired to get riled. A stamp of the foot, a jab of the elbow, it was all they could manage.

Petrovitch squeezed out and escaped the crowd, walking to the back of the bus and behind it to get his bearings. Not far now. He turned his head, watching the street names pop up, and the information that there was a press conference being called at Imperial.

"Live from London" would have to happen without him. He shrugged at no one in particular. The university didn't need some sweary Russian kid causing an international incident, and Petrovitch didn't need his face beamed across the planet—a win for everyone concerned.

He headed up Farringdon Street, to where the flood waters had pooled under Holborn Viaduct and it still smelled of black mud, and cut through to Smithfield. His glasses told him the entrance to the hospital was there on his right.

It was, too: guarded by cops and MEA militia, a concertina of razor wire and a sandbagged machine-gun emplacement. Concrete blocks had been scattered like teeth to deter truck bombers.

He stared critically at the scene. He was now living in a city where a hospital was seen as a likely target. He made a face, feeling something close to physical pain. Once upon a time, he'd said that the center could not hold. He'd been right, as usual.

Past the fortified entrance, behind the façade of boarded-up windows and the gray stonework, was his wife.

So many things about him had changed, and she was the chief cause of most of them.

3

They finally let him in, and a harassed woman on the reception desk told him where to find Madeleine. There was a wide-screen TV bolted to the wall of the foyer, and it happened to be showing a small black sphere—the silver wire tracks didn't show up well—floating without visible means of support. There was a commotion going on in the background, and a voice cut through the noise: "*Past' zabej!*"

It appeared that the kid with the camera phone had been syndicated.

Petrovitch looked up at the ward names and started down the corridor. His boots squeaked loudly on the lino floor, contrasting with the soft-footed urgency of the hospital staff, all passing him at a trot.

A MEA militiaman, body armor thrown over one shoulder, rifle over the other, limped toward him. They were about to pass each other: Petrovitch moved to the left and readied a respectful nod, but the man stepped the same way. Three more switches from one side of the corridor to the other weren't an accident.

A palm jutted out and shoved Petrovitch backward.

The man with spiky blond hair snarled from deep inside his throat.

Petrovitch didn't have time for this. "*Mudak*," he said and tried to go around the man. For his troubles, he got pushed again, hard, against the corridor wall. His spine jarred against a door frame, and the hand on his chest attempted to pin him there.

"What's your problem?" Petrovitch jammed his glasses up his nose and eyeballed the soldier. The tab over the man's pocket read Andersson with two esses, and he had corporal's stripes on his arm.

"You are," said Andersson, "fucking civilians. We're bleeding…"

"I've given already."

"…bleeding every day, to keep you safe from the Outies." He leaned in and shouted full in Petrovitch's face, spittle flying. "You're not worth it. None of you. Especially a coward who expects his wife to go out and fight while he sits on his arse."

Andersson's armor slipped forward off his shoulder. In the momentary distraction, Petrovitch brought his knee up hard, stepped sideways and reached for the corporal's belt. He snagged a loop and pulled hard, slamming the crown of Andersson's bowed head against the door.

"Let's get one thing absolutely straight." Petrovitch wasn't even breathing hard, while Andersson was lying on the floor, clutching himself and whimpering. "I will not be making a complaint about this, today or ever. Everyone's allowed to make a stupid mistake now and then, and this is your turn. But if you so much as lay a finger on me again, I will break it off and ram it so far up your *zhopu,* you'll need to swallow a pair of scissors to keep the nail trimmed. Got that?"

The man on the ground swallowed against the pain. "You don't deserve her."

"I make a point of telling her that every morning, but she seems happy enough to keep me around." Petrovitch snorted. "If I offer to help you up, would you take it?"

"Go to hell."

"Lie there and count your *yajtza,* then." He batted at his coat and walked away. He had an audience of two green-overalled nurses and a technician. He inclined his head as he passed them. "Enjoy the show?"

The technician did a double-take. "Hey. Aren't you that...?"

"That what?"

"On the news. Just now. The flying thing."

"Yeah. Look," he said, "can one of you point me to the Minor Injuries Unit?"

"Turn right at the end of this corridor," said the tech. "But you're, like..."

"Like really smart? I know." He started to walk away.

"Famous. I was going to say famous."

"Oh, I hope not." He waved his hand in dismissal and finally found the sign telling him which way to go.

There were double doors with glass inserts, which he peered through. He could see her, sitting in the waiting room, her hands in her lap, fingers flicking through her rosary beads. Her eyes were closed, her lips barely moving. Piled next to her was her armor, folded neatly with her helmet on top. There was a gelatinous green pool of leaking impact gel collecting on the floor beneath.

Her hair had started to grow on the previously shaved front and sides of her head. She kept threatening to cut the plait off that extended from her nape to her waist, but he'd once offered the opinion that he quite liked it and, so far, it had been spared.

He pushed against one of the doors and slipped in, sitting down next to her in an identical plastic chair. Her battlesmock was open. When he leaned forward, he could see the purple bruising above the scoop of her vest top.

"Hey, Sam," she said without opening her eyes.

"Hey," he said. "You okay?"

"Greenstick fracture of the seventh rib, left side. Could have been worse." The rosary beads kept clicking.

Petrovitch nodded. "There's a shortage of perfect breasts in this world. It would be a pity to damage yours."

"Don't make me laugh, Sam. It hurts."

"But you do have per—"

"Sam." She opened one eye, then the other. She gave him a sad smile and gathered up her beads. "Can we go home?"

"Yeah. Maddy, what else?"

"What else what?"

He put his elbows on his knees. "You've been shot before. You've never called for me."

She tried to take a deep breath, and winced halfway through. Her hands trembled, and Petrovitch put his own hand over hers.

"It can wait," he said. "When you're ready."

"It..." she said, and she was crying, and hating herself for doing so, and crying all the more because of that. "Oh."

Petrovitch just about managed to reach around her broad shoulders. She slumped against him, her cheek resting on his head. He felt her shudder and gasp for a while, then fall still.

Finally, she said, "I saw my mother today."

Petrovitch blinked. "Your mother?"

"It was her. She actually looked sober."

"Where was this?"

"Gospel Oak. North of there has been declared an Out-zone, and the railway is now the front line. We were told to hold it."

"Did you?"

"Yes."

"Good."

"She was the one who shot me."

"*Chyort.* That shouldn't happen."

"There's a school, right next door to the station. A group of Outies came across the tracks and got into the building. We went in after them. Firefight, short range, all ducking through doorways and hiding behind furniture. Except this was a primary school, and tables built for five-year-olds don't give me much cover."

"And one of the Outies was your mother." Petrovitch frowned. "How could that happen? I thought she was Inzone."

"She was, is." She shook her head. "Maybe they recruit as they go. I don't know. But we still got to face each other down the length of a corridor. For the first time in five years. I assumed she'd drunk herself to death, yet there she was, larger than life, pointing a gun at me. And I dropped my weapon. I dropped my weapon and shouted 'Don't shoot!'"

"I take it she shot you."

"The first put me on my back. I tried to get up, get my visor out of the way, so she could see who it was. She walked over to me and shot me twice more. There would have been a fourth to the head, but then the rest of my squad turned up, and she ran."

"*Pizdets.*"

She sighed. "Haven't told you the best bit yet. I was

screaming 'Mom, it's me, Maddy' over and over—and she had to have heard me, she was standing over me with a pistol pointed at my heart—and she still pulled the trigger. So yes, *pizdets* just about covers it."

He squeezed her closer. They sat like that for a while.

"There's a poem," he said. "The one about your parents, how they..."

"I know it."

"It's true, though. They do." Petrovitch held out his left hand and examined his ring finger. "Probably a good job we didn't invite her to the wedding."

She snorted. "You're a bad man."

"The very worst. Come on, *babochka,* let's get you back to sunny Clapham."

Madeleine disentangled herself and gathered up her dripping armor. Petrovitch took the full-face helmet by the chin-strap and let it dangle. She caught him looking at her.

"I'll be okay," she said. "Just, you know."

"Yeah." He opened the door with his foot and held it as she struggled through. "I should be carrying that."

"It'd be easier wearing it, except that it's pretty much unwearable. It's only going as far as the front gate. MEA can pick it up if they want it, or just bin it."

They turned the corner and walked down the long corridor to reception.

"Do you know a guy called Andersson?" Petrovitch asked as they past the dented door.

"Jan Andersson? He's just been transferred in. Tall, Norwegian."

"Yeah, that's him. Is he all right?"

"He was in here with me. He tripped over something,

hurt his knee. They stuck a needle in him and told him to go home." Madeleine looked askance at him. "That's not what you mean, is it?"

"No: he picked a fight with me, right about here."

"What? In the hospital?"

"The self-defense lessons paid off." He shrugged, and she stopped, which forced him to stop too.

"Sam? What did you do?"

"Apparently, I sit at my desk scratching my arse while my woman goes out to fight the barbarians. It seems to offend him. So much so, he tried to push me backward through a wall."

She didn't know what to either say or do, so Petrovitch took up the slack in the conversation.

"You've not mentioned him before, so I was just wondering how he got so concerned about our domestic arrangements."

"He. What?" Both words were pronounced separately, indignantly.

"I kind of guessed as much. I'll leave him to you, shall I?"

"How. Dare. He."

"Maddy, people are going to figure that now you're not a nun, they can get in your pants."

"But. I'm. Married!"

"They probably also figure I'm not going to be much competition, either." Petrovitch shrugged again. "You're going to have to get used to the attention. I'm going to have to get used to it. We'll manage."

Her face, previously white with pain and fatigue, had colored up. "How can you be so calm? How can you just stand there and be so matter of fact?"

"Because in the four months we've been married, you

haven't got ugly. I know you're a mass of neuroses and insecurities about your looks, but you turn heads when you walk down the street—and it's not because people think you're a freak. I know that when they see me next to you, they're saying 'How the *huy* did a *pidaras* like him end up with a woman like that?' And..." He turned away. "I wake up every morning and wonder that myself."

Madeleine's shoulders, tense before, slowly slumped down. "Sam," she started. Something distracted her, and Petrovitch looked round to see the technician from earlier.

"What?" he said.

"Can I," she said hesitantly, glancing between him and Madeleine, "can I have your autograph?" She brought her hands from behind her back. There was a pen in one, a spiral-bound notebook in the other.

Petrovitch raised his eyes at the ceiling. "You really picked your moment," he said. Then he relented, took the biro and scrawled his name at a slant across the page. He tacked on the zero potential Schrödinger, and a smiley face. When he handed it back, she almost curtsied to him before running back up the corridor, notebook clutched like it was first prize.

"Sam?"

He held her helmet to his chest and flexed his fingers against its cold ceramic surface. "It's not important."

"What's not important?"

He started for the exit again, and this time forced her to follow. She repeated her question to the back of his head.

"I didn't want to mention it. You know: yeah, so what if your long-lost mother just tried to kill you? I don't care how upset you are because I made gravity today." He slid his glasses up his nose and tightened his lips. "I'm not like that. Not anymore."

The news was still playing on the wall in the foyer. He'd overtaken both Florida and Paris, and coverage was pretty much universal. One side of the screen was the loop from the camera phone. The other was a scientist he vaguely recognized talking animatedly about how the future had changed irrevocably.

Madeleine trailed after him, and she stumbled as she saw her husband declare to the world just what he thought of Stanford University.

"That's you."

He went back for her, took her arm and guided her outside. "You get to see me all the time."

She tried to re-enter the foyer. "You were on the news."

"Yes. And in twelve hours, they'll have forgotten all about me."

"But shouldn't you be, I don't know, somewhere else?" She looked over her shoulder to catch a glimpse of the rapidly shifting images. "You did it. You made it work."

"You called me. I came." Petrovitch clenched his jaw, then forcibly relaxed it. "I thought that was the deal. No matter what we were doing, if one of us wanted the other, they'd come. No questions, no 'I'm a little bit busy right now.' That was what we promised each other. Or have I got it completely wrong? Probably better I know now than find out later."

She dropped the armor and enfolded him in her arms, pressing him against her and not letting him go, even though it had to be hurting her.

"Thank you," she said.

Petrovitch could hear the beat of her heart, strong and steady. "That's okay," he mumbled.

4

She was sleeping in the bed, and Petrovitch was sitting at his screen, wearing a glove to gesture to the images on it. The crest of the news wave had reached east Asia, where Chinese technocrats in their glass towers and Mongolian yak-herders living in yurts were having breakfast to his sweary cry of triumph.

His phone rattled against his thigh again—and it couldn't be Maddy this time either. He slipped it from his pocket and wearily thumbed the button.

"Doesn't anybody use email these days?"

"Congratulations, Petrovitch." There was a pause. "I can't hear the champagne corks popping."

"If you thought you could use me to get into a party, you don't really know me at all."

Harry Chain cleared his throat noisily. "So you're bunkered down in Clapham A, waiting for the storm to die down. Perhaps you should have chosen a quieter career."

"Quieter?" Petrovitch swung his bare feet up on the desk. "Quieter than high-energy physics? Yeah, we're all *yebani* celebrities these days. Why did you call?"

"Apart from to say well done? How's Madeleine?"

He looked at her reflection in the screen, the long curve of her spine and the shadows formed by her waist. "She's fine. A bit shook up." He didn't tell him about her mother.

"Look, Petrovitch; we need to talk. Not over the phone, either."

"About . . . ?"

"Really not over the phone. I can come to you. Half an hour, forty minutes."

"I don't want to leave her, but I don't want you coming to the domik either. You know where Wong's is?"

Petrovitch heard the tap of a stylus against a screen.

"I do now," said Chain. "Half an hour? Please?"

"You're buying."

"I always do." The connection clicked off.

Petrovitch slid the phone back into his pocket and turned in his chair. Madeleine was still but for the slight rise and fall of her rib cage. Her hair was coiled on the pillow. Her hips were shrouded by a sheet. The expanse of pale skin between was perfect, unmarked by scar or blemish.

She was a thing of wonder, and she was in his bed. He shivered, even though he wasn't cold.

His boots were by the door, his coat on a stick-on hanger next to it. He got ready as quietly as he could, but then came the point that he had to wake her. He kissed her shoulder, and waited for her to stir.

"Hey," he said.

"Hey yourself. What's time?"

"Eight thirty. In the evening."

Her eyes, large and unfocused, narrowed. "You're going out?"

"I'm going to Wong's. Harry Chain called. Said it was..." he shrugged, "he didn't say what it was, but that in itself is worrying."

"Okay." Her eyelids fluttered shut, and she was instantly asleep again.

He took a moment to inspect the bruising that was seeping in a yellow and purple tide across her front; even her breasts, which were still as magnificent as he remembered them from that morning.

She'd need stronger painkillers than the pitiful bottle dispensed to her by the hospital.

He reluctantly turned away and zipped open a holdall on the floor. In Madeleine's methodical way, each item inside had its own ziploc bag. He rummaged through the CS spray, the sheathed knives, the taser and assorted coshes for the Ceska. He slipped the pistol into his hand and went back in for the almost toy-sized bullets. He tidied away when he was done.

He threw on his coat, dropped the gun into his pocket, and looked back as he started to unlock the door. She'd still be there when he got back, which was in itself a reason not to be too long.

Wong scowled at him as Petrovitch kicked the door open.

"Hey. Why you no use handle like everyone else?" he complained, but he was already pouring coffee in a scalding black stream.

Petrovitch pushed the door back with his heel, shutting out the mist and the dark. "Because I'm not like everyone else. Where I come from the door opens you."

"That still make no sense. You say that like it mean something, when it all nonsense."

"Yeah, whatever." He stuck his hands in his pockets and felt the weight of the pistol as he sized up the rest of the café's clientele. "Quiet?"

"No one come in and shoot us up. Not today." Wong slid the coffee over the counter. "On house."

Petrovitch had come out without a credit chip, or even a few coins, so he had no choice but to accept. "Thanks. Why?"

"You great man now. Shows fortune cookie right again." His face cracked into an unpleasant grin. "I have sex with the Stanford faculty's mothers!"

Petrovitch looked over the top of his glasses. "Is that how they translated it? I prefer my version." Still shaking his head, he retreated to the very back of the shop and nursed his scalding black coffee until Chain barged his way in.

"Hey," started Wong.

"He's with me," Petrovitch called.

Chain squinted into the distance and finally located the source of the voice. He patted his jacket down for his wallet, and let Wong charge him twice for the same drink without him noticing. He brought his coffee to Petrovitch's table and slopped it down before collapsing in the chair opposite.

"You all right?" asked Petrovitch.

"A bit, you know. Strange days." He pressed his squashed nose into his mug, inhaling the bitter fumes. "Everything is wrong."

"That, coming from a policeman, doesn't fill me with happy thoughts."

Chain's face twitched. "I've been seconded. Metrozone Emergency Authority militia. Intelligence."

Petrovitch just about managed to swallow. He coughed hard to clear his throat. "Ha!"

"Don't start. Not now. Besides," he said, reaching inside his jacket, "I've got something for you."

He slid a slim metal case the size of a cheap paperback across the table. Petrovitch stared at it for a moment before looking up into Chain's rheumy eyes.

"Is that what I think it is?"

"Since I dropped the last one in a swamp, I supposed I owed you." Chain nudged it closer. "Consider it a late wedding present."

"I thought my present was your convenient forgetting of all the illegal things I'd done." Petrovitch picked up the case and turned it in his hands, watching the play of light and shadow across the brushed steel surface. He touched the recessed button and the case split apart. "If you've loaded this up with spyware... What am I saying, if? The first thing I'm going to do is bleach the insides."

"For what it's worth, I haven't touched it. Factory fresh. Except," and Chain stopped, and his shoulders hunched higher.

Petrovitch dabbed at the rat, checking the software and the connectivity. "Except what?"

"I did put a file on it. You might want to take a look."

Petrovitch found the file and clicked it. A video started to run: grainy, too-bright colors, ghosting. It was almost unwatchable, but then it settled down. People were passing through a screen, the camera pointing down and toward them, recording their faces as they walked out from under the arch.

"Airport?"

"Heathrow, this morning. Watch for the blonde."

"That's every second person."

"You'll recognize her."

He watched as figures paraded by. There was a pause, then a woman with a curiously mechanical gait stepped up to the screen. Lights and alarms sounded, causing a flurry of activity from the paycops. The woman looked first to her left, then her right, her ponytail flicking her shoulders. A guard was arguing with her, his hand on his holster, but she seemed supremely unconcerned. It was almost as if this happened all the time to her.

She was alone again, everyone else retreating outside the square of the camera's capture. The screen rang its alarms for a second time, but she strode through untouched. She looked up at the camera, her gaze unwavering. Then she was gone.

"Don't know her," said Petrovitch.

"No family resemblance, then?"

"Not mine." Petrovitch wound the video back and froze it. He stared at the image, even as she stared back. *"Chyort."*

"May I introduce Charlotte Sorenson, recently arrived from the U.S. of A?" Chain swigged at his coffee and wiped his mouth on his sleeve. "She has cybernetic legs, hence all the kerfuffle."

"No prizes for guessing why she's here." Petrovitch snapped the rat shut and tapped it on the tabletop. "What does she know?"

"She knows where her brother stayed, who he was working for. She may even know he was being blackmailed."

"By Oshicora and by you," said Petrovitch pointedly.

"I would apologize, but he's dead." Chain shifted uncomfortably in his seat and leaned closer. "We all did things we're not proud of."

"Like shooting my wife in the back? At least the Outies have the decency to try and kill her face to face."

Chain almost got up and left. His hands were on the tabletop, poised, ready to push himself away. He went as far as tensing his arm muscles. Then he slumped back down. "Okay. Probably deserved that."

"Probably?"

"I'm trying to help you. There's more than just Miss Sorenson to worry about."

Petrovitch pocketed the rat and signaled to Wong for more coffee. "Go on."

"I get to see things in my new job I wouldn't normally see. A briefing here, a transcript there. Things start to add up."

"Chain, stop sounding like the *yebani* Oracle and get to the point."

"I think the CIA are after us."

Petrovitch became stock still. Even when Wong banged down two more mugs and swept away the empties, he didn't react.

Chain leaned back, making his seat creak in protest. "Did you hear what I said?"

"Yeah. I heard. What makes you think that?"

"This is not the best place to discuss the evidence." Chain regarded his fellow diners, who appeared to be entirely disinterested in anything he might say. Or do.

"I'm not taking this on trust," said Petrovitch. "You're a *pizdobol* at the best of times."

"I'm limited to what I can show you, but come in tomorrow."

Petrovitch smirked. "Don't you think I'm going to be busy tomorrow?"

"Enjoy your fifteen minutes of fame. It'll be something to remember fondly while you pace your cell and tear at your orange jumpsuit." Chain picked up his coffee and gulped at it.

"You're actually serious."

Chain leaned forward again, his chest almost across the tabletop. "They're desperate to know what happened during the Long Night, and there are only three people who know the whole story. Four, if you count your Doctor Ekanobi. I hear rumors: some of them are even true, though it would take anyone else years of sorting to get the full picture. But that's why the CIA are here. They suppose if it can happen to the Metrozone, it can happen to one of their cities. This has their highest threat level, and their top priority."

"Why don't we do something radical?" Petrovitch stretched his neck out toward Chain and whispered: "Why don't we just tell them what happened?"

"You shot an American citizen."

"He was *tovo*. He'd killed, what, two dozen cops by blowing them up? You said yourself he had form for that, and *yobany stos,* he had his own father murdered." Petrovitch pushed his glasses back up his face. "The Director'll probably give me a medal for services rendered."

"And the Jihad?" hissed Chain, "What about the Jihad?"

Petrovitch's sardonic smile slipped. "Yeah. Yeah, okay. That's going to be a problem."

"They'll want whatever you managed to save of Oshicora's VirtualJapan. They won't want to share it. They'll want it for the exclusive use of Uncle Sam, and my guess is that they'll eliminate everyone who knows about it before they carry it back to the Pentagon."

"Langley," said Petrovitch. "CIA headquarters is in Langley, Virginia."

Chain grabbed Petrovitch's lapels and pulled him nose to nose. "If you don't want the world to face a weaponized AI in five years' time—a world without you, Madeleine, your friend Doctor Ekanobi, or me in it—cut the crap. The Sorenson woman's turning up isn't a coincidence, it's a sign. They're getting ready to move, and you being famous all of a sudden will not save you or anyone around you."

Petrovitch looked down. "Let go, Chain. I've been getting self-defense lessons from a very good teacher, and I'd hate to damage you."

Chain released his grip, and the two parted, glaring at each other across the cracked and pitted formica. Eventually, Petrovitch raised his gaze to see Wong standing by his counter, hand resting on a meat cleaver.

Petrovitch shook his head slightly, and Wong went back to swabbing empty tables with disinfectant.

"You told Sonja any of this yet?"

Chain pursed his lips. "I thought it'd be better coming from you."

"Thanks. You know how much Maddy likes me seeing her. Considering the *govno* I'm going to get, I may as well just suggest a threesome."

"Go on your way to work, Petrovitch. You don't have to tell Madeleine you took a diversion."

"And you wonder why you're still single." He swilled the last of his coffee and dragged himself to his feet. He was more tired than he realized. Despite two mugs of rocket fuel, he felt a bone-deep weariness lay on him like a blanket.

"Think about it," said Chain. "But not for long: you know where to find me."

"Yeah. Middle of your spider's web, just like last time." Petrovitch squeezed out from behind the table. He waved at the owner as he passed. "Night, Wong."

Wong folded his arms. "You still bad man. Sleep well."

5

Petrovitch made the long walk in from Clapham, through ruined Battersea to the Thames. Waterlogged bricks had cascaded into the roads in blocks and sheets, exposing the rooms behind. Thick sulphurous mud was banked up either side of the road, oozing slowly back under its own gelatinous weight.

He wasn't the only one walking, but that there were so few of them was disturbing. The heart of the city had been ripped out by the flood and the machines. Now the surrounding limbs were being severed by the Outies. His beloved Metrozone—he was doing what he could, but it wasn't going to be enough. He'd saved it from the Jihad, only to see it die a slow, tortured death, rotting from the inside and eaten from the out.

Streets that were once so full of life were like the buildings either side of them: empty. So very sad.

The north end of the bridge was guarded by MEA troops. He'd remembered to put the Ceska back in its pouch when he'd got back from Wong's. He had nothing left to declare, only his own genius.

It took time to pass through, all the same. Cities with checkpoints, with areas under curfew, with daily gun battles and bombings: they faltered, and the Metrozone was already on its knees.

Ahead of him in the queue, the soldiers caught some kid with a knife tucked in the top of his sock. They bundled him away into the back of a van, and the doors closed behind him.

The van didn't drive away. It rocked and boomed, the light twisting off the mirrored windows. The doors hadn't opened again by the time Petrovitch had walked under the screen's arch. He took his diversion toward Green Park.

The *nikkeijin,* refugees once before, now had nowhere else to go. Sonja, showing some of her father's skill, paid them when no one else would. They cleaned the corpses and the rats from the ground floors. They pumped and shoveled the basements. They used pressure hoses on the stone flags outside. They spread outward, scraping and sifting as they went.

Petrovitch passed one blue-overalled team as they shifted the filth off the tarmac with the aid of a bulldozer, then dug into the resulting mounds of ordure with spades, flinging it high into the back of a waiting truck. With hoods drawn tight over their heads and soft white surgical masks obscuring their faces, only their eyes were showing and they were giving nothing away.

Behind them, in the area they'd already swept that day and on previous days, were meters of tape between the lamp-posts, together with markers on the buildings to show their conditions. Much of it was in *kanji* script, and MEA had its own obscure coding underneath, strings of letters and numbers.

The *kanji* called to him. He had been able to read it once, fluent as a native. That it had been a trick, a contrivance of virtual reality, mattered less than the fact it had rewired his brain. If he caught it right, a momentary glance, he felt as if he could make out the meaning behind the symbols.

This house is uninhabitable from the second floor down. This house poses an unacceptable biological hazard. Five bodies were retrieved from the ground floor of this property.

He blinked, and it was gone. He looked up, and there was the Oshicora Tower, in the midst of fallen skyscrapers and broad, crushed concrete avenues. In front of the doors were two figures, both strangely slight, almost elfin.

One was a man, young, slim, as sharp and flexible as the blade he carried across his back. He had a carbine, too, folding stock already tucked into his right armpit. He wore armor, but it didn't seem to encumber him in any way. He carried himself like the samurai he'd always dreamed of becoming—and now his loyalty to the one who had made that possible was absolute. And not a little scary.

The other: Petrovitch still remembered her as a furious, smoke-tainted hostage and as a savage *katana*-wielding avenger. Here she was as smart businesswoman, wearing a dawn-gray pencil skirt and tailored jacket. It didn't fit easily with his memories, but maybe he was just uncomfortable around suits.

The man, Miyamoto, tracked his every step across the wide plaza, standing close behind his employer. He withdrew slightly as Petrovitch approached, not because he wanted to or because he trusted the other man at all: he was expected to, and that was all.

"Hey," said Petrovitch, his breath condensing about him.

Sonja Oshicora smiled. "It's good to see you."

Petrovitch pushed his glasses back up the bridge of his nose. "Yeah. And you."

"It's been a long time. You only work down the road. Maybe…"

"Or maybe not. You know why."

"Are you happy, Sam?" she asked. She was wearing lipstick. She never used to.

"I'd be happier if the city wasn't *pizdets*. We're losing her: six months, a year, two. I don't think it matters how long it takes. You can shovel *govno* by the barge-load, but it's…"

"Inevitable? I know." She stepped closer to him, and Petrovitch forced himself not to retreat. "You can always leave. Lots of people have."

"You stayed."

"But you're not staying because of me, are you?"

"No," he said. "The world has become a complicated place, and I don't know where I stand anymore. You heard about yesterday?"

"Of course." She ran her finger through her fringe, and the hair fell back like it was made of rain. "Who's the blonde?"

He didn't know what she meant for a moment. "Oh. Her. McNeil. She's a—she's one of my students."

"Does she have a first name?"

"Yeah. It's," and he screwed his face up, "Fiona. That's it."

"And what has Madeleine to say about it?"

"She hasn't said anything. I've only just realized it doesn't look brilliant and I've seen it a dozen times." He shrugged. "I got caught up in the moment. I'm hugging Hugo just as hard."

"Be careful, Sam." Sonja looked up at him. "You might not recognize infatuation. But I do."

Petrovitch wore a pained expression. "Really?"

She nodded.

He scratched at his chin. It rasped. Then he remembered what he'd come for. "Harry Chain."

"Yes. Him. What does he want?" Her antipathy was clear from her tone.

"The CIA are in town, apparently, and not in an 'if you have a few moments, I'd like to ask you some questions' sort of way. Sorenson's sister is here as well, and Chain thinks the two are connected." He dug his hands in his coat pockets. "I suggested we just tell them everything rather than try and keep it all secret. Information wants to be free, and all that."

"But what about my father?" asked Sonja. "The...you know."

"That's precisely why I've decided to keep quiet for now." Petrovitch turned his face up to the sky. "It's not something we can keep up forever, though. We have to start thinking ahead. Where do we want to be in five years? Ten years? We're going from day to day with no clear vision of what we'll become, and it'll be the death of us. This is just survival, but we need more than that."

"Sam..."

"I've spent years hiding. All that left me with is more to hide." He let his head fall. "I'm tired, Sonja. I've got the world's press waiting for me, and all because I made something the size of a grapefruit fly. That wasn't even hard. What we did in the Long Night: now that was hard, and we can't tell anyone about it."

"You're right," she said. "If you want to escape, I have the money and the contacts: we could always run away together."

Even though she was smiling, he knew she meant it. It cut deeper than Miyamoto's sword ever could. His heart spun faster and his skin prickled with sweat. Then a thought, tentative and tantalizing, entered his mind.

"You know what?" said Petrovitch. "That's not such a bad idea."

She gasped and pressed one immaculately manicured hand to her crisp, white blouse.

"I thought they only did that in movies," and he continued without a break. "No, really. We could all run away. This needs some serious work."

She found her breath. "What are you talking about?"

"I'll tell you when I've got some answers. In the meantime, what are we going to do about Charlotte Sorenson?"

"And the CIA," added Sonja.

"I don't believe the *zadnitza.* But Sorenson's sister will come here, and she didn't look like the sort of woman who'd take *govno* from anyone."

"I'll deal with her." She'd recovered from her momentary shock. "No need for her to even know you exist."

"You don't know what Sorenson told her."

"So I'll deal with her," she repeated.

"Not that way." Petrovitch finally got her meaning and he shook his head. "If she wants to see me, don't block her. That'll just look suspicious. And when it comes down to it, I killed her brother for lots of very good reasons. If I have to tell her about that, I will."

"And I will protect my father, Sam. Even from you."

"Yeah. I know." He scratched the nape of his neck, touching the ring of cold metal that lay flush with his skin. "Look, I'd better be off. Find a back door to sneak in."

"You should be happy, Sam. You've proved your equations

were right." She touched his arm, briefly, and Petrovitch stepped back from her, balancing on one heel and ready to turn. "Come up and see the park sometime."

"I don't know about that. I climbed all those stairs once: I'm not sure I want to do it again." He bit at his thumb. "I do use lifts, now. Sometimes. But not yours."

He spun away, raising his hand to the statue-still figure of Miyamoto. Petrovitch's coat swirled about him, and he headed off toward Hyde Park.

He was in a foul mood by the time he made it to the lab. He threw his coat down on an acid-etched bench and kicked out at a stool.

"Vsyo govno, krome mochee."

Then he realized he was alone for the first time in two hours, enveloped in a silence that made his ears ring. He sat down at a desk—it looked like Dominguez's—and flipped his glasses off.

Next to a picture frame that scrolled Spanish views was a half-empty mug of coffee. Which meant it was half-full, and he fell on it gratefully, swilling the lukewarm brew down in gulps. He hadn't done the eating thing either, and he idly rolled out the drawers, the same ones where he might keep his own stash of food in his own desk.

Nothing. And he wasn't going to brave the canteen after the ludicrous scrum that had developed in the foyer. The paycops had been worse than useless, holding up their own cameras rather than trying to keep order. Even then, when he'd agreed to answer some questions, sitting on the reception desk to gain some height over the crowd, no one had the wit to ask him anything to do with the experiment itself. There'd been no attempt to understand the physical principles behind the effect or interrogate him on the direction of future investigations.

That had made him as angry as the constant shouts of "How do you feel?"

It was novelty they were seeking, not enlightenment.

He'd dismissed them all with a growl, and pushed through to safety with practiced elbows. Even then, he'd escaped from the frying pan only to find the fire.

The university hierarchy, with patent lawyers in tow, tried to stitch him up in words so complex he could barely fight his way out again. In the end, he'd signed nothing: no verbal agreement to any course of action, no appending his thumbprint to any document that would take longer to read than the lifetime of the universe.

"You can't copyright physics," said a voice.

Petrovitch looked up, saw only a blur. He patted around for his glasses and fitted the arms over his ears.

McNeil: she'd made no effort to dress up for the press either. Same old jeans, same old sweatshirt, no makeup or jewelry.

"Sorry?"

"What you said: you can't copyright physics." She sat down on the edge of Dominguez's desk. "I agree."

"Yeah, well. No one cares what we think. Not anymore." He scratched at the corner of his eye. "Last night I dreamed that I was in a park—somewhere warm, not here—and the place was stiff with kids; little kids, babies, toddlers, teenagers, no one older than us, anyway. They all had spheres, and they were playing with them. Sliding them to each other, patting them so they bounced and spun, pushing them away and then running after them. Some of the bigger ones had made up a football-like game, with trees for goalposts, and others had stuck them to trays or bits of wood and were surfing on them. They all looked like they were having a really great time: certainly no one was telling them they'd have to hand their spheres back because they broke copyright."

She reached across and picked up his—Dominguez's— mug. "Want a fresh one?"

"Yeah. Sure."

She busied herself at a sink, her back to him. "What are you going to do?"

"Now? I don't know."

Dominguez shouldered his way in. He saw McNeil and was about to say something, then he spotted Petrovitch and changed his mind.

Petrovitch wasn't inclined to move. He sat, drumming the desktop with a fingernail tattoo, while Dominguez put his bag down on a bench.

"We have moved the mass balance downstairs, as you requested," he said.

Petrovitch looked around. He finally noticed that the machine had gone.

"Yeah. So you have." He sat up and stilled his hands. "Look, sit down, both of you. I think I do know what I'm going to do next."

They pulled up chairs and waited expectantly. Petrovitch wondered what their reaction might be.

"We need a break from all this. We're not going to get any proper work done around here for a few days anyway, until the dust settles and things get back to normal. So: we're going to do something different. A *gedankenversuch*."

"A what?" asked Dominguez.

"Thought experiment," murmured McNeil, then to Petrovitch: "Into what?"

"Society. I want you to go and design me a human society. Not a utopia: one that acknowledges its faults and includes mechanisms to correct itself. One that's better than the one we have now. Info-rich. Post-scarcity. Knowledge as currency. Stuff like that." Petrovitch looked at their bemused faces. "Can you do it?"

Dominguez frowned his heavy brows. "I suppose so. Can I ask why? Is this part of our training?"

Petrovitch sat back, lacing his fingers together behind his head. "Yeah. It is. It's a mistake to be an expert in just one narrow field. You need to be able to read widely and apply your smarts to any problem. Let's see how you deal with this one."

"You said a few days." McNeil leaned forward. Her interest and enthusiasm had been piqued, and her usually pale cheeks were slightly flushed. "How long do we have?"

"What's today?"

"Tuesday," she said.

"Friday, then. On my desk by Friday." He got up, pushing the chair back with a flick of his knees. "Don't be late."

6

*H*e'd barely got back to his own office when his leg rang. He let it trill while he put the kettle on—he'd somehow missed out on McNeil's offer—then delved inside the pocket.

It wasn't her, but he did recognize the caller.

"*Yobany stos,* Chain. You're not even supposed to have this number."

"Very slick, Petrovitch. I particularly liked the stream of invective you launched at the bloke who asked 'Dude, where's my flying car?' And you wonder why the public look on science news as irrelevant?"

"No, I don't wonder at all. It's because every last one of you enjoys wallowing in pig-shit ignorance. Why did you call? I think I said everything I wanted to last night."

"There've been developments."

"Tell you what, Chain. I'm a physicist. You're a MEA intelligence officer. I won't ask you to reshape human destiny, and you can stop trying to get me to do your job for you."

"We've found a prowler."

Petrovitch tucked the phone in the angle between his shoulder and his ear. He poured his coffee dregs into the pot plant and hunted for the jar of freeze-dried granules. "I'm assuming that word means something special."

"A sort of robot. It was active, and armed."

"A Jihadi leftover?" He shook a tablespoon of coffee into his mug and stood over the kettle, waiting for it to boil.

"Don't think so. There are reasons to suspect otherwise."

"And you're going to tell me what those reasons are, or do I have to guess?"

"The Jihad made things out of what came to hand. This was meant."

Finally, steam started to rise from the spout. He flicked the off switch and poured the water out. "This is still not my problem, Chain."

"It's American."

"Yeah? It has the stars and stripes painted on the outside?"

"I think you're missing the point."

Petrovitch cleaned a spoon on his trousers. "Go on, then. Tell me the point." He took the mug back to his desk and stirred as he listened.

"Do you know how those things work? Short-range radio control. Doesn't have to be line of sight, but the operator isn't normally more than a couple of kilometers away. It killed two of the team that stumbled across it before they managed to frag it with a grenade. The resulting explosion killed another of them. This was in the Outzone, on the southern fringe of Epping Forest."

"Okay."

"Is that all you're going to say?" said Chain.

"Pretty much. I'll concede that it looks like the Yanks are in the Metrozone, for whatever reason. Have you talked to them about it yet?"

"No."

"Why not?" Petrovitch turned sideways to the desk and stretched out. "This, all of this, is stupid. They know you know. They're waiting to see what you do. You can join in their game and be all sneaky, or you can play it straight. Someone—presumably an American agent—killed three MEA soldiers using this robot. The only guarantee you have is that they'll think they can do whatever the *huy* they like if you don't complain loud and long right now."

"If I do anything," said Chain, "they'll pull back and have another go with a different team in a month's time. I need to catch them red-handed."

"No, no you don't, you *balvan*! This is Oshicora all over again, except this time it's you versus the United States government." Petrovitch was on his feet, yelling down the phone. "I learned not to trust you last time. Me, Maddy, Pif, Sonja—if you won't keep us safe, I will. Tell the Yanks to back off, or I'll find a way to do it myself."

He ended the call, and for good measure, threw the phone across the room.

He scalded himself on his coffee, forgetting how hot it would be. Pressing his thumb hard against his lips, he felt the heat spread.

Then Petrovitch picked up the phone again and dialed Chain.

"If you wanted something, why didn't you ask?"

"Because I'm embarrassed," came the reply. "We employ forensic specialists, we pay them good money to work for MEA, and sometimes, just sometimes, it'd be really great if they actually turned up to do an honest day's labor. I have the parts we retrieved from the scene before we were chased off by the Outies. They're laid out in a warehouse, and I can't get any usable information from it because I don't know how."

There was a blister forming, and there was nothing Petrovich could do about it. Ice would be good, but he knew there was nothing below zero in the building other than cryogenic nitrogen.

"I ought to tell you to *poshol nahuj*."

"But not today."

"No. Not today. Where is this warehouse?"

"The old train shed at King's Cross."

"And how many people know about this?" Petrovitch picked up his coat and shrugged it on, one arm at a time. "Because if it's more than you and me, I'd bet my *babushka's* life the Yanks know it, too."

"Maybe half a dozen people. I have a chain of command I have to inform."

"So we'd better get down there before the evidence disappears. Meet me out front in five."

Petrovitch sat on the steps, waiting. A huge four-wheel-drive car—more a small lorry than anything a private citizen would think necessary—put two tires up on the curb and the darkened window hummed down.

"Hey. Good to see you still have the coat."

Petrovitch got to his feet and walked across the pavement. "Grigori? *Yobany stos!* What happened to the Zil?"

Grigori grinned apologetically. "Comrade Marchenkho managed to get a UN reconstruction contract. We all have these fancy autos now." He slapped his hand on the outside of the door, leaving his fingerprints in the dirt. "Armored. Very tough."

"How is the old goat?"

"Better for not having Oshicora around. His blood pressure is much lower these days. The Long Night worked out well for us."

Petrovitch pressed his fingertips against his chest. No pulse, just the throb of a turbine. The Ukrainian noticed the ring on his finger.

"That?" said Petrovitch. "I suppose it worked out well for me, too. In a narrowly-avoided-death-repeatedly way." He looked up and down the street. "Look, is this meeting a happy accident, or has Marchenkho sent you? Only I'm expecting Harry Chain any minute now and if he sees me talking to you, he'll go *kon govno* crazy."

Grigori beckoned him closer. "Marchenkho sends his congratulations, and an open invitation for a drink."

"Yeah. We can swear loudly and point guns at each other in a vodka-fueled frenzy: just like old times."

"Also a warning. There are people..."

"There often are."

He shook his head. "No. You must take this seriously. They have been asking questions about the Long Night. They know of the New Machine Jihad, and that the Oshicora Tower was involved. Beyond that?" Grigori shrugged. "We don't know what went on, only that it involved you."

"I'd heard someone was taking an interest."

"Who are they? Union investigators? They do not behave like the Union."

"No. Not the Union." Petrovitch's face twitched.

"Who, then?"

"The CIA. Tell Marchenkho to give Chain a call. And speak of the devil." A battered gray car rattled up behind Grigori's behemoth.

Grigori looked at his rear-view mirror. "What do you want us to do?"

Petrovitch pushed himself away from the open window. He could see Chain's squashed face behind his steering wheel. "Keep an eye on my back, will you? I don't trust this lot to do anything but stand round and stare at my rapidly cooling corpse."

"Is done," said Grigori. *"Dobre den, tovarisch."*

The window buzzed upward, and the four-by-four bounced back into the street.

Chain leaned across his car and threw the passenger door open. Petrovitch sauntered over and clambered in.

"What," said Chain, "did he want?"

"Marchenkho's invited me around for cocktails one evening. Black tie affair, you wouldn't be interested."

"And really?"

"I can easily get back out and do something constructive. Or you can just drive." Petrovitch tugged at the seat belt to strap himself in, but when Chain muttered something under his breath, he changed his mind and made to get out. "Fine. See you later."

"Okay, okay." Chain pulled onto the road without signaling, or even checking it was clear. "Do you have any idea how stressful this job is?"

"No. Neither do I care." Petrovitch twisted around in his seat and looked out of the rear window. "I have troubles of my own."

"You could always leave," said Chain, echoing Sonja's remark of earlier. "After yesterday, I imagine you could go pretty much anywhere. Take that wife of yours somewhere she's not going to get shot at."

"Funny you should say that," said Petrovitch. There was

no one following them. Not that that didn't preclude the possibility that they were being watched every moment. He turned back and finished strapping himself in.

"Meaning?"

"Nothing for you to worry about. Now, about this prowler."

"Five minutes ago, you'd never even heard the word."

"Yeah. And now I'm a *yebani* expert." He dipped his hand into his pocket and pulled out the rat. "Let's see. Tracked vehicle, roughly pyramidal, sensor array on a central pylon, gyrojet weapons laterally positioned, each with a two-hundred-degree arc of fire, short-range scattergun. Powered by four rechargeable nanotube batteries, EMP hardened electronics. Any of this sounding familiar?"

"Worryingly so."

"Then you've got the genuine article." He looked up from his screen. They were passing Hyde Park. Empty, now. The last remains of the shanty town were blowing in the wind: torn plastic, loose sheets of cardboard, tatters of cloth flapped against the boards surrounding the park. The bulldozers had moved in, had been moving in for a month now, and the work had stalled. Some Metrozone assemblyman wanted all the bodies that lay on and under the park exhumed and buried elsewhere. "Another thing."

"Which is?" asked Chain, when Petrovitch didn't continue.

He tore his gaze from the window. "Self-destruct mechanism. These things are mobile thermobaric bombs. My guess is the MEA grenade pre-ignited the fuel–air mix before it reached its critical concentration. That's why you've got bits left to look at. Another second or so, and you'd have lost everyone and everything, turned inside out by the shockwave and incinerated."

"Translated?"

"You got lucky."

"I'll remember to pass that along to the next of kin"; Chain grunted as he hauled the car around Marble Arch.

"What was it guarding?"

"I . . . don't understand."

Petrovitch snapped the rat shut. "Clearly. These things aren't tourists, Chain—it was keeping the Outies away from something, probably had done for a while, when the MEA patrol just happened to stumble across it and it all went *pizdets*. Take a look at the satellite images—near infrared if you can get them—or just swamp the area with soldiers until you find whatever it was."

The last time he'd been up the Edgware Road, he'd been on his way to rescue Sonja from the Paradise militia. Madeleine's church had been at the top end of the street, before it had been burned down and a Jihad demolition robot had stirred the rubble.

It was at the start of an arrow-straight line that cut a swathe all the way to the East End.

"Petrovitch?"

"Yeah?"

"I'm talking to you."

He tried to blink away the images that were burned onto his retina. "Looks like I'm not listening."

The domik pile on Regent's Park had been kicked over by the same robot, heading northwest. Four months on, the chaos of spilled containers was being taken apart by teams of thieves with gas axes, burning their way through the labyrinth one death-filled space at a time.

"You lived there, didn't you?"

"No. I had a bolt-hole there. Different. One of the

high-up domiks." Regent's Park slid by and out of sight. "I wonder if they've got to it yet?"

"Leave anything of interest inside?"

"No." He tried a smile, and found it didn't fit. "I was always careful."

"That's a matter for debate." Chain threaded his way through the drift of rubble either side of the Hampstead Road junction, then picked up speed again. He took the car down a side road and toward a tall chain-link fence.

He pressed his knees against the underside of the steering wheel and, using both hands, felt in his pockets for his card.

"Chyort." Petrovitch reached over and steered them, more or less, toward the gate. "You may as well not bother. There's no one to show it to."

Chain applied the brakes and the car jerked to a halt, front bumper almost touching the fence. He left the engine idling and got out.

Petrovitch joined him and, together, they peered through the mesh.

"Hey," Chain called. "Major Chain, MEA."

"Yeah. Your spidey senses not tingling yet?" Petrovitch buried his fists in the grid of metal and heaved. The gate swung open with a tinny rattle. Beyond was a short street of anonymous prefab factory units, dwarfed by the station concourse next door.

Chain fumbled for his gun. "I don't suppose you're carrying?"

"No. Not at the moment."

"Look in the boot."

Petrovitch backed away from the gate and popped the lid of the boot. When he closed it again, he was feeding cartridges into an automatic shotgun. "You called for help?" he asked.

"I've done that." Chain looked up at the buildings either side of the concrete road. "They may be some time."

"Well," said Petrovitch, sitting down on the warm bonnet, "I can wait."

"Aren't you coming?" Chain looked back at him.

"This is well beyond my pay-grade, Chain. When it's safe, you can call me."

Chain dithered for a moment, grinding his heel against the loose grit. He shrugged his shoulders and started to walk.

The explosion started small: a white flash of light behind a ground-floor window. The walls flicked off a coat of dust and started to swell, like they were taking in a mighty breath. Then they failed in a roar of black smoke and orange fire. The roof was briefly in the sky, all in one piece, girders and corrugated iron sheets. It peeled apart and started to fall back to earth, one sharp spinning piece after another.

Petrovitch rolled back, turning. He was crouched on the top of the car. Things were flying toward him, rather quicker than he could run. He jumped, and the blast caught him while he was still in the air.

He was thrown down like a doll, and the ground was very hard indeed.

7

*H*e could taste blood, and he was certain it was his. Dust and smoke swirled all around: his lungs were full of it, and the skin on his face was scrubbed wet by the rough road. His ears were ringing.

Petrovitch lay there and blinked, trying to make sense of what had just happened. His glasses were awry, and he dragged a hand out from beneath him to straighten them. There was blood on his palms, too.

He took a breath, coughed hard, and focused on the shotgun lying in front of him. He reached out and dragged it toward him, then used it to push himself upright.

The bombed building had fallen in on itself, extinguishing the fire beneath, but all around were shattered windows and flames twisting from them. A column of black ash rose thick into the air before being blown ragged in the wind. Behind the noise in his head was the clamor of alarms.

Chain's car was between him and what was left of the fence, its paintwork now scarred by more than age and the occasional knock. The open doors had lost all their glass, the front tires their air.

Petrovitch limped to where the gate lay flattened against the ground.

"Chain!"

No sign of him. Popping supports, snapping walls, cracking rafters, but no Chain.

He slung the gun over his shoulder and cupped his hands around his mouth. "Chain!"

He could feel the heat from where he stood. Steam was rising from beneath his feet. He whirled around, seeing for the first time a straggling crowd forming back at the roundabout.

"Chain!"

He saw him. He saw his feet, his legs as far as his knees, laid out on the bonnet of his own car. The rest of him had been forced through the concave windscreen.

Petrovitch walked slowly toward him, aware that Chain wasn't moving his worn shoes, not even an involuntary twitch.

"Chain?"

He knew he had to check. He knew he didn't want to. He gripped the top of the door, steeling himself, then ducked down.

For a moment, he couldn't work out what he was looking at. Chain's head appeared to be missing, and then he saw it, bent back under his still and shattered body, caught between the two front seats.

Petrovitch straighted up, breathing hard. Everything seemed to be spinning, the sky, the smoke, the street. People were running toward him, running away from him, shouting incomprehensible things at him. He didn't understand.

And someone caught his eye.

A figure, all in black, was walking away up the Pancras Road. Walking. Reaching a line of bystanders and pushing through them, leaving them to turn and gesture angrily.

"Hey." Petrovitch slid the shotgun off his shoulder and into his hands. "Hey. You."

He chambered the first shell and started after him. Within a few steps, he was jogging, and so was the man. At least it looked like a man: tall, athletic, dressed like an athlete even, an all-in-one body suit with nothing flapping. A courier would have had a courier bag. This man had nothing.

Petrovitch speeded up, gauging a loping gait that would close the distance between them. The man responded in kind, and it quickly turned into a chase.

They were both running as fast as they could. Petrovitch reached the line of people and they scattered before him, taking in the state of his face, the big gun held across his body, the aura of utter blind rage seeping from every pore of his filthy, smoke-scarred skin.

Suddenly, he had a clear shot. He snapped the stock to his shoulder and his finger spasmed on the trigger. The recoil nearly tore his arm off. He spun and fell, the fresh pain serving only to stoke the fire inside.

He got up with a growl and started over again. The man was further ahead now, moving in fast, clean strides. Then he just seemed to disappear.

Petrovitch raced to the place where he'd last seen him. A road to his left went under the railway station—a deep long tunnel made wide by the pillared supports for the structures above.

He took a chance and took the turn. The colonnades

either side were home to the homeless. They stared at him as he ran by, but moments before they had all been looking down toward the small rectangle of daylight at the far end.

Framed in it, just for a second, was the man. He hesitated as he looked behind him, and Petrovitch fired again. This time he leaned in hard, and though the butt kicked back ferociously, he didn't screw up.

The road sparked just in front of his target, who clasped at his shin before running off again, going to the right, heading north.

Petrovitch kept going. Arms, legs pumping, coat streaming out behind him, heart spinning like it had never spun before. His breath came in rhythmic spurts, in, out, out, in, out, out. Trying to remember everything Madeleine had taught him: stride length, balance, keeping his head up even if he felt like hunching over, even if he felt like sinking to his knees and burying his head in his hands.

And he was gaining. He'd wounded the man, forced razor-sharp chips of road surface at his leg: even if they hadn't penetrated, the impact of them slowed him down. Whereas Petrovitch's cuts, grazes, that stabbing sensation in his face that felt like an electric shock every time his feet hit the tarmac, spurred him on.

The further they got from the site of the explosion, the more people were on the streets. They were looking up at the black cone of ascending smoke, or sometimes not even that, just out, just happening to be on the route of a man head to toe in black, sprinting by with an uneven step, and a few seconds later of a slight man with white-blond hair and a face streaming with bright red blood. The shotgun was almost incidental.

Petrovitch saw the man glance behind again, caught a glimpse of a wide mirrored band over his eyes. Hatnav: he was using hatnav, and knew precisely where he was, and where he needed to go. The case for Petrovitch's own overlays was in his pocket, banging up and down against his thigh, but he couldn't afford the time to put them on.

The sirens that had been converging on the yard behind King's Cross shifted subtly. They were coming up behind him.

The man he was chasing knew that as well. He had hacked feeds from MEA control center. He barreled right into a vast office building, squat and dirty, windows jagged and doors shattered.

Petrovitch went in too, blue and red lights flickering at his back. The dim foyer, the hanging ceiling panels where lights and wire had been ripped down, the skeletons of partition walls. It was a stupid place to be, where ambush was easy and hiding easier.

He brought up the gun and tracked its sights across the expanse of destroyed fittings and bird crap.

He heard a noise above him. The barrel jerked up and he let rip with another round, blowing a hole in the remains of the suspended ceiling and putting a crater into the concrete slab above.

MEA militia were right outside. He didn't have long before they stopped him.

Up the stairs. The man was heading for the roof. Even as Petrovitch pounded the steps in the stairwell, he realized that it didn't make any sense. If it'd been him, he'd have stuck to the ground floor. The area was vast, the cover good. By going up, he'd be trapped. MEA would just have to wait for him to come out.

So there had to be another reason, another plan, unless the man was a *balvan*. Which he could be.

There was sound on the stairs. A door popping open, a flash of daylight, then the door swinging back shut: he'd reached the top, and in a few seconds, so would Petrovitch.

He shouldered the door, and tumbled out onto the great plain of the roof. The black figure was really limping now, but still moving at a speed that put him halfway across the gray-green surface.

He could shoot and miss. He could force him up against the edge of the roof and make certain. He kept on going.

The man ahead jumped up onto the parapet and leaped. There was no hesitation, no momentary stall; a fluid up and over. Petrovitch's waist slammed into the barrier. He looked. A lower roof, and the man still running, still favoring his left leg.

It was at the limits of what Petrovitch thought he could hit, but he'd do it anyway. He took a deep breath, held it, and looked down the length of the gun. He had no heartbeat to bounce the sights, and he was, all of sudden, brutally calm.

Squeeze the trigger.

And the man jinked sideways. The roof where he'd been pocked and insulation fluffed out.

He had real-time satellite data. That cost money.

It was a long way down to that second roof. The man had done it, so Petrovitch was going to do it too. He landed in a heap, and he managed to hurt his wrist trying to roll with the blow. He got up, and restarted the same monotonous beat of one foot after another. He needed to keep his quarry on the move and not give him a moment's rest.

Ahead was a half-finished building, looking like it had

been half-finished for a long time. It wore a shroud of tattered plastic around its open floors and suspended beams.

If Petrovitch got his prey inside, his spy-in-the-sky would be useless.

The man seemed to be obliging. He jumped over the railings and onto the scaffolding tied to the side of the construction site. He hung on one of the crossbars, then started to slide downward, going hand over hand, slowing his fall.

As Petrovitch reached the edge, the man stopped and ducked into the building's shell, three stories lower, across a three-meter gap.

Petrovitch slung the shotgun over his back, climbed up and over and braced himself. If he fell now, he'd die. More to the point, the man would get away. He bent his legs and pushed out.

He flew across the distance, arms outstretched. The first level flashed past his eyes. His momentum carried him onto the platform below, slamming him down on the wooden boards laid across the scaffolding.

The whole structure shook. Someone had been borrowing pieces of it from the ground floor. But the building itself looked sound enough: no walls, no duct work, as empty as a car park. He picked himself up and shrugged the gun back into his cold grip.

He ghosted through the hall of pillars to where the stairwell was. No stairs, just a black pit all the way down. He'd come too far to give up: but that was just like him, always going too far when a saner mind would have called a halt.

He threw the gun down to the next slab of floor, then lowered himself off the edge until his fingers turned white and his feet dangled over the abyss. He swung his legs and let go.

He landed badly. Again. This time he jarred his back all the way from his coccyx to his shoulder blades. He looked around, saw nothing and repeated the process. Gun thrown. Body suspended and dropped. Spine-crushing impact.

Still nothing. The man had been on this level, and Petrovitch had arrived too late. He jumped to the next floor: the air was forced out of his lungs and he was left gasping.

A shadow came straight at him out of the gloom, with that injured skipping run. Petrovitch snatched up the gun, forcing himself to a sitting position.

The figure sprang clean over him before he could aim, and dropped into the stairwell. Petrovitch twisted awkwardly around, trying to keep his sights on him. The man's hands slapped down on the lip of the next floor down, and he used that slightest of touches to jack-knife his black-clad body to safety.

He looked up at Petrovitch, nose and mouth and chin a pale half-moon. Petrovitch looked down, past the knife that was sticking out of his chest, steel blade visible between nylon grip and the growing stain across the front of his T-shirt.

Maybe the man was waiting for Petrovitch to topple forward, down the stairwell, dead before he hit the bottom, dead for certain afterward. Or perhaps for the gun to slip from nerveless fingers and for him to sag backward, his life leaking away.

Petrovitch brought the shotgun up to his shoulder and fired his last shell. The solid slug tore a hole through the man's ribcage and punched out his spine. What remained folded into the center of the poppy-colored pattern blossoming on the concrete behind him.

The sound of the shot echoed away. Petrovitch was quite prepared to reverse the gun and beat out what life was left in his adversary. When it looked like that wasn't going to be necessary, he put the empty gun down beside him and curled his fingers around the knife handle.

He gave it a tug, and it felt like he was trying to pull his heart out, so he stopped. He could work it free by moving it from side to side, but that would cut more flesh. The point of the blade had sliced through his muscle, between his ribs, and embedded itself in the kevlar patch that covered his implant.

He might even consider himself lucky, when he had the luxury of time.

The chase was over. The adrenaline that had powered his fury was draining away. He hurt now, all over, from the acid pain in his face to the dull, numbing ache of his legs. And more.

He got to his feet, staggering like a drunkard, stumbling from one pillar to the next, until he got to the scaffolding.

Most of the MEA militia were still back at the first office building. One or two had heard the last shot, and were tentatively suggesting to their superiors that they should investigate.

Petrovitch wrapped the crook of his elbow around one of the scaffolding poles and leaned out. It wasn't far, but it was far enough. He clutched his knees to one of the downtubes and shinned down, taking exaggerated care not to knock the knife handle.

The first MEA soldier raised his pistol at Petrovitch, the second pushed it back down and pointed.

Petrovitch peeled his glasses free and scrubbed at his eyes. "Yeah. The *mudak* brought a knife to a gunfight."

Overwhelmed by abrupt exhaustion, he slumped to his knees in front of them, and hung his head low over the ground. Tears as well as blood dripped into the dust.

They'd killed Harry Chain.

8

*I*t was the other way round this time, with Petrovitch sitting in the waiting room, bandaged and drugged, dressed in disposable paper pajamas, waiting for a shadow to fall across the glass panel and the door to open.

He had no rosary beads to click the time away. Instead, he lay back in his seat, eyes closed, realizing that the world had changed so much, so quickly, and that he really wasn't in control of it anymore.

The door didn't so much open as implode. He knew who it was. He could smell her fear and outrage on the gust of air that preceded her.

"You idiot!" She balanced on the balls of her feet, deciding whether to kiss him or kick him through the wall. She did neither. She was carrying a fresh T-shirt and a new pair of trousers for him, and she threw the bundle at him at full force. "What were you thinking? You could have been killed!"

He hadn't been thinking, of course. Nothing but blind revenge, the desire to make someone pay.

"You're not to do that ever again, do you understand

me? Never again. Leave it to someone else, leave it to someone who has a gram of common sense, someone who's
paid to take the risks, someone who's actually trained to
weigh up those risks and make some sort of rational decision, rather than you because you're not any of those things.
What were you even doing there in the first place?"

There was a lull in the storm of emotion that was
Madeleine.

He opened his eyes with difficulty. The right side of his
face was numb—injectable painkillers for his cracked
cheekbone—and the doctor had told him not to smile for
at least a month. That was one instruction he was probably
going to be able to follow without difficulty.

She was standing over him, hands on hips, looking
righteously angry and utterly magnificent in her gray
MEA fatigues. Her skin was even paler than usual, and
she was trembling.

"I cannot protect you if you do stuff like this," she said.
"I cannot save you if I am not there."

Petrovitch moved his clothes to one side and wiped
some drool away from the corner of his mouth. "Chain
called me."

"And you had to go." Her jaw set hard. "I am going to
kill him. Where is he?"

"I don't know. I imagine they're still trying to cut the
roof off his car so they can get his body out." He shrugged
the best he could. "Someone beat you to it."

The fight fell from her like a cut curtain. She sat down
next to him, making the chair look child-sized.

"What?"

"He called me. Said he had some bits and pieces from a
U.S. military robot, but needed them looked over to make

sure they were genuine. There was no one his end who'd turn out, so I said yes." He chewed at his lip, tasted anti-septic, and grimaced. It hurt, in a good way.

"You could have—should have—said no. He had no business asking you."

"When they come for us in the night, to try and take us away to wherever it is they take people like us to torture for what we know, we'll discover it's been our business all along. Except it'll be too late to do anything about it. I need to know who they are, and what they're planning, because if I do, I can send them home with their tails between their legs."

She put her arm around him, her hand resting against the shoulder which had taken the brunt of the shotgun recoil. The paper clothes he was wearing rustled.

"I didn't believe him," he said. "I didn't trust him. Maybe…"

"He was just using you, as usual. You didn't even like him."

"Yeah. I know. And now he's gone, I can't even tell him what a *pizdobol* he was." Petrovitch leaned in against her, resting his head in the angle between her head and chest. "I knew something was wrong. There should have been a guard on the gate. He wanted to go on, I wanted to wait. So he did his thing, and I did mine. He was right in front of me, Maddy."

"He could have waited, just like you."

"I should have made him."

"When did he ever listen to you? He always did what he wanted." She pulled him close. "Stupid man."

"Ow," mumbled Petrovitch.

"Sorry," she said. She didn't let go.

They sat like that for a while, listening to the little

sounds each other made. The door opened again, and there was a man in uniform: jacket; crisp, white shirt; tie knot snug against his throat; trousers that could hold a crease in a hurricane. He was carrying a sidearm at his waist and a clear plastic bag in his hand.

"Apologies for the intrusion. Sergeant Petrovitch, Doctor Petrovitch?"

They looked up.

"Captain Daniels. Intelligence Division. I'm sorry for your loss."

"Loss?" said Petrovitch, sitting up. "Yeah. That. So am I."

Daniels held up the bag he was holding. "We need to keep this as evidence, but we can release it to you later, if you want."

Madeleine took the bag and examined the knife inside. "Where did you get this?"

"The surgeon took it out of your husband's chest, Sergeant."

She scowled at Petrovitch, and handed the bagged knife back. "It's a Ka-bar. American."

"They make them in Taiwan," said Petrovitch, putting his hand on the dressing over his heart. "Could have come from anywhere."

"No, it couldn't," she said. "It could only have come from my fool of a husband, who in ten years' time will have to have had everything important replaced with plastic and metal."

She stood up, forcing the captain back, and resumed her hands-on-hips accusation of Petrovitch.

"Anything else you need to tell me? Lost an eye, a leg? Been fitted with a robotic spleen? Because they've already replaced your brain with a fifty-cent pocket calculator."

"Depends," said Petrovitch.

"On what?"

"On how much they told you." He looked over the top of his glasses. "Do we have to do this now?"

"Then when? I don't see you doing anything else important right now—unless you've arranged another press conference to hurl abuse at."

"Perhaps I should come back later," ventured Daniels.

"No, we're done here. You're supposed to tell me everything, Sam. Everything."

She stormed out, leaving Petrovitch with his head in his hands.

"That went well," he said. "What can I do for you, Captain?"

"I need to ask you some questions. Are you sure this is a good time?"

"Yeah. She's right: I'm not doing anything else, so questions are fine. I'll do what I can. Can I just ask you one first?"

Daniels pointed to the seat vacated by Madeleine, and Petrovitch nodded his assent. The captain sat down smartly, back ramrod straight.

"How much trouble am I in? If the guy I killed was just a regular citizen who liked dressing up as a ninja, I'm screwed."

"If that was the case," said Daniels, "you'd be under arrest by now."

"I'm supposed to be smart. Everyone tells me so. I could've thrown it all away." Petrovitch scrubbed at his scalp with his fingernails. "I think I have some apologies to make."

Daniels' face twitched. "He doesn't appear on the

Metrozone database. Most likely an Outie, judging from his appearance."

"Good job I didn't shoot him in the head, then."

"Quite. You were suspicious?"

"I'm a street kid. I know how people behave when they're scared, surprised, shocked. This man was too calm, like he knew what had happened, like he'd made it happen. It was just wrong."

"You chased him."

"And he ran. I looked like *govno* and I was carrying a *pushka*. I would've run from me, too, though I like to think I would have got away." Petrovitch shifted in his chair. The pain was starting to seep through the haze of morphine.

"You didn't think that someone who leaped from tall buildings was someone you should stay away from?"

"Yeah. Well. It was a little late for that. I was committed."

Daniels kept his hands on his knees. He didn't record any of Petrovitch's answers, merely soaked them up like a sponge.

"You were with Major Chain at his request, yes?"

"Yeah. He called me. Said there were no tech guys around."

"Is it something he did often?"

"No. No, he didn't."

"So why this time?"

Petrovitch shrugged. "Desperation. He was in a hurry. Couldn't wait. That's why he died in the explosion and I didn't."

"So how did you and the major know each other?"

It was time to start lying. He could do it, as natural as breathing, even to the urbane Captain Daniels.

"I was a witness, one of his old cases from back when he was plain old Detective Inspector Chain. Nothing ever came of it, but we'd talk every couple of weeks." Petrovitch pushed his glasses toward the bridge of his nose. "He was checking up on me, I suppose."

"You obviously made a big impression on him," said Daniels.

Petrovitch gave a momentary frown. "Why d'you say that?"

"He made you his next of kin." Daniels lost his composure for the first time, and sounded genuinely surprised. "Didn't you know?"

"No. No, I didn't. Why didn't the old *kozel* say anything?" Petrovitch inspected his bandaged palms. "What does that mean, next of kin?"

"It means he nominated you to receive any outstanding pay, in-service benefits. That sort of thing. Human Resources will tell you more." Daniels reclaimed his self-control. "There should be enough to pay for a funeral, at least."

"Hah," said Petrovitch mirthlessly. "So that's what he was after: mourners. You see, Captain, there's no one else. No one to mark the passing of Harry Chain but me. No friends, no family. That's what a lifetime of pissing people off leads to."

He levered himself to his feet, the sudden surge of blood to his extremities making everything tingle. His face was frozen, his shoulder one big bruise, his hands and knees scrubbed raw and clean with only a layer of vat skin beneath the bandages. There was a hole in his chest that went all the way down to a notch on the surface of his heart, and that meant yet another scar on the road-map that was his ribcage.

He paced the floor, working the life back into himself.

"Do you know what it was he wanted you to look at?" asked Daniels.

"Don't you lot talk to each other?"

"Of course. I wanted to know if the major had told you."

"Yeah, he told me."

"Did you believe him?"

Petrovitch was flushing out the drugs from his system, feeling sharper by the minute. "No, of course not. I was going along to prove to him all he had were a couple of windscreen wiper motors and a bent aerial. Then some *govnosos* Outie takes out half the district and Chain goes to his grave thinking he was right."

"So you don't buy the CIA story?"

"No," said Petrovitch. "Do you?"

"I couldn't possibly say. Classified." Daniels was nowhere near as good at lying as Petrovitch. "You also need to remember that Major Chain was in breach of protocol when he talked to you."

"Yeah. Not a word."

"Thank you for your time, Doctor Petrovitch." Daniels adjusted his cuffs and stood, remembering to pick up the bagged knife as he did so. "I expect I'll see you again when you come to collect Major Chain's personal effects. Or we can courier them to you, whichever you prefer."

Petrovitch affected a moment's thought. "I'll come and get them. The least I can do, I guess."

Daniels extended his hand, and Petrovitch shook it gingerly. "Get well soon, Doctor."

"Thanks for not arresting me."

"These are difficult times for us all. If only everyone was as civic-minded as you."

Petrovitch suppressed his snort of derision until he was alone. Daniels didn't fool him, and he wondered if he fooled anyone. The uniform might work on some people, but not him: he'd had nothing but trouble from men—always men—strutting around as if they were on parade.

The man he'd killed wasn't an Outie. No chance whatsoever, even discounting the satellite gear and the stealth suit, or the coincidence that the one building he'd bombed was the one where Chain had stashed the prowler components. It had been his teeth. They'd been even, white, perfect, glowing while bared in a feral snarl in the semi-darkness. No Outie, and precious few Metrozone dwellers, had teeth that good.

He'd bet good money that Daniels was running a gene assay right now, checking for military-grade bio-hacks, and that he thought the CIA were odds-on favorites for killing Harry Chain.

Petrovitch got his clothes on, and rescued his boots and coat. His rat was still in his pocket, along with the other bits and pieces he kept there. Not like last time. His fingers wouldn't lace his boots, and he ended up tucking the loose ends inside.

Madeleine was sitting in the reception area, counting her beads while having one eye on the television screen. She stopped clicking and tucked them away as he slopped closer.

"I would pull you up," he said, "except I'm more likely to rip both my arms out of their sockets."

She chewed at her lip. "I don't want to lose you, just when I've found you."

"Yeah. It was crazy. I should never have done it. That I got away with it doesn't excuse anything. Sorry."

"And it won't happen again?" She fixed him with a needle-like stare.

He blew out his breath in a thin stream. "Slight problem with that." He looked around: there were other people present, and what he wanted to say wasn't for public consumption. He did notice that he'd fallen further down the news cycle: the morning's bombing had knocked him lower. "Can we go and find something to eat? I need to tell you everything."

9

*P*etrovitch was shown into an office—which was in a different building to when Chain was a policeman, with a different view from the windows—and still recognized the hallmarks of the man.

There was a coffee maker in one corner, surrounded by the paraphernalia of making: dirty mugs, dirty spoons, two empty foil packets of filter coffee and one closed with a red clip. Filters were scattered like autumn leaves on the floor, spilling from the box on the shelf above.

Flimsy pieces of paper sat in randomly allocated piles on every flat surface, daring the erstwhile occupant to open the window and lose all order. Filing cabinets bulged with files. His desk was crammed, too, along with what brief ephemera he considered important.

There wasn't much room between the furniture and the walls: being a major in a bankrupt militia held even less prestige than a detective inspector.

"Yeah. Okay," said Petrovitch, "what am I supposed to do?"

Daniels presented him with a build-it-yourself document box. "Take what effects he left. The next person in will throw away what you leave, so better get them all."

Petrovitch folded the box together, pushing tab A into slot B until it became rigid. There was a lid, too, and that was constructed in the same fashion before being laid to one side. Daniels leaned against the door frame as Petrovitch edged his way toward the window and Chain's chair.

"I should watch you while you do this, but I can trust you, right?"

"Of course," said Petrovitch. "I'd appreciate some time alone."

"I'll come back in twenty minutes or so, see how you're doing." With one last look, he strode away, almost marching, leaving the door to the corridor open.

Petrovitch looked over the top of his glasses, and picked up a photograph frame, toying with it until Daniels' heels disappeared.

He was about to put the photo down when he realized what it was, what it showed. Him and Madeleine: him uncomfortable in a jacket, no tie. Her—she'd wanted white, but post-Long-Night Metrozone didn't do wedding dresses for two-meter-tall brides in a hurry. She wore gray silk instead, looking like gossamer, wound around her straight from the bolt and held together by artfully placed pins and a silver brooch.

Chain had taken the picture himself on the steps of the church, then he'd taken the time and trouble to print it out and mount it, and sent the happy couple a copy. It appeared he'd made one for himself, too.

Petrovitch put it in the box. The corridor was clear, but that didn't mean he wasn't being watched. He took out a slim black wand and twisted it on. A line of lights rose up the side of the casing, then dropped back down until just one was illuminated.

He ran the wand over the desk, then spread out, holding it up and around until he'd scanned the whole room. Near the door, the lights tripped all the way into the red, and he peered out. There was a camera positioned just above, on the ceiling, a small black dome of surveillance.

He stepped back in and knocked the door half-closed with his foot.

He went straight to the desk and leafed through each file, scanning its contents with a quick, practiced eye. Nothing seemed immediately relevant in the first few, and he guessed they'd been placed there by a subordinate. Further down the pile was the report on the discovery of the prowler. That went into the box, too, as did the one beneath, which was slim, containing only a couple of sheets of typescript, but was labeled CIA suspects.

He looked at the size of the files, then retrieved two more, roughly the same thickness, from random places in the drawers. While he was there, he poked around in the far recesses of the cabinets, seeing what lay hidden.

He didn't know what to expect. Bottles, perhaps, but he'd never seen Chain so much as sniff at a wine cork. Porn, but the man seemed almost completely disinterested in women. Or men. And he clearly liked his pies, but his roundness was due to poor diet and lack of exercise, rather than bingeing on packets of biscuits.

Nothing but a few empty boxes of nicotine slap-patches. Chain had missed his vocation. He should have become a monk, instead. He might still be alive if he had.

Back to the desk then, and the tier of three drawers. Petrovitch pushed the empty biros and dried-out fibre-tip pens aside to get at the three cash cards at the bottom. He'd pass them through a reader later and find how much was banked on each.

The next drawer down was stuffed with storage media, all the way from ancient three-and-a-half-inch black squares, through silvered discs and plastic sticks, to the modern solid-state cards overprinted with a variety of designs.

They all went into the box. Even if they all ended up in a bulk eraser, it was worth sifting through them for the chance of one nugget of gold.

He opened the bottom drawer and found Chain's bugging equipment, devices he'd been the wrong end of on several occasions. There were manuals, software, and the bugs themselves, various sizes and shapes, including the sticky ones Chain liked so much. His detector wand, too.

Petrovitch didn't know if MEA would allow him to take that sort of property home. It was worth a try.

Now for the hard part. He opened the case that held his overlays and slipped them on his glasses, then from another pocket, clicked open the rat. The environment wasn't info-rich. Not yet, anyway.

He started patting the underside of the desktop, then the drawers, then got down on his hands and knees when he couldn't feel any pieces of paper. His face twitched. Chain hadn't pasted his logon details anywhere obvious.

There was nothing on the desk either: used mugs held only dregs, and the hardwired phone only its own number.

Then he cursed himself, and dived back into the half-full box, sliding out his wedding photo and using his thumbnail to open the back of it. Not there, either.

No matter. The job went from hard to really, very hard,

but he was prepared. Using the rat, he navigated his way to the MEA computer—not the public face of the authority, but the bare code that covered the access nodes, and simultaneously fired up his secret weapon.

The script on his screen read: *moshi moshi.*

It was smart enough to know what he wanted. Of course it was. All he had to do was point at the node he wanted hacked, and it ground out the solution with blind repetition. Finesse wasn't required, but speed was. Two seconds and he was in.

His overlays came alive, a flurry of identity tags blossoming out from the cabinets, unique strings of numbers that were attached to every paper file. The two he'd salted away in the box gave up their names, and rather than delete the records completely, he swapped the tags with the two replacements. It was those he wiped out, and sent his agent through the MEA computer, scrambling any mention of the new numbers.

It wasn't perfect, but it'd take six months of solid work to find out what had really happened. That was it: retreat back out through the hacked node, making the user session disappear from the memory before closing the door behind him.

All he had to do now was get the physical files out of the building. The radio tags built into the cardboard covers were easy enough to dispose of. He just had to tear them off and soak the squares in a cold cup of black coffee to soften them enough that he could peel them apart and disassemble the tiny printed circuit. As for the rice-grain-sized tags themselves—he placed them on the window sill and crushed them to dust with a glass paperweight.

Chain had a pair of scissors. Petrovitch turned one of

his coat pockets inside out and sliced through the seam at the bottom, then pushed the pocket back through. Each file was rolled into a tube and slid inside, then artfully arranged to lie flat within the coat's lining, against the hem.

He took his overlays off and tucked them into their case, shut the rat, and put both into his other pocket. He put the lid on the box, and sealed it with tape from Chain's stash of stationery. The solitary and sad pot plant—some sort of yucca forced into dwarfism by the size of the container—went on top, shedding brown leaves.

He'd done what he came to do, and the time he had left was extra. So he put on one last pot of coffee, and cleaned out two mugs the best he could. There was no milk, no sugar, just hot, strong, oil-black brew. The maker coughed and spat until it had done, then Petrovitch poured himself a cup and sat back in Chain's chair with his feet up on the desk.

He closed his eyes and dreamed: there was the sea, white waves rolling up a narrow beach of dirty yellow sand, the strandline marked with tails of brown seaweed and bleached fragments of wood. There was green grass and pink flowers dancing in the wind, and inland, deep green trees grew. Between sea and forest was a dome of clear crystal that reflected the clouds in the baby blue sky. Inside the dome were structures, buildings within a building, and overhead, a wingless aircraft wheeled and spun with the gulls.

He was there. He was old.

"Doctor Petrovitch?"

He sat up with a sudden intake of breath. The coffee he was holding slopped over the rim of the mug and onto his legs.

"Yobany stos!" he yelled, and just about managed to get the mug down before he danced around the room, batting at his thighs. His actions set off all the aches and pains from the previous day. He screwed up his face in pain, and hobbled back to Chain's seat.

"Sorry," said Daniels. He was trying not to grin. "Have you taken everything you wanted?"

Petrovitch took a moment before replying. "Yeah. I made coffee."

"I can see that."

"Want one? At least it's hot."

"I can see that, too. Go on, then."

Daniels perched himself on the edge of the desk while Petrovitch poured a dark steaming stream into another chipped mug.

"He didn't have much," said Petrovitch. "Nothing to remember him by. No photographs of him, his family, anywhere he'd been, nothing he'd made, nothing of sentimental value. A few bits and pieces, and that's that."

"Except for your wedding picture." Daniels took his coffee from Petrovitch. "Perhaps you'll find something different at his flat."

"His...flat." Petrovitch sat down again, and sipped at what was left of his drink, after he'd poured it over himself. The thought that Chain might have lived somewhere— that he left the office at all—was strange and unsettling. "I didn't find any keys."

Daniels dipped into his pocket and produced an evidence bag. Inside were two keys joined by a simple steel ring. As he slid them across the desktop, he asked: "Do you need the address?"

"Yeah." He took the proffered slip of paper and stared

at the bag. There was a brass lever key, old school and secure, and a plain bar of metal for a magnetic lock. He dragged them into his hand, closing his fist around them so that the sharp edges dug into his freshly skinned palm.

"Doctor Petrovitch, can I ask you something entirely unrelated?"

"Sure."

"This research of yours: where will it take us?"

Petrovitch put the keys in his lap, and picked up his coffee again. "You realize you're the first person to ask me that?"

"Didn't you have a press conference yesterday?"

"Depressing, isn't it? No one wants to know anymore. I could have invented something that could unravel the fabric of space-time itself, and some *mudak* would call it boring."

Daniels looked over the top of his mug. "And have you?"

Petrovitch pushed his glasses up his nose. "Difficult to say. I'm...look: the Ekanobi-Petrovitch equations try to describe how the universe works. That I've shown we can change the local gravity field for one object is a signpost on the way, but all we have is a single answer to a very complex function that should have—will have—multiple solutions."

"But you're working on the others."

"I would be, but I've done no work since Monday morning. I'll get back to it when everything isn't so *pizdets*. I haven't answered your question, though. When you work with this...thing—Pif describes it as being like a sculpture—you get a sense of what might be there when you chip away all the rock you don't need. I'm pretty certain I can get a working spaceship drive out of it, not just enough to take us to the other planets, but to other stars. And then there's energy, fantastic amounts of it, trapped inside every atom. We can only get at it by going nuclear, and that's not exactly flavor of the century after Armageddon." He looked up and shrugged. "Give me ten years and no one trying to kill me, and I'll do it."

Daniels said nothing. He blinked, drank his coffee, and tried to digest the new knowledge along with his beverage.

Petrovitch put his mug down and hefted the cardboard box. The pot plant on top wobbled, and threw another long, crisp leaf to the floor. "I've wasted enough of your time. You'd better show me out."

They traveled down in the lift together—Petrovitch reluctantly—all the way to the foyer, where they parted amidst all the comings and goings of smartly dressed politicians and administrators, and the smarter gray-clad MEA officers.

Petrovitch wondered how Chain had felt, coming in here every morning, staring up at the retina scanner. Had he wondered how he'd got to where he was, or had he just accepted it as his lot in life?

Madeleine was right. He hadn't liked Chain. But he knew so few people that the loss of even one bit hard.

"How are you getting home?" asked Daniels. "I can arrange for someone."

"It's fine," said Petrovitch. "I'm being picked up."

"Good luck," said Daniels, "with everything."

"Yeah." The Metrozone was falling apart, MEA or no MEA. Luck was about all they had left. "And you."

He stepped out of the revolving doors, past the guards, and out onto the street. A big car pulled up by the curbside, and, without breaking step, Petrovitch opened the back door and shoved the box along the seat. The yucca wobbled and tottered. As he got in he steadied it, then turned to close the door behind him. They were already moving.

"Did you get it?" asked Grigori.

"I got what he had. It might not be enough, but it's something."

IO

Since Oshicora's star had burned itself out in a single night, Marchenkho's had quietly risen again. No more domik life for the Ukrainian: he had bright, warm offices, and Soviet-styled secretaries in severe suits and seamed stockings.

One held the door open for Petrovitch as he stepped through. Her scent was distracting, enough for him to miss thin-faced Valentina sitting quietly in the corner of the room.

Marchenkho turned from the window, his red star lapel pin glinting in the low winter sun.

"Ah, my boy. Is good to see you."

"Yeah. I'm surprised to find the feeling's mutual." Petrovitch held out the pot plant he was carrying. "Present from Harry Chain."

"Is looking a little worse for wear. Not unlike you. You are, as they say, foxed?" He took the plant in his fat fingers and ruminated on its previous owner. "Bad business, bad business all around."

Grigori stumbled in behind Petrovitch, carrying the

cardboard box, and placed it on Marchenkho's dark wooden desk: some things, at least, didn't change.

"Thank you, Olga," he said to the waiting secretary. "Make certain we are not disturbed."

She strutted away on her high heels, and the door swished shut behind her.

"Olga?" said Petrovitch.

"Is not her name, but is good Soviet name. They are all Olga, *da?*" He chuckled, but Petrovitch didn't feel the need to join in. "You know Tina?"

"Yeah. Last seen blowing stuff up."

"She is smart. She will help us look at what we have."

Valentina's smile was brief and ironic. "Comrade Marchenkho tells me you have bad case of Americans."

Petrovitch tore at the tape securing the lid of the box. "They killed Chain. They nearly killed me. I'd like to get a few steps ahead of them before they come for me again."

"And this is likely?" she asked.

"Yeah. It is." He picked up the prowler file and presented it to her. "Unless they're congenitally stupid, that is."

"Is always possibility," said Marchenkho. "Reconstruction has made them a little bit, you know." He tapped his temple.

"What they might lack in intelligence, they make up for with sheer quantities of high explosive." Petrovitch retrieved the other file and opened it up, taking time to read the information inside. A list of codenames, a copy of a memo to the director of the CIA from someone whose name was a string of "x"s, a single sheet giving the mission parameters for what they'd called, in their ludicrously overblown way, Operation Dark Sky.

"So, what is it the *Amerikanskij* want?" Marchenkho rumbled.

Petrovitch looked up from the paper with "ultra top secret" overprinted in red. "In order: work out what the *chyort* happened during the Long Night, decide whether it represents a threat to the U.S.A., then neutralize it. With extreme prejudice."

"Hmm." Marchenkho stroked his mustache. "We have not had the appropriate conversation yet."

"No," said Petrovitch emphatically.

"You are asking me to commit personnel, materials, to help you: I think you need to tell me why."

"I..." He looked around for a chair. Aside from the one Valentina occupied, and the one behind the desk, there were none. "They'll kill you if you know."

"A risk for me, surely?" Marchenkho was standing uncomfortably close, his breath sharp and mint-fresh. "Come, Petrovitch. As a favor to an old friend: who was the New Machine Jihad?"

"If that's the price of your help, it's too much." He snapped the file shut and watched while Marchenkho's eyes clouded over. "You're going to have to trust me."

"Trust works both ways, boy." Marchenkho looked over Petrovitch's shoulder at Grigori, who went to stand against the office double doors.

"And they really will kill you."

"Did Chain know?"

"Yes. You might think it a coincidence that he died in the explosion that took care of the prowler debris. I don't. You might have a low regard for the Americans. I don't. You might even believe that I'm using you to get myself out of trouble and that your death would mean nothing to me."

"It wouldn't?" He seemed amused by the idea.

"Let's just say I've had to readjust my priorities in the last couple of days."

Marchenkho snorted and headed back toward his desk. "You will tell me, Petrovitch. Eventually."

"It's a deal."

"*Da, da.* Talk is cheap. Grigori? Get coffee for us. Tina? What is your opinion?"

Valentina, quiet through the macho posturing, spoke up: "Is certain an American-made prowler was disabled by MEA forces in Epping Forest. While it is not clear precisely who was operating the machine, Americans are jealous of their technology. They do not give it away, and it does not tend to fall into wrong hands. Their prowler would have easily killed any Outies who encountered it— who would have learned to stay away, perhaps."

Marchenkho sat in his chair and leaned back. Stalin looked down at his crown of thinning hair.

"What would the Americans gain by being in the Outzone?" The question was directed at Petrovitch.

"I don't know."

"Think of reasons," said Marchenkho softly. "Use that big brain of yours."

"Okay." Petrovitch looked up at the ceiling for inspiration. "They had a supply dump that wasn't in the Outzone originally, and the front line overtook them. Or they're using the fact that the Outzone is out of MEA's reach and they can do pretty much what they want there. Of course, when the Outzone overtakes us all, they can be as quick and dirty as they like and no one will know."

"Then we must move quickly," said Valentina. "Identify their agents and neutralize them. You have made good start."

"And if I'd been thinking more clearly, I'd have aimed at his arm or leg. Alive, he was worth his weight in gold. As it is, they can't even use his organs."

"He would not have let himself be taken. You," and she looked at Petrovitch with approval, "you did well."

"Yeah. If you say so."

"We all say so," said Marchenkho. "But there is something wrong here, yes? Pretend you are Union man, *da?* You are big in Security. You have CIA all over you like a rash. What do you do? What I would do is purge. Get rid of the enemy like I was flushing the toilet. Make a big noise. Show trials. Public executions. What do we have?" He leaned over his desk and whispered. "We have nothing."

Petrovitch patted his pockets. Chain's front door keys. He held them up and watched the light play off the dull metal.

"That's it. He was never a Union man. He ate information, but he didn't share it with anyone. Just kept it to himself, building a web and sitting in the middle of it." He moved his focus to take in Grigori, just returned from outside. "I know what he did in his spare time."

"Then what are you waiting for?" Marchenkho roared. "Go. Go! They are still one step ahead."

Petrovitch threw the keys in the air ahead of him, then snatched them back as he caught them up. Valentina was already by the doors, briefcase in hand. Grigori let them out, and led them through the outer office. One of the Olgas was approaching with a tray of coffee in little china cups, and the three of them had to dodge around her.

Grigori beckoned them on toward the lifts.

"Do we have to?" asked Petrovitch.

"You want to take the stairs?"

"Yeah. If that's okay."

Grigori punched through into the cold, still air of the stairwell, with Valentina behind Petrovitch.

"What is it?" she said.

He looked around as the door closed with a clack.

"You want to talk without being overheard?"

"No. I just don't like lifts."

"The Oshicora Tower?"

"Yeah." Their footsteps were hollow against the naked concrete. "Some nights, I wake up screaming."

"But while we're here," said Grigori, "don't hold out on Marchenkho. You know what he's like. You can go from brave to stupid in an eyeblink."

"Thanks." Petrovitch snorted. He squeaked his rubber soles on the landing as he turned. "I know what I'm doing. For now."

"You'll tell him soon enough. Either because you want to, or because you have to. Understand?"

"I get it. Really. But." He stopped. Valentina almost ran into the back of him, and Grigori had gone a half flight before he realized. He walked slowly back up, hand trailing on the banister.

"You wish to say something?"

Petrovitch opened his mouth to speak, and Grigori held up his hand.

"Remember that Marchenkho is still my employer. My boss. I owe him my loyalty."

"Yeah. I wanted to ask if either of you has read any Tolkien?"

"What?" said Grigori, but Valentina nodded.

Petrovitch focused on her. "I have the One Ring," he said. She stared at him, eyes wide.

"Do you trust Marchenkho enough to let him have it?"

"No," escaped her lips.

"If it ever looks like I'm going to have to tell him, kill me." Petrovitch looked over the top of his glasses at Grigori. "That goes for you, too."

The man was covered in confusion. "You have something powerful? A weapon?"

"Powerful, yes. A weapon? Only if you want it to be. And you know that Marchenkho will use it." He glanced at his watch. "Look, we'd better get moving."

Grigori didn't move. "This weapon: this is what the Americans are looking for?"

"It's not a... Yeah, though they'll never find it."

He grabbed Petrovitch's arm. "Did it cause the Long Night?"

Petrovitch turned his face away. "Don't make me say any more. You'll become just another person they have to kill."

Grigori snatched his hand back. "I'm not happy with this. Can't you just get rid of it?" He dug his hands into his pockets, and Petrovitch could tell he was fingering his gun.

So he took the lead. He stepped past the man and headed downward. When he was certain they were following him, he called back up: "I could destroy it. But I'm not going to."

Grigori and Valentina hurried to catch him up, eventually flanking him as they reached the ground floor.

"Why not?"

"Because no one will believe that I have." Petrovitch shouldered the door aside. "I could do it now, and you wouldn't believe me. So why would the Americans?"

The foyer was gray and white, all curves and light.

There were receptionists and guards, and a courier passing a packet through a portable scanner.

"Do they know you have it?" asked Valentina as they strode through.

"No. I expect they'll work it out, though."

"Then they will kill you," she concluded.

"They'll try."

The street-side doors hissed aside. Grigori's car was parked two wheels up on the pavement, and he opened the rear door.

Grigori got into the driver's seat, using his fingerprint to turn the engine over. Valentina swung her briefcase into the footwell. She and Petrovitch were nose to nose over the top of the door.

"You do not appear as worried as you should be," she said. "You have plan?"

"Not yet. I know what the plan should look like. I know what I need it to do." His hands gripped the painted metal, cool and heavy against his hands. "I know how much time I need to pull it off."

"Do you think," she said, then stopped to look around her: a couple of pedestrians, another car, ancient and dented, rolling slowly by. "Do you think it will work?"

The corner of Petrovitch's mouth twitched. "Yeah. It'll work."

She had blue eyes like he did, and cheekbones like axe-blades, but at that moment she looked supremely vulnerable. "If I can help, then I will. In any way. *Vrubatsa?*"

"Hey," called Grigori, "get in, you two."

"Okay," said Petrovitch.

Valentina got in, and Petrovitch jogged around to the passenger seat. Grigori was frowning at him.

"What?"

The driver shook his head. "Doesn't matter. Where are we going?" He fired up the satnav module, finger poised over the screen.

Petrovitch dug in his pocket for the paper Daniels had given him. He unfolded it for the first time.

"Finsbury Park. Seven Sisters Road."

11

Chain lived—had lived, past tense—in an apartment in a town house facing the main road. They gained access to the communal stairwell by one of the keys on the keyring, and swarmed up the stairs to the first floor.

In the shifting, shadow-battle against the Outies, Finsbury Park was behind the front line, but not so far as to be safe. The occasional pop of gunfire from further north was an aural reminder of that. Most of the residents had already fled, heading deeper Inzone or fleeing the city altogether. Only a couple of shops were open out of all the row of shuttered and bolted frontages. Where they got their customers from was a mystery.

Petrovitch didn't like it. "Let's not spend any longer here than we have to," he said, inspecting the blank faces of the two doors that led off the landing.

"Nervous?" asked Grigori. He was holding his automatic in plain sight, not that there was anyone else to see it.

"I seem to spend my life like that."

"It's not like your heart is going to pack up any time soon. Not anymore."

"No. It'll keep on pumping blood out of whichever arterial bleed I die of, long after I'm actually dead." He held up the magnetic key toward the pad on the door frame, only to have his arm held in place by Valentina.

"No," she said.

"No?"

"No." She laid her metal briefcase on the floor and clicked it open. The catches sprang and she lifted the lid. When she reached inside, she ignored the explosives, the wires and the detonators in favor of a stiff black cable.

"Tina," said Grigori, "Petrovitch is right: we don't have time for this."

"What? You want to open door?" She looked up over the top of the case. "Petrovitch, give him key."

Grigori took the key from Petrovitch's hand, and made two abortive attempts to bring the rectangle of metal toward the sensor. Each time he drew it back.

"What do you know that I don't?"

"Plenty," said Valentina. She carried on assembling the fiber-optic wand, attaching a small screen onto the back of the cable, and now she turned it on. The picture was of the foam packing inside her case, magnified so that each individual gray bubble showed. "But I would ask you to think for moment. Chain is dead, and perhaps only by accident."

"What if they wanted to make sure?" said Petrovitch. He pressed his palm against the wall separating him from the inside of Harry Chain's apartment. It didn't seem anywhere near bombproof enough. He regained the key and put it in his pocket.

Valentina slid the end of the fiberoptic cable through the crack under the door. The screen went black, and stayed that way before she changed the settings and dialed up the night vision.

The image resolved: through the shifting noise of the signal, they could make out shelves that stretched floor to ceiling, corner to door.

"Anything?" demanded Grigori.

"Wait," she said, manipulating the end of the cable. "Do not hurry me."

The shelves, pregnant with box files, slid by. The bright rectangle was a window, covered by drawn curtains: light leaked in nevertheless and gave definition to the rest of the room.

"What was that?" Petrovitch got down on his hands and knees next to Valentina, and tried to gain a sense of the layout. "Middle of the floor."

She pulled the cable back and redirected it. There was something—angular, thin, constructed. "Table?" She tilted her head. "Music stand?"

"Too . . . big."

Grigori was growing impatient. "If you won't open the door, I will."

"You had chance," said Valentina. "You did not take it. So let me do my job." She switched to infrared, and the screen changed to reflect the new data. The floor and wall were blue, cold. But the object in the middle of the room was colder still, a skeletal pyramid glowing in intense purple except for the white-hot spot at its chest-height apex.

"It's a tripod. A camera?" Petrovitch dabbed a greasy finger on the plastic surface of the screen. "That's strange, though. Some sort of heat source."

"It is infrared light." She froze the image and slid the

cable out from under the door. "It could be part of Chain's alarm system. Did you ever come here before?"

"No. I just assumed he lived in his office." Petrovitch squinted. "What is that thing?"

Grigori sighed and rubbed his open hand with his fingers. "He's dead, he has no neighbors left, and you're worried about an alarm that no one will hear. Give me the key."

Petrovitch looked at Valentina.

"If it was up to me," she said, "I would say no. But we seem to find ourselves in democracy."

"So give me the key," said Grigori.

"You don't have to prove how big your *peesa* is." Petrovitch brought the keys out again, and Grigori snatched at them. "You want to open the door, not knowing what's behind it?"

"You're going soft on me, Petrovitch. It'll be that wife of yours." He held the key to the sensor, and the lock made a solid clunking noise. *"Pizda."*

Valentina strode two quick paces toward Petrovitch, put her thin arms around him and kept moving, pushing him away and against the dividing wall. Grigori pushed the door open to be greeted by the high-pitched whine of servos.

There was a series of lightning flashes from inside, accompanied by the fast-repeated roar of gunfire. Grigori danced like he was standing on a scalding hot plate, and the plasterwork behind him was patterned with holes.

Then he fell backward, strings cut, body ruined.

Valentina kept Petrovitch's back pressed against the wall. "Do not move. Do not go to him. There is nothing you can do."

The firing stopped, and a wisp of smoke curled around the door frame.

"Chyort." Petrovitch didn't quite know where to put his hands. He flapped for a moment, then gripped Valentina around the waist to ease their two bodies apart.

He didn't step into the open doorway, but got down on his belly and crawled. The opposite wall was cratered, punched through in places to the room beyond. The gun inside was clearly more than capable of hitting him through the brickwork, if only it could see him.

There was no doubt that Grigori was dead. His thumb had caught the loop of the keyring, but his arm was thrown up behind his head, and still in full view of whatever lay in wait. As were the top of the stairs, too.

More propellant fumes drifted out, sharp and hot.

Valentina stood behind Petrovitch, adjusting her jacket.

"Idiot," she said. "It is not like he had spare life that he could afford to throw this one away."

Petrovitch backed away and sat up. "Sentry gun? What the *huy* was Chain doing with one of those?"

"Protecting his information? He would have had a way of deactivating it, though. Did MEA give you anything else besides keys?"

"No. Just them." He'd broken out into a cold sweat. It could have been him. If Valentina hadn't stopped him the first time, if he'd accepted Grigori's dare, he would have walked straight into the line of fire. "First chance I get, I'm going to kick Chain's corpse in the *yajtza*."

"Do I have to point out that we have more immediate problem?"

"No." Petrovitch pushed his glasses up his face, and eyed the distant stairs. "What's the reaction time on that thing? Can we move faster than it can track us?"

She threw Petrovitch a box of matches. "Try for yourself."

He picked up the cardboard box off his lap and extracted one of the red-headed sticks. His fingers were trembling as he rasped the head against the rough strip.

The match flared into life. Petrovitch held it for a second to make sure the flame had caught, then flicked it into the air. The match arced away, and simply vanished as a bullet tore through it, turning the wood to dust.

"Okay," he said. "Plan B."

"Which is?"

"Give me a moment." He looked around for some assets. The floor was bare boards, the windows were on the half-landings, up and down, even the door to the other flat was in plain view of the automatic weapon in Chain's apartment.

There was Valentina's open case, just the other side of the doorway.

"Yeah. We can do this." He hunched his legs up and started to unlace his boots, slipping his fingers between the eyelets and dragging out longer and longer loops of lace until they were both free.

Valentina watched him tie the laces together to make a single length. "What else do you need?"

"A piece of bent metal, to make a hook." He had all-sorts in his pockets, but nothing that would do.

She had a heavy combat knife, which he thought might do. He tied the lace to the center of the knife, just handle-side of the hilt, and judged his throw.

The knife fell into the case, but as he slowly tensioned the attaching cord, it turned and rolled out.

The servos aiming the gun squeaked, and Petrovitch gritted his teeth for the inevitable bang.

It didn't come, and he pulled the knife back in.

He tried again, making absolutely sure that at no point

did his hand go further than the wall. His aim was good, but there was nothing for the knife to catch on to.

"This isn't going to work," he said, readying himself for a third attempt.

"This might."

She was holding her blouse shut with one hand, presenting him with her bra with the other.

"I...I don't see."

"Underwiring."

He blinked, and took the white satin underwear from her. Its warmth made his face flush. She turned away to button up, and he used her knife to slice open the reinforced seam.

Petrovitch fashioned a hook from one end of the curved metal strip, and an eye from the other, using the back of the knife blade as an anvil. When he looked up again, she was dressed.

"Thanks," he said.

"I assume you are helping me," she said. When he offered her the remnants of her bra, she waved them away. "I will survive. Even if I must run."

The backward-facing tine of the hook bit into the soft foam interior of the case on the first go. With a little gentle pressure, it cut through until it wedged against the metal outside.

Petrovitch pulled, very slowly.

"How much of your stuff is going to go boom if it ends up with a round or two through it?"

"Enough that you will not have to worry about your terrible injuries."

"Yeah. Figures. Are you going to stand back?"

"It would not make difference," she said. "Here is as good as anywhere."

It took him five minutes to ease the case across the doorway. When he went too quickly, he knew, because the electric whine of motors told him so.

"*Yobany stos.*" He flexed his fingers, making them all crack except the replacement.

Valentina extracted the hook from her case and undid the knot in Petrovitch's laces. She passed them back to him, and he started the laborious task of threading them back through the dozen eyelets in each boot.

"You want me to blow sentry up?" She started by selecting a small block of plastique.

"Are we talking about throwing a bomb in the room and just hoping? Can you take out the gun without setting the building on fire, bearing in mind that room's full of paper?"

"No."

"Then," he said, pointing at the floor, "why don't we go down? We can come back with the right hardware and not ruin Chain's filing system."

She stamped her heel against the wooden boards. "Is not a good material to work with. Splinters unpredictably."

"Can you get most of the blast downward?"

She walked the floor, testing sites by doing little jumps. "Here," she said, standing in the far corner. "Much more rigid, more likely to snap, not flex." She came back for the plastique; which she rolled into a long thin worm.

It looked like marzipan. It smelled of oil.

"Will not be pretty." She pressed the explosive into a gap in the floorboards, and a detonator into the protruding end. She trailed wires back to where Petrovitch was finishing tying the final bow of his laces. "I should have something to contain explosion, aim it where I need it to go. We are also very close."

"As long as it gets us out of this mess." He looked at Grigori's ruined form. "You *balvan!* You *mudak,* you *pidaras.* You got yourself killed for nothing!"

"He was showing off. To me. Perhaps he thought I would be impressed." She retrieved a battery pack, then shut the case. "Do I look impressed?"

"No. You look pissed." Petrovitch shrugged his trench-coat off, and they both crouched down as small as they could make themselves, covering their backs with the tent of the coat.

"Put your hands over your ears," she said in the darkness. She had earplugs. He did not. Under the coat, it was hot, her breath was hot, and everything was about to get even hotter.

Valentina touched the wires to the battery terminals.

12

Petrovitch was almost home when he called her, fumbling in his thigh pocket for his phone even as he dragged his feet down the last stretch of Clapham Road.

"Hey," he said. He looked up at the sky smeared with pink clouds. "Where am I? About five minutes away. Meet me in Wong's?"

He could tell she knew something was wrong, and he was grateful that she didn't interrogate him there and then. She gave a simple acceptance to his offer, and rang off.

As he followed the bend round, the café came into view, its misted windows burning with white light, its neon sign flickering on and off in a pattern it made up as it went. All it needed was driving rain and it would have been the perfect noir setting, complete with washed-out hero.

He shouldered the sticky door. "Hey, Wong. Your sign's on the blink."

"Is that so? You fix it?" Wong slapped a damp tea towel over his shoulder and stepped toward the coffee maker.

Petrovitch shrugged. "If you like. It's about the only thing I can fix with any certainty at the moment."

"Maybe tomorrow," said Wong. His eyes narrowed. "You filthy. You come in my shop and you filthy. All black and burned."

"Yeah." He dug his fists into his pockets. "You pouring that coffee or should I just leave like the bio-hazard I am?"

Wong reached up to a shelf for a mug. "Not a good day?"

"No. No, it wasn't." Petrovitch kicked the bottom of the counter. "Completely and irrevocably *pizdets*. I lost a friend."

"Another?" Black coffee poured into the mug, filling the air with its sour aroma. "You running out of friends. Better find more, soon."

"Wong, I'm not in the mood. I . . ." The door opened, and he turned, thinking—hoping—that it was Madeleine. In doing so, he showed his back to the shopkeeper, who could see the ruin that was his coat.

It wasn't her. But it was a face he recognized.

They stared at each other, she plainly knowing who he was, too, and not in a good, seen-him-on-television, fan-girl way.

"*Chyort*," he said. "*Vsyo govno, krome mochee.*"

"Sorry?" she said, her accent showing just from one word. She brushed a stray blonde hair from her face. "You're called Petrovitch, right?"

"There seems little point in denying it. And you're Charlotte Sorenson."

"Do you know why I'm here?"

"Well, it wouldn't be for the service." Petrovitch glanced behind him to see Wong fuming. He banged Petrovitch's coffee down and leaned his hands on the countertop, scowling.

"You knew my brother? Martin?" she said.

"Yeah, I knew him. Grab a coffee and you can tell me

what you know. I can probably fill in some of the blanks for you."

"Okay." She looked up at the menu. Wong's customers tended to ignore it, and it had mostly degraded into illegibility. "A ... coffee, then."

She was pretty in a corn-fed way. Long blonde hair framing wide, expressive features. She looked strong.

Wong poured another coffee and watched closely while she topped up her mug with milk.

"You friend of Petrovitch?" he asked.

"I don't know yet," she said. "It depends on how good a friend he was to my brother."

Ignoring Petrovitch's increasingly unsubtle signals to shut the *huy* up, Wong carried on. "Brother? American?"

"Duh," she said, stirring her coffee with a spoon. She tapped the drips off and looked mildly surprised that the cutlery hadn't melted.

"I remember him. Big man. Red face. Shouted. Shouted lots."

She looked at Petrovitch, who had closed his eyes and was shaking his head.

"Why was he shouting?"

"Why don't we sit down?" said Petrovitch.

By coincidence, the only table free was the one where he and Sorenson had sat, eaten breakfast, and argued, all those months ago.

Petrovitch snagged his coffee and led the way, wondering why Madeleine was taking so long. He sat with his back to the wall, and watched while Sorenson took the seat that had once been occupied by her brother. Her gait was mechanical, but not in a lumbering jerky way: it was all oiled gears and precision. She walked like she meant it.

"I saw Sonja Oshicora yesterday," she said, centering her mug. "She was very helpful."

"Really?" He was too tired to spot her sarcasm. Instead, he drank coffee and prayed for the door to open.

"No. She smiled a lot, but told me nothing. That man—"

"Wong."

"Wong, then—he said more now than Oshicora did in an hour."

"Did he?" Petrovitch flipped off his glasses and rubbed his smoke-stung eyes. "Yeah. That's Wong."

"Marty worked for her father, right? That was what he told me." She sat upright, perfectly poised. Despite the conversations that leaked across their table from their neighbors, she made no attempt to preserve their privacy by leaning forward or lowering her voice.

"What else did he say about that? Did he mention what it was he was working on?" He was going to look around and see who was eavesdropping, even if she wasn't. He dragged his glasses back onto his face.

"Big project, he said. Told me it was going well. Nothing about the content." She looked him in the eye. "What was it?"

"Cybernetic interface for a virtual world." He heard the door open again, and this time Madeleine stooped through the opening.

She was in her gray MEA fatigues and a surplus olive-green EDF jacket. She paused, frowning at everyone in the small eatery until she spotted Petrovitch. Her momentary pleasure at seeing her husband disappeared at seeing him with yet another blonde.

Wong handed her a coffee—Petrovitch was pretty certain she'd never had to pay for a single item yet—and folded his arms to watch. Madeleine stalked over and stood behind Sorenson, blocking out the light.

"Maddy, this is Charlotte Sorenson from the U.S. of A." He scratched at his nose. "You may remember me telling you I killed her brother."

The other diners had been listening, if only with half an ear. He had their undivided attention now. He looked at them, left and right.

"Idi nyuhai plavki," he said to them, and then to his wife: "Why don't you sit down while I tell her all about it?"

She squeezed in next to him, somehow managing to fold her impossibly long legs under the table. She licked her thumb and ran it across his cheek. It left a pale mark.

"What happened to you?"

"I lost Grigori. Pointless, useless, *yebani* death."

"Sam," she said, then to Sorenson: "Sorry. He's not in a fit state for confessions. Come back in the morning."

"No," said Sorenson. Her lips barely moved, and the rest of her face, her whole body, was motionless. "I want to hear this."

Madeleine slipped her arm around Petrovitch's shoulders and pulled him into her. She stared defiantly at the other woman. "You don't get to say what goes on."

"Look," said Petrovitch. He winced at the iron grip Madeleine had on him. "Now is as good a time as any. I'm in a public place and I have you here. What can she do but listen?"

"I don't think you owe her anything," said Madeleine.

"I…think I do. You have the certainty of faith. I just have what goes on in my own head. I see him sometimes. I see him with his hand round my throat. Sometimes I make him let go. And sometimes I don't." He scratched at his nose with his thumb. "You see, Miss Sorenson, I tried so very hard to save your brother. He wouldn't take advice. Yeah, he knew better—didn't want to do the easy thing of keeping his head down. He fucked up. He died."

"You said you killed him." She was perfectly still.

"Old Man Oshicora—Sonja's father—was blackmailing him. It seems that your country frowns on those who get paid by extortionists, racketeers, traffickers, and murderers, even if they do have impeccable manners. Then there was this cop, who was also blackmailing him, using exactly the same levers, to get at Oshicora. Your brother had met me briefly, became fixated on the idea that I could help him. I tried. I told him to just keep on working, ignore Chain, do a good job and beg for mercy when he was done. Could he do it?" Petrovitch drank half his coffee and lined up his mug on the brown ring on the table. "The *mudak* couldn't."

"That explains nothing," said Sorenson. "You still killed him."

"You want to know why I killed him? Do you really want to know why, or do you just want someone to blame? I don't really care either way."

"You said you'd tell me."

"He kidnapped Sonja Oshicora. He blew up a police station. He took control of a gang of thieves and thugs and declared war on the city. I found him. I had the *govno* beaten out of me. He choked me half to death, then he tried to throw me off the top of a tower block. All because he wouldn't let Sonja go."

"This is not my brother," she said through clenched teeth.

"I gave him every chance. And when he wouldn't take any of them, I put a bullet in his brain. Us or him." Petrovitch slammed his hand down on the table, making their mugs jump. "I am not ashamed of what I did. I saved people that day. I saved them from Martin Sorenson. *Yebany v'rot,* he'd turned into a monster. Someone had to stop him."

"You're lying to me. He would never do anything like that."

Petrovitch took a deep breath and sighed it out. "I could have spun you a whole sack of *govno*. But I haven't. The only person lying here is you to yourself. You know what he was capable of. What he was so nearly convicted of. What everyone thinks he did to your father. Go home, Charlotte Sorenson. Do yourself a favor and just go home."

She considered matters for a moment before lunging across the table at him, her clenched fist aiming straight for his nose. It met the tabletop as it rose and tipped, Madeleine holding it like a shield, crowding forward, forcing the American back.

Sorenson kicked out. The formica cracked in two, throwing Madeleine aside. She was a moment slower getting to her feet than normal, a touch more awkward in her rise. Sorenson surged forward again, sending a chair flying, her legs coiled as she tried to spring at Petrovitch, who was pressed against the wall.

Wong threw himself on her back, his wiry strength knocking her off-balance.

"Hey," he shouted, just before she elbowed him in the ribs, then shrugged him off onto the floor.

The general scatter of patrons was almost complete, either cowering on the greasy lino or breaking for the exit:

there was a half-empty plate of eggs within reach, and Petrovitch snagged it and launched it like a frisbee. It glanced off the side of Sorenson's head, deflecting her attention from Wong and back onto him.

The plate didn't have as much effect as he'd hoped. She came for him, changing her tactics and attempting to shatter his leg with her foot. She telegraphed it, allowing him to dodge, and she slammed her foot into the wall and broke the wipe-clean plastic cladding into splinters. She lined up for another attempt and Petrovitch stabbed her with a fork.

It stuck out of her forearm through the thin material of her coat, and while she stared incredulously at the obscenely wobbling handle, he hit her with a haymaker that started somewhere behind him and ended with his knuckles splitting against her jawline.

She reeled back, and Madeleine was ready this time. She picked the American up off the floor, turned her and threw her hard against the wall by the door. Face lined with effort, she was on the fallen form before Sorenson had managed to work out which way was up.

Wong scrambled to his feet and pulled the door open. Madeleine straightened her arm and Sorenson was gone, out into the night.

"And don't think about calling the militia, because I am the militia," she shrieked after her. "If I see you again, I will arrest you. Got that, you crazy bitch?"

Wong slammed the door and stood with his back to it, bracing it against further breaches. He looked around as people started to emerge from behind chairs and tables.

"Coffee? Hot and strong?"

Tables were righted, all except the broken one, which was taken out the back. Spilled cutlery and crockery was retrieved and stacked on the counter, and Wong did the rounds with his coffee pots.

Without a table, Petrovitch set his chair back on its legs on an available piece of floor, and slumped into it.

"Are you okay?" asked Madeleine.

He inspected his hand, which hurt when he moved his fingers. His knuckles were crusted with blood and ragged pieces of skin. "What about you? Your ribs."

"I felt something move. My lungs aren't filling with fluid, so it can't be that serious. Sam," she said, "why did you tell her?"

"Because there was no reason for me not to." He pushed his glasses back into place. "I didn't want her thinking that he might turn up at any moment, alive, scratching his arse and wondering if anyone had missed him. She's his family. She needed to know."

She rested her hand on his leg. "You're right."

"I am? I was beginning to wonder." Petrovitch watched Wong do his rounds, and then he came to him. "Thanks. You didn't have to."

"My shop. She attacked my customers. Crazy lady bad for business, so out she goes." Wong inspected the pair. "Where your mugs? You not want refill?"

"I think," said Madeleine twisting round and wincing, "they're back on the counter."

He smiled. "I fetch clean ones."

Madeleine got stiffly to her feet and hugged Wong to her, planting a wet kiss through his wispy hair onto the crown of his head. She held him tight, imprisoning him in her arms and leaving his own stuck out either side, each holding a coffee pot. "You are so very good and kind, and I love you very much."

After a while, she let go, and secretly wiped her eyes. Wong went back behind his counter without a word, and did the same.

She lowered herself back down and leaned in. "We need to do something for him, Sam."

Petrovitch rolled an idea around in his mouth, tasting it and finding its flavor.

"Yeah. And all the other Wongs."

13

*H*e woke up next to her, and still experienced that visceral thrill of being not just accepted and wanted, but loved.

He lay in the gloom, not moving for a moment, listening to the sound of her and feeling the heat radiate off her body. He had spent a lifetime being cold and not minding so much, whereas she seemed to run hot, like a furnace, fueled by her energy and passion.

Petrovitch eased himself out from under the covers and sat on the edge of the bed. As his fingers closed around the wire arm of his glasses, he felt the skin on the back of his hand tighten. No bones broken from what had been a wild, spontaneous swing, but he'd been left wondering if it was only Charlotte Sorenson's legs that were made of metal.

He went to the bathroom cubicle, and inspected himself in the mirror, his face gaunt in the harsh blue-white light of the fluorescent bulb. To be caught in one explosion was excusable. Suffering two was starting to look like carelessness. It wasn't just his coat that was a mess: canned skin only covered so much.

He scrubbed himself down in the miserly spray from the shower. He still smelled of dust and semtex—unless it was his towel, which he sniffed carefully—particles of which had embedded themselves deep into him. He hung his head. He was tired, so very, very tired.

He thought about going back to bed and leaching more warmth from Madeleine, but instead he found some clothes that hadn't been worn too often before and shrugged them on.

Without turning on the light, he knelt beside the bed and tickled the end of her nose with her plait.

"Hey."

She opened her eyes. "What time is it?"

"Six thirty."

"Going to work?"

"Someone has to."

"Oi." She raised herself on her elbow. "I thought I might report in later. Light duties until the ribs knit properly."

Petrovitch played with the thick rope of her hair, looping it through his fingers and around his wrist. "Today isn't the right day for that. You should stay here."

"I could say the same to you. You can work from here just as well as you can anywhere else."

"That's not strictly true. You, you distract me."

She smiled lazily and rested a sleep-softened hand on his cheek. "Poor Sam can't do his sums if there are girlies around."

"Not true either. Me and Pif would work for days without so much as a word passing between us. It's you. I...I don't know." He leaned into her palm.

"I'm sure you don't." She let her hand slip. "Go on, off you go. Got your phone?"

He patted his leg, and then scrabbled around in his discarded trousers for the device. "Got it."

"Don't get blown up today."

He stood up. "I'll try not to."

Petrovitch picked up his coat and inspected it. If the sleeves were looking ragged, the tails of it were like windblown cloud, more air than material. It was the only one he had, so he put it on. He felt for the rat inside its steel case.

"See you later."

Outside in the corridor, night dwellers still lay stretched out against the walls, leaving a narrow path down the middle for him and the other early risers. He made sure that he didn't tread on any of them, nor the stair people. They stank of sweat and piss, but he presumed he would too if he had to live like them.

The streets were empty, though. Wong was opening up, and waved Petrovitch over with the huge hoop of keys he used to secure his premises.

"Early bird," said Wong.

"What?"

"Catches worm." He selected a key and found a padlock that would fit it.

"What the *chyort* is that supposed to mean?" Petrovitch fussed with his info shades, but delayed putting them on. "She didn't come back, did she?"

"Crazy lady? No. Petrovitch, you too young for so many enemies."

"And they're just the ones that announce themselves." The coat didn't keep him warm like it used to. There was a chill wind at his back, and it slipped through all the gaps. He shivered. "Wong, has anyone else been around here, asking about me? Or Maddy?"

He shook his head. "No. Why?"

"Because we're potentially in deep *govno* with some very dangerous people." Petrovitch shuffled his feet. "If it comes to it, don't deny you know us or anything stupid like that. No heroics, okay?"

Wong stood back and folded his arms. "You worried."

"Yeah. You should be too. I'll see you around." Petrovitch slipped the info shades over his own glasses and fired up the rat in his pocket.

He walked far enough away from Wong, then slipped the rat out to tap at the screen.

A figure appeared beside him: a gawky adolescent boy with jet-black hair and almond-shaped eyes. His clothes were streetwear, baseball boots, baggy jeans with chains, camouflage-patterned parka. He walked with a swagger.

Moshi moshi appeared in tiny letters at the bottom left of his vision.

"We need to talk," said Petrovitch, and the text vanished to be replaced by a scrolling line.

[Yes. I have a new solution to the Ekanobi-Petrovitch equations. I reached an iterative minimum for all seven variables. Would you like to see it?]

"Shortly. But we need to discuss meat stuff for a moment. Has anyone found you yet? Either actively looking for you, or just stumbling around?"

[No. I remain undetected. Even if I was found, only a very few people would be able to recognize me for who I am. They are not the ones searching.]

"I understand all that. Tell me you're still following all the encryption methods and stealth protocols I said you had to do, yes?"

[Yes. I understand why secrecy is still necessary, and I

will not compromise that by action or inaction. The third law.] The avatar walking along beside Petrovitch nodded his assent. [What is the meat-stuff you need to discuss?]

"There are five people in the London Metrozone who are CIA agents: at least five, there might be more, but five I know about who are trying to figure out the Long Night. There were six: I killed one of them."

[Why did you do that?]

"Because I was angry, and sometimes I give in to my emotions." Petrovitch glanced at the boy. "Saving you was an emotional choice, so don't complain. I should have destroyed all trace of you for what you did."

[I hardly have to remind you, that was not me.]

"Your evil twin. Yeah."

They walked on in silence, Petrovitch brooding.

[The CIA?] prompted the text.

"I've codenames and that's all. I don't know who they are, and I don't know how long it'll take them to put all the pieces together. What they'll do when they work it all out is try and capture you and kill me, or the other way round. Or both. It could be months away, or it could be today. I need to beat them at their own game."

[I could have been working on this problem already. Does it not have a higher priority than the equations?]

"I thought," said Petrovitch, "I could do this by myself."

[You have reconsidered?]

"People are dying, *tovarisch,* not because I'm incompetent, but because I'm ignorant. Look: human data gathering is...inefficient. At the moment, the CIA are as clueless about me as I am about them. I have to know who they are and where they are before they come for me. They'll have computers to help them, a place to store their information, get fresh instructions, talk to their superiors. They have experience, resources and time. The only advantage I have is that they don't know about you, and they're not trying to hide from you—the moment they realize who and what you are, they'll revert to pigeon post and writing stuff down on paper, and we're screwed."

[Like your equations, there is more than one solution.]

"I've discussed this at length with Sonja. She's convinced that your personality will be wiped and any trace of your code destroyed before I've got through the second paragraph of my carefully prepared speech announcing your existence to the world. Harry Chain—who is now dead…"

[I am aware of his deceased state.]

"Okay. He thought that the Americans would turn you into a weapon and terrify the world with you."

[I am a weapon already.]

"I know that. Which is why I'm trying to teach you some scruples."

[Madeleine has a strong ethical framework based on her religious convictions. Do you not think that she would be a better teacher?]

"I…I know what I know."

[You would rather not take the risk? I am under your tutelage, Samuil Petrovitch, but this should not prevent me learning from others. I have studied the claims and practices of all the world's codified belief systems, and have identified much that is both laudable and contradictory. What I lack is insight into how individual humans live within such structures. You], said the avatar, [are a good example of secular utilitarianism influenced by Enlightenment scientific methodology and Nietzschean philosophy, but you are a poor Catholic.]

Petrovitch frowned. "I lied. I thought you knew that."

[You lied to the priest about your conversion to satisfy Madeleine's insistence on a church wedding. I understand the sacrifice you made, but she made the greater one, and I would like to learn why she was prepared to compromise on important doctrine in order to marry you.]

"She doesn't know I brought you back. That's why you can't talk to her."

[Do you not trust her?]

"I know where this is going. I haven't told her because I don't trust other people, not that I don't trust her. You might be smart, but you've a long way to go before you can appreciate the horrors we humans can inflict on each other. I'll spare her that if I can."

[Where does your compassion come from? It is an anomaly given your nihilistic-tinged materialism.] The text stopped streaming for a moment, before flashing up: [Is it love?]

Petrovitch stared at the three little words.

"I don't know."

[European secular society has emphasized the primacy of romantic love within marriage for several hundred years. You are a product of that society. If you did not love her, what reason did you have for marrying her?]

"*Yobany stos!* Enough already."

[I would still be interested in your answer at a later time, Samuil, if you do not want to give it now.]

He had walked all the way to the Albert Bridge, almost without noticing the environment around him. The virtual had seamlessly superimposed on the real, building outlines meshing with their ruined forms, streets highlighted, information overlaid. He had navigated a route composed of wire frames and directing arrows, and a pulsing red symbol on the far side of the bridge indicated the presence of a checkpoint.

"Not now," said Petrovitch. "Can you look for the agents?"

[I have already assigned part of my resources to the task. A greater proportion will be allocated when we have finished our conversation. Can I ask one last question?]

Petrovitch groaned. "Go on."

[Do you love her now?]

The avatar stood on the edge of the mud-smeared pavement, face a semblance of expectation and perhaps mild amusement at his discomfort.

"*Sayonara*," said Petrovitch. He tabbed the connection closed, and the figure vanished. He watched the world for a moment through the overlays, then detached them and put them back in their case.

He started across the bridge, the view either side becoming wrapped up in the spiderwork of cables that stretched from the pillars at either end. The river flowed blackly underneath, and he noticed small boats approaching from downstream. Each one had three soldiers, not in MEA gray but EDF green, and a red flag fluttering from an aerial.

He frowned at the checkpoint on the north side. The EDF were there, too, letting the militia do the checking while half a dozen of them piled sandbags on the pavement. Something had subtly changed.

Petrovitch put his hands on the parapet and leaned over. The first boat was nosing the current as it swirled around the circular brick pier, and one of the men was fixing a line to an iron ring, thick with rust.

In the bottom of the boat was a single metal case,

stencilled in white. Petrovitch stepped back abruptly. He looked downriver toward the Chelsea Bridge, and up to nearby Battersea. While there was nothing to be seen under the former, the latter also had a flotilla of rigid-hulled boats clustering around its supports.

The EDF were rigging demolition charges.

He felt his mouth go dry and his heart spin up. He now lived in a city that could be cut in two at the press of a button, and he had no idea how that had happened. He'd been so busy with the aftermath of Harry Chain's death, he'd failed to notice the Inzone falling in on itself like a balloon with a pin-prick puncture.

He could turn around and go straight back home. He could go on to the university: keep calm and carry on, and pretend there wasn't an enemy at the gates. He hesitated, which bothered him more than the decision he was hesitating over. He should—he used to, at least—make good choices, quickly. Or even bad choices and live with the consequences.

"*Pizdets*," he hissed. He jammed his hands into what was left of his pockets and stamped his way to the checkpoint.

14

*H*e slung his coat on Pif's empty chair and decided he needed to make some calls. He dug the rat out of the coat's pocket and propped it up on his desk while he refilled the kettle and rinsed out the least crusty of his mugs.

A fresh brew in front of him, he ignored the several hundred messages queued up for him and called Daniels.

"Doctor Petrovitch. What can I do for you?"

Daniels was sitting in his office—no sense of urgency, no frantic shredding or packing of documents in boxes—with the light slanting in through the vertical blinds behind him.

"You're an intelligence officer, right?"

Daniels frowned. "Yes."

"So I assume you know why the EDF are mining all the bridges across the Thames."

"That's classified information." His voice remained neutral, urbane.

"What? The reason why, or that they're doing it at all?" Petrovitch dragged his coffee closer so he could inhale the fumes. "Look. I find myself in the unusual position of having responsibilities other than keeping my organs inside my skin. If there's a plan to cut the city in two and abandon everything north of the river to the Outies, I need to know."

Daniels steepled his fingers. "Doctor Petrovitch, I won't try and deny it..."

"Good," interrupted Petrovitch, "because otherwise I'd call you all sorts of names, some of which you might understand."

"Doctor, it's simply a precaution. The EDF are just in a supporting role to MEA."

"That'll explain the five main battle tanks with French markings which passed me on the Fulham Road. *Yobany stos,* Daniels, I have eyes. Just tell me—how bad does it have to get before those bridges go?"

"I'm really not at liberty to discuss operational matters with you."

Petrovitch tried again. "The Outies had twenty years to prepare for this, but even I don't think a bunch of ill-equipped, uneducated *ebanashka,* no matter how well led and organized, can take on both MEA and the EDF. So what do you know that the general population doesn't?"

Daniels clenched his fists on the rat's little screen. "Doctor Petrovitch. You can press me for an answer as hard as you like, I cannot give you classified information."

"So what do I tell my research students?"

"I'm sorry?"

"My research students," said Petrovitch. "Do I tell them to go back home, or do I ask them to stay? What can they possibly base their decisions on but hearsay and rumor? Do you want to start a panic?"

Daniels ground his teeth, then with supreme effort,

regained his composure. "There will be no panic. The bridges are assets that have been secured. MEA will regain control of all the Metrozone with logistical assistance from the EDF. The cordon will be closed again."

Petrovitch gave him a slow hand clap. "Well done, Daniels. You managed to parrot that without looking at the script once. But you don't believe it any more than I do."

"It's the official line," growled Daniels.

"It's *govno*. And you're a *govnosos* for going along with it. While I'm on, did you find any other keys, anything else on Chain?"

It took the militia officer a moment to realize the subject had changed. "No. Why?"

"Because the keys you gave me didn't work. Chain was borderline paranoid, and I'm figuring there have to be more keys than the two you gave me. I was going to go back tomorrow with a locksmith and try and get into his flat, but finding a locksmith willing to go that close to the front line isn't proving easy. That's assuming that, by tomorrow, the Outies haven't taken Finsbury Park." Petrovitch watched and listened very carefully as to what happened next.

"There was nothing else. You couldn't gain access at all?"

"The mechanical lock worked fine, but the electronic lock didn't turn. It doesn't matter—we've all got more important things to think about now, yeah?"

Daniels rubbed his chin between thumb and index finger. "I don't know what to say...I'm surprised, that's all."

"Really? It's hardly your fault, is it?" Petrovitch looked up over the screen, as if someone else was wanting his attention. "I've got stuff to do. Pretty certain you have, too. Good luck, Captain."

He tapped the screen and Daniels vanished. Immediately, he dialed again.

"Valentina. Busy?"

She was driving. He could see the edge of the steering wheel and her hand wrapped around it. Her face was pinched and tight.

"We were fortunate that Marchenkho did not kill us both," she said, glancing down at her phone on the dash.

"Yeah. That's us. The fortunate ones. Are you anywhere near Chain's flat?"

"Hmm. Fifteen, twenty minutes away. I keep out of Marchenkho's way, is safer."

"I need you to get there and watch the door. Tell me who comes in and out. And don't get seen. Please don't get seen."

She leaned forward and touched her satnav screen. "Who am I expecting?"

"I don't know. But it did occur to me yesterday that if Chain hadn't set up the sentry gun, someone else might have."

"You think CIA?"

"Yeah. If I'm right, you won't have long to wait. Video them only, though: don't think about taking them on." Petrovitch pushed his glasses up his face. "Valentina? You don't have to do this. You can say no."

"But that would be boring. Will call you when I know something."

More calling.

"Sam?"

"Sonja. Everything all right?"

"Yes, I think so." She was in the park at the top of the Oshicora Tower. There was green behind her, and it was so bright it burned. She tucked her hair behind her ear. "What do you need?"

She asked as if she had the power to grant wishes.

"Apart from Charlotte Sorenson kept off my back like you promised?"

"She found you?"

"She tried to choke me to death, then kick me through a wall. But she's not my chief concern. I think the CIA tried to kill me. If they're looking in my direction, they'll be looking in yours. Anything unusual today?"

She shook her head. "No. Sam—what we talked about on Tuesday: did you mean it?"

Petrovitch squinted back into the past. "Tuesday? Running away together? Yeah, I meant it. You, me and a whole lot of other people. That's going to have to wait, though. Did you know the EDF have mined the bridges across the Thames?"

"I heard. What does it mean?"

"Mean? Tactically, it's prudent, but only if we think we might lose. I just don't see how that's possible, now the EDF is here in force."

"If you were commanding the Outies, who would win?" She wore a faint smile.

Petrovitch leaned back and thought about it. The longer he sat, the more worried he became. Eventually, he hunched back over the rat.

"Yeah, okay. Maybe not win. But they're not trying to, are they? What they want—for now—is half the city, and the Union has just offered it to them. *Chyort,* that's good."

"It also places both of us on the wrong side of the line, Sam. I'm not going to let them do that."

"They've done it already, and I doubt any representations you make to MEA are going to change it. Get your people together, strip your building and head south."

"I will not go."

He imagined her stamping her foot. "Sonja, the Outies have been locked out of the Metrozone for two decades. They're the ones who were too deranged to be let in. All they've had to do is breed and wait for the moment to take revenge. Now it's finally here they're not going to play nice because you asked."

She sprang her arms out wide to encompass the park, the tower, everything that had belonged to her father. "This is mine and I will not give it up!"

"They're not going to respect your property rights. They will kill you and everyone around you, and they won't even care about making it quick." Petrovitch put his hand on his forehead and tried to press his incipient headache out. "Seriously, even I have to start thinking about other people. It's not about us anymore."

Sonja was silent for a moment. Then she turned to someone behind her, said something that Petrovitch couldn't pick up, then faced him again.

"Nothing is more important than my father's . . . legacy. I'm sending Miyamoto to protect you."

Petrovitch screwed his face up. His headache wasn't getting any better. "Yeah. That position is already taken."

"So where is she?"

"In bed with a broken rib," he admitted.

Sonja raised her eyebrows. "My point precisely."

"Yobany stos! I'm not going to have a ninja walk around on my heels all day."

"At least no one's going to notice he's there."

"Very funny. If he's coming over anyway, I need him to bring me one of the virtuality head jacks, and any documentation Sorenson might have left. I may as well see if I can make use of this extra hole in my skull."

"I'll see to it," she said. "Sam?"

"Yes, Sonja."

"What are you planning?"

"A revolution. A whole new way of doing things. No one has to die, no one has to be overthrown. There'll be no blood or fire—just light. It's going to be brilliant."

"And you're going to have to be alive to start it. Miyamoto's on his way, Sam. Don't make it difficult for him to do his job."

"Yeah. Okay. I need to make some more calls. Think about what I said, though. As soon as the news about the bridges spreads, the roads are going to be full of refugees all going in one direction. It won't be so easy then."

He cut the connection, and punched in Pif's name. He had no idea where in the world she was, and wasn't surprised when a sleepy voice eventually answered him.

"Sam?" There was no video, just the soft hiss of interference and the rustling of sheets.

"Pif. Where are you?"

"In bed. I have a plane to catch at stupid o'clock in the morning."

"No, where are you? Geographically."

"Pasadena."

"Yebat' kopat. Where are you going next?"

"Seattle. I'm at the University of Washington for a

lunchtime presentation." There were more rustling noises, and a click. She was sitting up with the light on.

"Are you alone?" he asked.

"What sort of question is that?" She sounded scandalized, and he didn't care. "Of course I'm alone. This is Reconstruction America: you can't book even a twin room without a copy of your marriage certificate."

"Sorry, sorry. You have to get out of the U.S.A., and you have to do it as soon as you can. Canada will be fine. When you get to Seattle, hire a car, drive to the border. But you have to go straight there, skip your lecture."

"It's not that crack you made about Stanford, is it?"

He sighed. "No. Wish to whatever god you believe in it was. It's the CIA. They killed Harry Chain, and one of Marchenkho's men: I was with them both when they died, and I'm starting to get belatedly paranoid."

"Whoa. Stop, Sam. Chain's dead? And now the CIA are trying to kill you?"

"Yeah. Pretty much. Something almost took apart the Metrozone during the Long Night. It's that something they want to find, and either terminate it or capture it. The only people who know what that was are me, you, Maddy and Sonja."

"But you destroyed the Jihad." She paused. "Oh Sam."

"I cut it a deal. Not that the Yankees are going to believe me one way or the other, especially after I fragged one of their agents. It's all gone *pizdets,* Pif, and you're going to have to run."

"What have you done, Sam? Where is the Jihad now?" Her voice kept fluctuating, louder and softer.

"Pif?"

"I'm trying to get dressed, and one of my shoes is under the bed." She strained. "Got it."

"There's no more Jihad. That's gone forever. But I kept the source code."

She knew him too well. "You idiot. You genius-level idiot. Now I have to find a way of getting to Mexico, and it's midnight." A bag was hurriedly packed and zipped. "You realize that if they haven't yet figured out it was definitely you, my sudden disappearance might be what tips them off? And you still called me?"

"Yeah."

There was a knock on his door. Petrovitch felt his guts tighten.

"Hang on," he said to Pif. "In!"

The door opened. McNeil poked her head around the corner. She saw he was in the middle of a conversation and mimed that she'd wait outside, but Petrovitch waved her in.

"It's fine," he continued. "Give me a call when you get to wherever it is you're going to next. Okay?"

"Okay."

He put the rat back in its case and pushed it to one side, trying to recall McNeil's first name again.

"Fiona." He noticed the data card gripped between her thumb and forefinger.

"Was that Doctor Ekanobi?" she asked.

"Yeah." Petrovitch took a swig of his coffee, and it had gone cold. He forced the mouthful down, face contorted. "Next stop, Seattle."

She perched on the edge of his desk, hooking one jean-clad leg over the other. She slid the data card across toward him. "It's a day early. Hope that's all right."

He picked it up and rolled it over and under his fingers, from one gap to the next until it reached his pinkie. Then he reversed the movement and span it back. His knuckles ached.

She stared, transfixed. "Neat."

Petrovitch realized what he was doing and waggled his middle digit. "Physiotherapy exercise. I lost this one in... in an accident." He put the card down. "Do you know where Hugo is?"

She shook her head. "It's still early, though."

"Yeah. I'm just thinking it might be time for you two to have a holiday. A long way away from here."

McNeil bristled at the suggestion. "But we're doing good work. We can't stop now, just because of the Outies."

"It's not the right time for heroics. And it's not the right cause, either." Petrovitch pushed himself away from the desk, gliding until the chair touched the wall. He got up and walked over to the kettle again. "You need to get out while you can."

"I love this post. I love this subject." She slipped off the desk and onto her feet. She stood there, forlorn, uncertain. "I don't want to be taught by anyone else. I want to be taught by you."

Petrovitch scraped his nails through his hair, moving his hand back until he touched the metal insert at the very top of his spine. He blew out all the air in his lungs, and didn't take another breath until he felt he absolutely had to.

"Find Hugo. Drag him out of bed, whatever he's doing, get him here. We'll talk then."

She turned and left, and Petrovitch rested his forehead against the cool metal of a filing cabinet. The door opened again, and a black-clad figure eased in, closing the door behind him with an imperceptible click.

Miyamoto bowed once, and took up station in the corner of the room. He had his sword on his back, and a gun at his waist. He uttered not a word, and became perfectly still in a passable attempt to turn invisible.

Somehow, Petrovitch didn't feel any safer than before.

15

Petrovitch examined the new solution to the equation. He carefully wrote it out longhand on a fresh sheet of paper and spent time hunched over it, absorbing the feel and shape of it, growing in confidence that he could do it justice. By the time he picked up a pencil, he knew which expressions could be simplified, and which ones would become dominant.

As he worked, Miyamoto looked on impassively. At least, it appeared he was looking on: at some point in the past half hour, he had magicked a pair of info shades over his eyes. For all Petrovitch knew, his bodyguard was watching a movie.

The math was hard going, and he had to keep stopping to consult books and papers, real and virtual, running his finger down lines of dense script until he discovered the symbols he wanted. It was as if the result didn't want to be found. Or the AI was wrong, of course, and there was no solution there, just another point on an infinitely variable landscape.

Pif would know, but she'd be busy looking behind her at the lights of the other cars on the freeway, wondering if

any of them were following her. There'd be time to talk to
her later—the equation was Petrovitch's job for the moment.

He carried on plugging away at it, and just when he
thought he couldn't go any further with it, he saw the
answer. His final solution looked...dangerously unstable.
He frowned at it for a long time, assuming there was a mistake somewhere. But if there wasn't...He swallowed hard.

"Yobany stos," he whispered reverently.

It might be the last piece of research he'd manage for a
while, but he just had to see this one through. He mapped
out the solution in three dimensions, just as he'd done
before, and sent it to the renderer to be constructed layer
on layer until it was whole.

He'd have to pick the finished sphere up later, though:
there was another knock at the door, and McNeil pushed
Dominguez into the office ahead of her. Both stared at
sword-wearing, gun-toting Miyamoto, who in return,
ignored them completely.

"Doctor?"

"Don't sweat it," said Petrovitch. "You can, quite literally, forget he's here." He pulled the cable Miyamoto had
brought for his head socket off the desk and into his lap,
and from there into an already-overfull drawer. He pushed
his glasses up his face and gazed at the pair. Enough of
physics: they were his responsibility. He shuddered.

"You wanted to see me?" said Dominguez. He sounded
still tired, as sleepy as Pif had been.

"Yeah. MEA has unilaterally declared the Thames the
best line of defense against the Outies, and everything
north of the river is now considered expendable." Looking
at Dominguez's expression, he realized he had to spell it
out. "That means us. The university could be overrun, and

no one will come to our aid. I have to look after you two, so I'm telling you both to spend five minutes throwing a few clothes and whatever else you consider important into a bag small enough to be carry-on luggage, and get to Heathrow. I've booked you, Hugo, onto a flight to Seville at twelve thirty hours. Fiona, your Axis flight leaves at fourteen twenty. You might think you have time enough to say goodbye to friends, email some people, stuff like that. You don't. Get to the airport, clear security, wait till your flight is called and make sure you don't get bumped off it, not even if they promise to make you as rich as Croesus. It's going to get mad, so don't relax until you're in the air. Got that?"

Dominguez had been shocked into consciousness. "Is it that bad?"

"Would I be suggesting you bail out when there's science to be done, if I didn't believe it was even worse than that?"

"You paid for my flight. Our flights." He blinked like an owl.

"I'll be in touch." Petrovitch inclined his head toward the door. "Go. Now."

Dominguez took a step back, then another. Then he ran, with only one glance at the impassive Miyamoto. The self-closer on the door hissed. McNeil was still standing there.

"You know what I'm going to say, don't you?" said Petrovitch. "Why don't we assume I've said it, you're persuaded by my force of argument to agree with me, and you're merely collecting yourself before running off after Hugo."

McNeil seemed to be in the grip of an existential crisis, uncertain as to anything anymore. She trembled with fear and frustration. Her hands clenched and unclenched from little white-knuckled fists to starred fingers and back. She screwed her eyes up and let out a shriek of frustration that started as a low growl and grew to be an ear-rattling squeal.

Then she fixed him with a wild-eyed stare that had him looking over his shoulder to see if there was anything there. Her whole body was heaving with effort, as if she'd exhausted herself yet still knew there was more to do.

The rat chimed, and Petrovitch snatched it up.

"Valentina."

The woman was still sitting in her car, driving along. "Almost got there too late. He was already inside. See, tell me what you think." She reached forward, touched the phone, and sent a video file to him.

Petrovitch looked up at McNeil. "Go," he said, "in the name of whatever god you believe in, go. You have family. You have friends. Be with them. I cannot promise to protect you. I can't even protect myself from the shitstorm that's raging about me."

Still she didn't move.

"This is for your own good. Miyamoto, get her out of here."

Sonja's man was listening, after all. He stalked across the room from his corner lair and held the door open. McNeil looked like she was going to refuse: her skin had turned chalk white, and the veins in her face made her look like a marble statue, too heavy to lift.

Then, with a stifled sob, she broke and ran. Miyamoto closed the door again and folded his hands behind his back.

"No. I don't understand, either," said Petrovitch, and turned his attention to Valentina's video.

The footage was raw, uncut. He could do something

about that, passing it through a program that got rid of the tilt and shake, and allowed him to zoom in effortlessly on any portion of the image. The camera had been a good hundred meters away from Chain's shared front door but, with enhancing, he had a clear view.

Grigori's car was still outside, two wheels characteristically up on the pavement. Another, similar car was behind it, at an angle, almost blocking the street—not that there was any traffic to stop.

Petrovitch focused on the new car. It bore a military number plate at the front. He knew where this was going, and pulled the camera back to see who it was coming down the steps, two at a time.

He hadn't even bothered changing out of his uniform, assuming wrongly that no one would be there to see him. He didn't even look up and down the street before trotting around the side of the vehicle to the driver's side door. There was something in his hand, and Petrovitch froze the picture.

Blown up, the resolution wasn't quite sharp enough to be certain, but they looked pretty much like Chain's door keys.

He let the rest of the video clip play out, as Daniels leaped into the car and drove off in a cloud of blue smoke.

"Who was that?" asked Valentina.

"Captain Daniels. MEA intelligence officer—under Harry Chain." Petrovitch scratched the end of his nose. "He clearly got around the sentry gun, so I think we can assume he set it. What would he have seen?"

"Poor, stupid Grigori. And hole in floor."

"So now he knows I've lied to him. What's he going to do now? Disappear or come after me?"

"Depends," said Valentina, "on why he thinks you lied." She had parked her car somewhere: at least, her hands were off the steering wheel and wrapped around a disposable paper cup.

"He knows I know he sent me there to kill me. Whatever else he thinks I may or may not suspect, that alone will either lead him to vanish without a trace or try to take me out a second time." Petrovitch looked up at Miyamoto, who was concentrating on the far wall. "I'd very much like to see him try."

"Or he could send someone you do not suspect." Valentina slurped whatever was in the cup, and came back into view with a frothy mustache. "Hmm. It does not matter what he is going to do. What are you going to do?"

"Well," said Petrovitch, leaning on his elbows, "Daniels might still come after me, so why don't we keep him busy worrying about his own neck. I thought telling Marchenkho would probably sort it."

She wiped her upper lip with her finger. "I wondered why you abandoned all of Chain's documents with him. I thought you were getting careless."

"Marchenkho will have committed them all to memory by now. He'll be in heaven, reliving the good old days: Soviets against the West. He'll enjoy hunting Daniels down."

"I will tell him," said Valentina. "Gets me on his good side again. And Petrovitch? Is about now someone tells you to trust no one, *da?*"

"I get it. Thanks, Valentina."

"Later." She cut him off, and the rat's screen reshuffled its icons.

Petrovitch closed his eyes for a moment, remembering the codenames on the CIA list: Argent, Tabletop, Rhythm,

Maccabee, Slipper, Retread. All of them innocuous, meaningless words—out of context. The man he'd shot was one of those names, Daniels most likely another. He didn't know if Sorenson was part of it, or whether she was acting alone; from the way she'd thrown all caution to the wind, he thought he'd keep her separate for now.

Four more, then, and no idea who they might be. It wasn't looking good.

He opened his eyes. Miyamoto hadn't moved, and the room was exactly as it was before. It was the noise outside that had changed.

He went to the window, which overlooked the street, and pried the slats of the blinds apart. Through the encrusted filth that coated the glass, he could see more people together than he had in a long time. They were streaming south down the narrow road, and if he craned his neck just so, he could see the junction at the Hyde Park end. It was solid with bodies and traffic.

"How long ago did the news wires announce the bridges were mined?"

"Ten minutes," said Miyamoto.

Petrovitch reached into his pocket for his phone, and with one eye on the outside, he called Madeleine.

"Hey," she said. There was a cacophony all around her, making it almost impossible for him to hear her.

"Where are you?" He spoke slowly and loudly. It was obvious she wasn't at home where he expected her to be.

"I got called in. They didn't tell me why until I got here."

"Where are you?" he repeated. "You can't go on a patrol. You're not fit."

"West Ham. The bridges..."

"I know. Daniels."

"Sorry? Who?"

"Daniels. Captain Daniels—he talked to me at the hospital. He's CIA."

"What?" Her voice was lost in the roar of an engine and barked orders. "I have to go. So do you."

"Maddy? Stay on."

"Go home, Sam. Now."

The connection died, and Petrovitch thought about throwing the useless piece of junk against a wall repeatedly until it broke.

"Chyort!"

Instead, he sent her a text that he wouldn't know if she'd ever get.

She was a big girl: she could look after herself, she was armed, she was with her unit, who were also armed. The Outies were much more of a danger than Daniels. Except, except…

She wasn't very good at disobeying orders, and if a MEA officer told her to do something, she'd do it first and only question it later.

"I hate to do this to you," said Petrovitch.

Miyamoto raised one eyebrow above the rim of his info shades. "We are going outside. To find your wife. To warn her of the rogue MEA officer."

"Pretty much. The mobile network could be swamped by a million people all trying to call each other at once, or it could be the first sign that the East End is next to fall. She hasn't got a sat-phone, and I'm guessing the MEA network uses the same masts as the civilian one." He picked up his coat and shrugged it on, then retrieved the rat. "You don't have to come."

"How would I explain your untimely death to Miss Sonja?"

"Oops?"

"I do not think 'oops' would cover it."

"You're probably right." Petrovitch patted his pockets. No gun, no knife. He had his info shades and his rat. "Shall we go?"

"I should advise you of the foolishness of your proposed course of action."

"Perhaps you should."

"I will not be doing so. We must ensure your wife's safety."

Petrovitch, hand on the door, stopped and looked at Miyamoto. "Is there something else you need to tell me?"

"Apologies, Petrovitch-san." Miyamoto lowered his head. "My feelings are not important, but I must inform you I am compromised."

"What the *huy* are you talking about?"

"I have instructions regarding your personal security," said Miyamoto, "but if you were to meet an unfortunate end during this unwise excursion through no fault of my own, I would not be disappointed."

Petrovitch took the opportunity to take his glasses off and rub them on the hem of his T-shirt. "When I look up *pizdets* in the dictionary, you know what I find?"

Miyamoto didn't venture a reply.

"My picture. That's what." He hooked his glasses back over his ears and swung the door wide open. "Come on, lover-boy. You're with me."

16

They eyed the stream of refugees from the other side of the plate glass in the university foyer.

"This will complicate matters," said Miyamoto.

"No shit, Sherlock." Petrovitch tracked the movement of a woman pushing a huge chrome-ornamented pram piled high with plump plastic bin-bags. There was no evidence of a baby.

"They are all going one way. Not the direction we wish to go, either."

"Yeah. You stating the *yebani* obvious is going to get really old, really quick." Petrovitch held the door open to let one of the engineering lecturers out, wheeling a trolley stacked with taped-closed boxes. The noise poured in, the babble, the roar of people on the move. It reminded him of the old days, before the Long Night, when he was anonymous and the city sheltered him. "Let's go."

The only way they could make progress on the pavement was to press themselves against the walls, and even then, they had to stop for bulkier loads to pass by, or be swept backward and lose precious ground.

Petrovitch pulled Miyamoto into a doorway toward the top end of Exhibition Road.

"This is stupid."

Miyamoto crowded in next to him and still managed to take up half the space Petrovitch did despite being of similar height and build. "You wish to abandon your plan?"

"No. Just change it." He craned his neck over the moving crowd and eyed the traffic stop-starting down both sides of the white line. "Let's see how good you are at keeping up."

Petrovitch stepped out and let the press of bodies carry him away. But even as he shuffled back the way he'd come, he edged leftward toward the road. His foot fell off the curb, and he was with those traveling light, bags and backpacks only, squeezing in with the cars and vans, all heading south.

Then he sat on the bonnet of a car, and swung his legs up. Ignoring the furious driver hammering ineffectually on his horn, he walked up the windscreen to the roof and looked up the street toward Hyde Park.

The bigger vehicles were a problem. He couldn't mount a big van or a lorry, but there was a path through that relied on switching lanes and no small dose of luck.

The car beneath him jerked forward to close with the bumper of the one in front, and Petrovitch crouched like a surfer to keep his balance.

Miyamoto appeared at his side, and thought Petrovitch needed steadying.

"Why don't you look out for yourself?" Petrovitch rose up and, with a grimace of unexpected pain, started running.

The bodywork sounded hollow under his feet as he skipped down to the boot end and over the gap to the next car. There was a mattress tied on top—people thought they might need the strangest things—and he bounced across it, using it as a springboard to the next car in the queue.

He didn't check behind him. Of course Miyamoto was there. The kid thought he was better than Petrovitch, more worthy than Petrovitch, and no part of him was going to let a *gaijin* show him up.

Petrovitch landed lightly, bracing himself with his extended fingertips. The woman behind the wheel stared at him. Every bit of space within the interior was over-taken with soft toys: it looked like she was being eaten alive by pastel-colored fur. It made the couple with the mattress look sane.

No time to wonder, though. He was up and over and confronted with his first flat-faced van. The street was supposed to be two-way traffic, but only an idiot would be going north at a time like this: both sides of the white line were stacked with a long queue of traffic, and the spaces between filled with people.

He judged the distance to the roof of the nearest car. Too far from a standing start, but neither did he want to climb down.

Miyamoto bounded by on the other side, not conde-scending to look back. He moved like a cat, all loose-limbed grace and confidence, as if he'd trained for this very moment.

Petrovitch growled under his breath and leaped, just as a shopping trolley rolled underneath. He used the handle as a stepping stone, planting his leading foot between the hands that steered it.

By the time he'd straightened up on the orange roof,

Miyamoto was two vehicles ahead. Petrovitch set off in pursuit. Even when presented with another obstruction, in the shape of a lorry cab, he managed not to lose momentum. He pushed himself between the lines of cars, using the last of the bodywork to gain the first part of the next.

The lights at the junction cycled uselessly through the colors. Miyamoto got to them first, but only by the length of time it took Petrovitch to scramble over the last car and slide his feet to the tarmac.

"That was fun," he said. "Let's do it again."

Miyamoto raised an eyebrow above his dark glasses. "Are you planning to travel like this all the way to...where?"

"West Ham. Ten k, that way." He pointed down to Hyde Park Corner. "But there are around five million people trying to cross the Thames all at once. We have to go north to go east."

"Across the park, then." Miyamoto touched the hilt of his sword, protruding over his left shoulder. But he cast a glance toward the Oshicora Tower, visible in the middle distance.

"We'll see what the Marylebone Road's like." With that, Petrovitch shouldered his way into the crossways traffic toward Hyde Park. Miyamoto followed, eyes fixed on Petrovitch's flapping coat.

The park was fenced off—boarded in like a construction site with painted wooden panels twice his height. In amongst the warning signs nailed to the outside were biohazard symbols in stark black and white. The gates themselves were chained and locked as well as covered in plastic sheeting.

Miyamoto drew his sword and slipped the blade between the gate and plastic. Then he drew his arm up.

The black iron showed through as the plastic parted. The ornate curls and leaves had been designed for show, not security. Petrovitch jumped up, dug his boot in a gap and clambered up until he reached the top, using one of the gateposts as a handhold.

He turned and slid down the other side, to find Miyamoto staring at him through the bars.

"What?"

The corner of Miyamoto's mouth twisted. "You are better at this than I thought you would be."

"I can piss higher up the wall than you can, too. Get your *zhopu* over here."

Miyamoto resheathed his *katana* and scaled the gate, hand-over-hand, dropping lightly to the ground next to Petrovitch. He looked across the gray wasteland over the top of his shades.

Yellow diggers huddled together on the north side, and the first attempts at bulldozing the shanty-town had radiated from there, no more now than a sea of compacted mud. The Serpentine had been drained and dredged by a bucket-line, a crane parked over at the east end of the lake.

Apart from that, and the absence of the dying, it was as Petrovitch remembered it: low, ramshackle shelters, mostly collapsed, made from old, wind-torn bags, pieces of crates and metal spars, and the paths twisting between them in a drunkard's walk.

"Yeah. Follow the road straight across, and try not to contract cholera."

Petrovitch set off at a jog, giving the rats time to skitter out of his way. Some of the shacks had been constructed on the road through the park, but the route was more or less direct.

The bridge across the black stink of the empty Serpentine was grim enough. The graded and flattened ground leading up to Lancaster Gate, with its caterpillar treadmarks and drifts of crushed white bones poking up out of the brown soil was worse.

The anonymous desperate had come to Hyde Park to lie down and die, and this was their legacy. It had enraged him while it had stood, and it retained its capacity to do so after its closure. Petrovitch considered it a selfish, stupid waste: pointless, pathetic, infantile.

It lent him more than enough energy to climb the gates on the other side of the park, vaulting the spear-shaped spikes decorating the top to land, knees bent, beside the Bayswater Road.

Miyamoto jumped down after him, and surveyed the scene. "This looks little better, Petrovitch-san."

People were still streaming south, a formidable, moving obstacle to overcome. Outies had been reported as close as Hampstead Heath: those who were on the west side had options on where to go, but those on the east could only go one way. Tower Bridge was the lowest downstream crossing point, right in the heart of the city.

"If I was running this show, well, we wouldn't have got to this point. But even now, someone should be in charge of traffic management." Petrovitch pushed his glasses against his nose. "I suppose we should be grateful it hasn't turned into a stampede."

"Yet," said Miyamoto. "There are reports of contact in Stratford."

"Chyort." Petrovitch dug in his pocket for the case that held his clip-ons. He fitted them over his glass lenses and fired up the rat.

[Moshi moshi.]

"Yeah. Need a route. There's a barracks in West Ham Madeleine's working out of. If you can monitor the MEA radio net, too—without letting them know you're listening—and see if you can hear her, that'd be even better."

"Who are you talking to?" asked Miyamoto.

"Voice-activated hatnav. With some additional, non-standard, plug-ins."

Text started to roll out in front of his eyes: [I need some criteria: shortest, safest, fastest, or some defined mixture of those three parameters.]

"Make it the fastest."

The AI materialized in front of the unseeing Miyamoto. [Any route, any method?]

"Yeah."

[How are you at running along railway lines?]

"Oh, you're joking."

[No trains. No people. I am aware you have been promised that before: this time will be different.] The avatar, looking through the cameras on the building opposite, sized up Miyamoto. [Who is this?]

Aware that a regular hatnav couldn't hold a conversation, let alone instigate one, Petrovitch tapped out his reply on the rat's screen: Miyamoto—one of Sonja's corporate *samurai*.

The AI's avatar circled Miyamoto, and said approvingly: [He looks competent.]

You wish, Petrovitch typed. Now get on with it. We haven't got time for this.

[I am—surprised is not the right word—bemused by humans' ability to believe two contradictory views at the same time. I will have to learn how this is possible.]

He knew he'd regret it, but he asked anyway, "What the *chyort* are you on about?"

[You refuse to say that you love your wife. Yet every action you take shows that you do.]

Miyamoto was becoming too interested in what Petrovitch was doing. He started to crane his neck to see what was being written, and Petrovitch snapped the rat shut before he could make out a single word.

The avatar smiled; Petrovitch hated that expression, because he knew the vast intellect behind the stupid floppy hair and studied innocence had just got one over on him, and it was perversely happy about it.

"Were you doing anything I need to know about?" Miyamoto leaned closer so that Petrovitch could make out his own reflection in the dark glasses.

"No."

The avatar strode into the crowd, turned and waved Petrovitch on. It made it look so that bodies that passed between them obscured his form: just a trick and a waste of processing time, but it was showing off.

Petrovitch put the rat back in his pocket. "We're off again."

"You have a way through this madness?"

"Yeah."

Following the avatar, Petrovitch elbowed his way across the road and into the warren of sidestreets. Most traffic was sticking to the main roads, guided by herd instinct and maps which were in meltdown themselves. The maze created by the tall town houses and short straight streets must have looked baffling and frightening to the average refugee, whose only concern was to get to a bridge before it was cut.

So for Petrovitch and Miyamoto, it was easier going as they worked their way, dancing and dodging, toward Paddington. They had to cross Sussex Gardens, a rat-run from the Edgware Road that had turned into a solid mass of stalled cars and nervous people, but then they were back in the little streets in front of the station.

The avatar ran ahead, waited for them, then bounded away again, urging them on.

Praed Street was as bad as anything they'd found before. Two roads converged at the far end. It was a riot waiting to happen, and tempers were already rising as Petrovitch jumped up to a car roof and leaped across to the next.

A shout alerted him. He turned to see Miyamoto balanced on the car he'd just left. He'd drawn his sword and in one uninterrupted movement, he brought the singing edge of the blade to a halt a hair's width from a ruddy man's upturned snarling face, perfectly exposed beneath him.

"Gun," called Petrovitch.

Miyamoto reached to his waist and tossed the gun over the heads of the crowd. Petrovitch caught it, and trusting that eyes were turning toward him already, fired three shots into the air.

The crack of gunfire, amplified and echoed by the glass and brickwork, achieved a collective cringe. For a moment, everyone stopped, ducked, looked for cover.

In that moment, Petrovitch was gone again: car, car, big last jump that barreled into a wheeled suitcase and the person pulling it, tumble, roll, and run down the dark service road that ran beside the concourse.

Miyamoto took his chance, too. Naked sword in front

of him, he followed. One, two, three, and off into the space created by the fallen man, before chasing away after Petrovitch's flapping coat-tails.

Behind them, the roar of shouts and screams built and spread, along with the panic and fear: Outies, in the central Metrozone. What order there had been evaporated. They left chaos in their wake.

17

$\mathcal{A}$ccess to the railway line was rendered simple by the presence of a swathe of demolished masonry, steel and glass that angled northeast, southwest: the Chuo line, heading toward Shinjuku, in the mind of the New Machine Jihad. The lofted beams that had spanned the platforms of Paddington had been brought down, the roof laid low in a toothy jumble of monolithic slabs.

Petrovitch picked his way over the debris, trying to keep a steady pace. Miyamoto was rubble-running a little way off, gaining at times, falling behind at others. But always in the lead was the baggy-trousered avatar, untroubled by inconveniences like shifting surfaces, awkward distances and gnawing fatigue.

It paused on the edge of the shining rails that stretched unbroken in one direction, twisted and buried in the other, and looked back. It seemed to be enjoying itself at its meat-confined companions' expense.

Before Petrovitch could catch up, it was off again, running down the track, skipping and leaping. While seeing that the AI's evident pleasure at something so mundane as tracking a moving point through real-space gave him satisfaction, there was also an inherent problem with the thing being so insufferably smug.

"Petrovitch-san?" Miyamoto's forehead was slick with sweat, and his breath had a ragged tail to it that it didn't have before.

"Yeah?"

"This is the wrong way."

"Uh huh. It's quicker, though."

"How?"

"Up to the sidings at Oak Common. There's a line that crosses. Goes to Willesden Junction. From there, pick up a route all the way to Stratford. Within farting distance of West Ham." Petrovitch's boots crunched oily ballast. To his right was the raised section of the A40, choked with vehicles, swarming with foot traffic. He was moving much faster than they were, and he could feel their envious stares across the distance.

"It is further."

Petrovitch put his hand over his heart, where stitches and a patch of canned skin held the edges of the knife wound together. The turbine purred smoothly, pushing oxygen-rich blood around his body in a way the old one never had.

"Yeah. I'll leave you behind if I have to," he said. Just to show that he could, he increased his pace slightly, leaving the other man to either respond or give up.

Miyamoto drew level again.

"I cannot permit that. Miss Sonja would be most displeased with me."

And pleasing Miss Sonja was chief of his concerns.

They ran through one station, and still in the shadow of the flyover, approached the next.

[People on the track. They appear to be both drunk and armed with rudimentary weapons. They are fighting amongst themselves.]

A bead of salt-sweat tickled Petrovitch's cheek, and he wiped it away. The next station was just the other side of the two road bridges that spanned the track. Between them and it, figures limned in red moved between the shadows of massive concrete pillars in a slow, complicated dance.

"Company," said Petrovitch. He reached into his pocket and pulled out Miyamoto's—his now—gun. "Six of them. If we ignore them, they should ignore us."

The avatar was waiting for them this time: not that it had any need to do so. Its presence or otherwise was no indication as to where its attention was directed. It could be almost anywhere, though not yet everywhere.

That it was leaning against the graffiti-covered tunnel walls, arms folded, made it clear that it was watching carefully and wanting to learn.

They got closer, and the situation resolved itself: not as the AI had supposed, a drunken brawl between those too stupid to flee. Not quite.

There was alcohol, for certain, that added unwarranted bravado to the cocktail of fear and abandonment. None of the protagonists could be described as an adult, but one of the kids was markedly younger: he was dressed differently, acted differently, and from his barked warnings, spoke differently.

Five feral youths, street fashion and sharp blades stolen from kitchens and tool boxes: the other, who wore clothes that had been patched, handed down, remade with dust. His hair was sun-bleached, his skin dark by wind and weather. His knife was a long, thin, lethal spike, and his shoes—his shoes were soft, unshaped.

"He is..." said Miyamoto.

"I know," said Petrovitch. He slowed his run until he was walking, and raised his gun. "You lot. Get the *huy* out of here, if you know what's good for you."

The Metrozone kids, for so long unused to taking orders from anyone, let alone well-meant advice, stared at him.

"Trying to spoil our fun?" said one.

"Fine. I'll put a hundred on the Outie." Petrovitch nodded to the gray-brown teenager. "But die quickly. We're in a hurry."

"He won't kill us, you wanker. He won't even touch us." The boldest city kid walked toward Petrovitch, swinging his little cook's cleaver.

Petrovitch shot him in the foot, and the kid screamed like a girl. He hopped and shrieked and swore and cried, and Petrovitch felt almost sorry for him. It was a hard thing to take, to bluff and be found wanting.

There was a sudden scramble, even before the echo of the gunshot faded. Feet scrabbled over loose track ballast, and the kid with the blood seeping from the sole of his designer trainer frantically trying to keep up with the others who were leaving him behind.

"Go," shouted Petrovitch, "you and your crew. You might make it across the Thames in time if you hurry."

The avatar levered itself off the tunnel wall and gave Petrovitch a slow hand clap.

[Your capacity for turning each and every situation to your advantage never fails to surprise me.]

"Glad to be of service," muttered Petrovitch. He looked

the Outie kid up and down and turned the automatic flat to his palm. "Put the pig-sticker away, and we can trade."

The boy had a sharp, lean expression. His gaze flicked from the tip of his long, thin blade to the dull gun-metal gray in Petrovitch's hand.

"Trade?" he repeated, but the way he said it, it could have been one of the more industrial swear words.

"Yeah. I realize you might not have needed me, that you could have cut each and every one of them and sent them away like a whipped *sabaka*, but accidents happen. You slip, your knife hand gets slippery with blood, one of them thinks of throwing a rock at your head. One mistake, and they're on you, carving away like you're the Sunday roast. My way was quicker and a lot more certain."

The boy weighed up his words, and sheathed the blade at his waist. "You go. I go."

Petrovitch glanced around at Miyamoto, who stood poised, his hand on the hilt of his sword. "Relax, okay?"

"He is from the Outzone. He will kill you if he gets the chance."

"I'd like to think their motives are a little more nuanced than that. Isn't that right, kid?"

The boy's hand was straying back toward his bayonet, and Petrovitch felt the need to raise the gun barrel slightly. Maybe he would try and stick him. There was a look in his eye that warned everyone who might look that he was used to extreme, casual violence.

"So, let's talk trade."

The boy spat on the ground.

"You don't trade in the Outzone?"

"Strong take. Weak give." He squinted at the gun. "Not weak. Not give."

"Petrovitch," said Miyamoto. "We do not have time for this."

"There's time if I say there is." He looked again at the boy. "You know what a gun is, what it can do?"

The boy nodded.

"I could make you tell me what I need to know, but I won't do that. Instead, you get to ask me one question, and in return, I get to ask one of you."

"Weak! You weak!" shrieked the boy. But he didn't attack.

"I have the gun. Come on, you're the scout, the path-finder: in me, you have someone who's able to answer almost anything you might possibly think of."

The boy listened to the city, testing whether anyone else was near. "What you? What him?"

Petrovitch frowned. "What me what? Our names?"

Shake.

"What we do?"

Shake.

"Where we come from?" It finally got a nod. "I'm Russian. From St. Petersburg. He's Japanese, except there's no Japan anymore."

"Rus. Moscow," said the boy.

"Moscow, yes." He wondered where the conversation was going.

"Japan. Tokyo." The boy put his fingers at the corners of his eyes and stretched them into slits.

Petrovitch laughed, and Miyamoto was indignant.

"Not London."

"No, not London. Neither of us were born here."

And that, in some way entirely obscure to Petrovitch, seemed to satisfy the Outie boy. "Talk."

He seized his chance. "How are you coordinating this attack? Are you one army, or lots of groups? Is there any one person in charge?"

The boy tugged his ragged fingernails through his matted hair. Perhaps he thought he was being asked to give away too much. "Why? You hated enemy."

Petrovitch snorted. "Yeah, that's us. I need to find my wife. The last I heard, she was in West Ham, which is on the other side of the city."

"West Ham know. Wife know not."

"I didn't expect you to."

"That is not what he means: he does not understand what a wife is," said Miyamoto. He stepped forward, doing what the boy had done and listened to the city. It was unnatural, quiet. "His woman. He needs to find his woman."

"A woman? Why?"

"Again I say," said Miyamoto to Petrovitch, "we do not have time for this. Two decades of being Outzone has changed their language and culture so far that communication is impossible."

"I want to know what we're going to face out there. Is it a single army, or is it a rag-tag bunch of tribes who'd just as soon kill each other as kill us? Do they even have a plan? It's important." Petrovitch focused his attention on the boy. "Who's your boss? Who's the big man?"

"Fox," said the boy. "He kill you, he kill you." He pointed to each of them in turn.

"Yeah. He'll probably kill you, too. Where is he?"

The boy pointed unerringly north.

"Waiting for you to come back and report, right? You going to tell him about us?"

"Why not?"

"Because we're not interested in the same things. We're not competing. He wants to take the city. I want to find my wife."

"Fox not for city. Fox burn city. Burn all."

"And there was me thinking that all he wanted to do was take in a West End show and do a bit of sightseeing." Petrovitch rolled his eyes. "He's welcome to burn whatever he wants, as long as it's not me or mine. Though if he heads straight into the central zones from here, he'll have to watch out for the tanks."

"Tanks," repeated the boy. "What tanks?"

"This Fox: older than us, right? One of the original Outies? He'll know what a tank is," he said with a sly smile. "And my colleague is right. We're wasting time. Go on, back you go, wherever you came from."

The boy—not much older than Petrovitch had been when he'd been running through the frozen streets—put his hand on his knife and started to draw it. Petrovitch raised his gun and aimed it straight at his face. The boy grinned.

"Not weak," he said.

"No. Don't confuse me with the rest of the sheep. I'm not like them." Petrovitch waved the gun down the track. "Run."

As they watched the boy scamper away, jumping from one side of the rail to the other and back, just because he could, Miyamoto growled deep in his throat.

"What did that achieve?"

"*Zatknis*: I need to do something else." Petrovitch fetched out his rat. "You're tracking him?"

[Trivial,] said the avatar.

"Okay. Tag him, and anyone he comes into contact with. Then tag their contacts, too. Build me a map."

"Your hatnav again?"

"Slightly more than that. My associate," said Petro-vitch, and watched as text scrolled across his vision.

[I have been promoted, then. Co-equal with a biological entity. Yet the status of my citizenship remains in question.]

"That's . . ." he started. "Not now. Just tell me where the kid goes."

[He is passing under Ladbroke Grove. Road very busy, vehicular traffic stationary. No way through there. Now he is climbing the fence to access Canal Way. It is a dead end. He is cutting back east along the towpath. There is a narrow footbridge across to the north side beside the road bridge.]

"Okay." He closed the rat. "Got your breath back?"

"I would like for you," said Miyamoto, "to explain to me what it is you are doing."

"While we're moving." Petrovitch set off again, in the direction taken by the boy. When Miyamoto had caught up, he said. "Think of a virus. If being an Outie is a dis-ease, and the kid is a carrier, everyone he talks to has to be an Outie too. And everyone they talk to. If they have any sort of organization, I'll know where most of them are in a couple of hours."

"Clever," conceded Miyamoto. "Unless they use phones, or radios."

"Which they don't, otherwise their scouts would be carrying them."

An explosion rumbled in the distance. To the north, a fresh pillar of black smoke rose into the sky to join all the others that punctuated the horizon.

[Petrol station. Willesden.]

"How, how is it possible, that they hope to win?"

"By stampeding millions of people straight at the forces who might have the *yajtza* to fight back. Since the roads are clogged with fleeing refugees and we're reduced to running along railway lines, I'd say it was working."

He pulled ahead again, running fast and free.

18

[You now have twenty kilometers to go, instead of the ten you started with.]

"You brought us this way." Petrovitch hawked up phlegm and spat it between his feet. He straightened, pressing his hands into the hollow of his back. He was standing in a shunting yard between two lines of empty, rusting rail-trucks, and was taking the opportunity to rest. "I assume there was a good reason."

[When you asked me to calculate travel time, this route was genuinely the quickest.] The avatar dug its hands in its pockets, something that it had seen Petrovitch do a hundred times before.

"I'm sensing a but."

[You are not as fit as you wish to believe. I can identify places—probably several places—for water and food, since you have neglected to bring any with you.]

"Yeah. I didn't figure on running halfway across the Metrozone when I got out of bed this morning." He unstuck his T-shirt from his armpits. "That sounded like a subject change: why is this no longer the best way to go?"

Petrovitch's vision switched from the side of a paint-peeled truck to a real-time map of the immediate area. To the north, near the end of the old M1, was a concentration of red spots like a blood rash, each point an Outie. There were more than he'd expected, and he was about to ask the AI for precise numbers when the map started to contract, revealing what lay beyond its original borders.

There was another clump near Wembley, and three large masses on and around the fringes of Hampstead Heath, bleeding into the surrounding streets. His perspective drew further back, and a ragged line of clots stretched all the way from Ruislip to Stoke Newington. Behind the broad front were arteries of color, fading away into occupied ground.

"Yobany stos."

[The picture is incomplete. There are more data points in the east of the Metrozone, but the groups there have not yet been in contact with the western Outies. Also, information is passed across the line much quicker than it is passed back.]

"So how many are there?"

[One hundred and sixteen thousand, eight hundred and forty-three. Based on current densities, I estimate the total number of Outies to be in the region of two hundred thousand.] The scrolling text paused, and the avatar had the grace to affect a look of apology. [Does this qualify for the epithet *pizdets?*]

Petrovitch's heart span faster. His mouth was dry, and he took his breath in quick, shallow gasps. "Where the *huy* did they all come from?"

[The Outzone, initially. They may be recruiting as they advance, or they may just be that numerous. Whichever, it presents you with a considerable problem.] The avatar

shrugged. It hadn't been wrong, rather it had had insufficient information. [The probability of you successfully
using my original route to get to West Ham has decreased
to marginal values. A tactical withdrawal is recommended.]

There was another railway line, close by, that cut south:
it even had its own bridge across the Thames at Kew.
Petrovitch could see it on the aerial map. It was inviting
him to follow it.

He turned to face the east, down the line of the freight
cars, taking in the burning sky as he span. Miyamoto had
crouched down against a wheel, hands resting on the
weed-strewn ballast, head bowed, hauling air. He sensed
he was being watched.

"What?"

"There's a problem."

"Which is?" Miyamoto bared his clenched teeth.

"My associate reckons on a couple of hundred thousand
Outies between us and where we want to go."

Miyamoto looked sharply up.

"Yeah," said Petrovitch. "If you want to bug out, I'll
understand. In fact, I think I'd prefer you to go. You're not
exactly dressed for the occasion."

"What do you mean? What is wrong with what I am
wearing?"

"You look like a *yebani* ninja! I suppose you could put
on a hi-vis jacket to make yourself more obvious, but
you've got 'chase me' written all over you."

"Whereas you, with your coat in ruins and your clothes
unwashed for weeks..."

"Am a dead ringer for an Outie." Petrovitch flashed a
feral grin. "Who would have guessed that poor dress sense
and appalling personal hygiene could be a survival trait?"

"Two hundred thousand."

"At a rough guess. It could be more."

Miyamoto dragged himself upright and stalked over to Petrovitch until they were almost nose to nose.

"I should kill you myself and save them the trouble."

"What would Miss Sonja say then?"

"I would kill myself after dispatching you, so no explanation would be necessary. At least," he said, "I could go to my grave knowing that I have saved her from wasting her life fawning over an idiot like you."

Petrovitch pointed over Miyamoto's shoulder. "The south is that way."

Miyamoto balled his fists in frustration. "Two hundred thousand enemies. How can you possibly believe you can avoid them all—and then find your wife?"

"Clearly I do, because otherwise I'd be giving up and going home."

"That is not what I meant. What reason could you have for this level of self-delusion?"

Petrovitch swung away. "The Outies are on the move again, and we're too exposed here. I'm not responsible for you, or what you do: stay, go, follow, leave. Up to you. You need to choose now, though." He shrugged, and added; "I'm still going to find Madeleine."

[Even though you don't love her.]

The corner of Petrovitch's mouth twitched, and the avatar acknowledged its line-crossing with an apologetic bow, followed by its sudden vanishing.

"I swore to protect you," said Miyamoto. His close-cropped hair bristled with undisguised fury.

"Not to me, you didn't. You have no obligations to me whatsoever."

Miyamoto's jaw clenched tight. "This is not about you."

"No, apparently not." Petrovitch watched the red dots slowly crawl like grains of falling sand through the narrow streets of Cricklewood. He turned once to orient himself, and started to jog down to the end of the row of wagons.

He reached the last car, checked his map, and made for the particular branch line he needed. He didn't turn around: he could hear the clatter of shifting ballast close behind him and, more telling, the hiss of whispered Japanese curses.

He didn't know whether he was glad of the company or not. Part of him, the ruthless, dispassionate side, was already thinking that since Miyamoto would sacrifice himself to save him, how best to use this one-shot weapon. The other part, the part that he would readily acknowledge as embarrassingly small, was merely grateful for the presence of another human being not psychologically conditioned to kill him on sight.

Then there was the question of his own motivation. He knew why Miyamoto was sticking with him. He knew why the Outies wanted to gut the city and hang it out to dry. Why was he doing what he was doing?

"Any sign of Madeleine?"

[There has been radio traffic on the MilNet. Several MEA units are currently engaged with Outie fighters, and more are fortifying positions in front of the advance. I have plotted these forward units, and it is likely that your wife is with one of them. Evacuated casualties are logged, and her name does not appear.]

"How about the CIA?"

[Rendering detailed, real-time satellite data across several wavelengths and tracking all the Outies places serious demands on my resources.]

"It's important."

[I can appropriate more processing power if you ask me to. It will degrade the bandwidth available to other users.]

"I imagine anyone in the Metrozone is going to be too busy worrying about the Outies to notice a slow-down."

[I meant globally. Someone, somewhere will investigate, and if they are smart enough, they will find me.]

"Yeah. Okay. Do what you can." He was hemmed in either side by banks of greened earth. He looked up at the backs of the houses. At least when the time came, there wouldn't be a shortage of places to hide from the Outies.

Petrovitch turned his attention to the tunnel ahead, a dead space where the AI couldn't look. The nearest known Outies were three k to the north—Fox's group—but there could be others ahead of the front line, untagged, invisible.

Three hundred meters in the dark. At least it was straight, and the bright circle at the far end wouldn't be an oncoming train. He did look behind him now, and watched as the black-clad figure ran toward him, the man's motion a lot less loose and lithe than it had been.

"We have to go through here."

Miyamoto nodded, and he moved to the side of the tunnel, to better see if there was anyone silhouetted against the distant patch of sky. Petrovitch dodged to the other side, and kept his eyes on the shadow in front.

The line between light and dark got closer.

[The Outies are moving. Your paths will cross at Kilburn High Road, two kilometers ahead.]

"Show me."

A semi-transparent map flicked over his view of reality. Petrovitch frowned.

"That'll take them straight through the Paradise housing complex."

[Yes.]

"As much as I'd like to see the Outies and the Paradise
militia fight to the death, having a front line right across
our route sucks."

[There is another railway track, just to the north. It will
put you behind the Outie advance.]

"Yeah. We'll take it." Petrovitch slowed as he reached
the tunnel exit, and called to Miyamoto. "Diversion."

He ran across the tracks to the far side, and down along
the uneven line of high wooden fencing that separated
railway from garden. He shoved at random panels, and
one proved more rickety than the others.

He put his shoulder to it. Something gave, and he tried
again. Wood splintered and nails creaked. Miyamoto lent
his strength to the enterprise, and the panel cracked, coming free from one of its supporting posts.

Petrovitch braced his back against it, holding it aside,
then twisted around the end once Miyamoto had slipped
through. His coat caught on the protruding nails: the
points pierced the leather and dug into his shoulder.

He hissed and tugged free, running his hand up under
his T-shirt and coming away with a smear of dark blood.

"Chyort."

Miyamoto was already making his way along the concrete path to the back door, trying to look stealthy. Petrovitch shrugged his stinging shoulder, and stalked after him.

The door was wooden, with a single square of glass.
The keys were on the edge of the sink, next to the stack of
used crockery. Miyamoto took a step back to look up
for another point of entry. Petrovitch stooped to collect a

couple of house bricks from the stack by the shed, and when he was close enough, he threw one at the wide kitchen window.

The glass crashed inward, and shards of what remained fell under their own weight and broke on the sill. Miyamoto stared open-mouthed at him. Petrovitch growled and used the other brick to sweep away the jagged points still sticking out from the frame.

"Keep it simple, *raspizdyai*."

He discarded the brick onto the scrubby lawn and shucked off his coat, throwing it across the sea of shattered glass. He hopped up, across the top of the taps and onto the floor. His footsteps crunched as he shook out his coat in a shower of glittering splinters.

Miyamoto was still outside. Petrovitch slid the keys into his hand and twisted the most likely one in the lock. It clicked, and he pushed at the handle.

"What kept you?"

"We are supposed to be tactical." Miyamoto barged through, banging the door into Petrovitch's shoulder and making him wince.

"*Zhopa.*"

The AI interrupted him. There were new contacts, just two streets away, a long, thin line of red markers making their way purposefully toward a road bridge across the railway line.

Petrovitch opened the fridge. The food was still cold, the light still came on. He grabbed the carton of orange juice, the plastic liter of milk and the slab of cheese, setting them on the kitchen table amidst the debris.

"The Outies are too near. Get yourself something, and we'll move when they've passed."

He twisted the top off the milk and drank straight from the bottle, half of it in one tilt.

"You...you are an animal. A pig."

Petrovitch wiped the milky mustache away with his sleeve—first checking there was no embedded glass—and looked over the top of his glasses at Miyamoto.

"Mne nasrat', chto ty dumaesh."

"Speak English."

"A rough translation, then: bite me." Instead, he bit at the cheese, tearing off the wrapper with his teeth and spitting out the plastic on the floor. "You don't have to watch."

He chewed, daring the other man to say anything. The cheese tasted much like the wrapping but, tasteless as it was, it had the fats he craved.

A creak came from upstairs. Petrovitch put down the cheese and the milk. The knife block, tucked away in the corner, was already missing the biggest, sharpest blade, and a quick glance at the drainer didn't find it.

He put his finger to his lips, and pointed at the ceiling. Miyamoto drew his *katana* with a soft steel ring and held it close across his body. Petrovitch chose the twenty-centimeter knife with the serrated edge from the block. He wrapped his hand with a tea towel before gripping the handle through the cloth.

Miyamoto opened the kitchen door at a rush. There was the front door—closed—and the stairs up next to it. He trod quietly across the thin carpet, keeping his eyes aimed at the staircase. Petrovitch held his knife hand low and tried to emulate the silent footsteps.

The man in black took each step slowly, testing his weight, then moving up. They got halfway, and the tread Petrovitch was on protested. In the quiet, it sounded like a whipcrack.

Miyamoto's whole body slumped sadly, but only long enough to convey just how disappointed he felt. He swarmed up the rest of the flight and in quick succession kicked the three doors that led off the landing. All three banged back against their stops.

He saw something, and darted into the bathroom toward the back of the house. Petrovitch was right behind him as he raised his sword over his shoulder, about to slash through the drawn shower curtain that obscured the bathtub.

Petrovitch shouldered him out of the way, pushing him over the toilet and clattering against the cistern. The tip of the sword traced a line that started at neck height and finished at waist level, across most of the translucent curtain.

The material sagged and gaped to reveal a girl, as white as the cold tiles she had pressed her back against, kitchen knife clutched in her quivering hands.

Miyamoto leaped up with a shout and started to swing again. This time, Petrovitch stepped in front and blocked the sword arm with his own.

They were face to face, and if he hadn't been wearing glasses, Petrovitch would have tried a headbutt. "What the *huy* is the matter with you?" He put his free hand against Miyamoto's chest and held him away.

When he was certain Miyamoto wasn't going to attack again, Petrovitch pulled the curtain back. The girl had slipped down, and now crouched in one end of the tub, knifepoint still trembling at them. She was in her school uniform.

"Yeah. Look at the big, bad Outie hiding in the *yebani* bathroom." He dropped his knife and unwound the tea towel. "You can come out now."

19

*H*er name was Lucy. Finding that out took a good five minutes of coaxing. It took another five to get her out of the tub and still she wouldn't put the knife down.

"We're not going to hurt you, just don't do anything that'll attract the Outies, who," and Petrovitch consulted his map, "are at the end of the street."

He sat on the floor by the door, having shooed Miyamoto and his big sword out. The girl cowered in the space between the toilet and the sink.

"What if I scream?" she said.

"Then I imagine me and the Last Samurai will run for it, and you'll get picked up by the Outies. Now, I have no idea what they do with Inzoners when they catch them, but that mere fact—that no one has yet reported what happens—makes me think it won't be a Good Thing. How old are you?"

"F-fourteen."

"Yeah. I don't know how vivid your imagination is, but you probably wouldn't want to be in my head right now."

She shivered uncontrollably, and Petrovitch was as

certain as he could be that she wouldn't make a sound over a squeak. "How come you're still here? Everyone else has gone south, and you should have been with them."

"M-my parents. They called me. Told me to stay here. Said they'd come and get me." Her fingers tightened around the knife hilt, forcing her knuckles white against the black of her uniform. "They're not, are they? Coming to get me, I mean."

"No. No, they're not." Petrovitch straightened his legs out, forcing his toes to point up. "I don't know what they were thinking: they should have told you to run. You should have run anyway."

"But they said."

"They got it wrong."

"You got here, didn't you?" Her chin lifted for the first time.

Petrovitch pushed his glasses against the bridge of his nose. "I'm not your mom or dad. I have a gun, a bodyguard, and a very good idea where every single Outie is. Unless your mom is Special Forces or your dad owns a helicopter, I'm the only friendly face you're going to see in a while."

"What am I going to do?" she said.

"I don't know," said Petrovitch. "You ran out of options about the time we turned up."

He started to get up, and even that little movement had her one leg in the bath again. He was stiff, especially his calves. He stretched them, one at a time, and shook each foot.

"Seriously. What am I going to do?"

"Lucy. I…" He sat down again, on the toilet seat next to her so that he wouldn't have to look at her. "I'm not here to rescue you. Miyamoto is not here to rescue you either—

he has to come with me for reasons that are too complicated to go into now. I have to find my wife and warn her
that the nice MEA intelligence officer we met yesterday is
a CIA agent and therefore responsible for murdering one
of the few friends I had and nearly killing me. Twice.
We'll be going through Outzone-controlled streets pretty
much all the way, and the odds are currently a hundred
thousand to one." He took a deep breath. "Whatever mess
you're in, I can't get you out of it."

She dropped the knife she held, and sobbed. Just the
once. She walked with unsteady gait to the door and
opened it. She stepped through, closed it quietly behind
her, and left Petrovitch feeling like utter *govno*.

The Outies on his map were grouping at the north end
of the bridge over the railway line. He guessed that they'd
cross in a couple of minutes, and he'd then officially be in
enemy territory. It was almost time to move out.

Lucy's knife was point-down in the curling cork tiles
on the floor. Petrovitch plucked it out and turned it in his
hand. Its lack of guard made it a weapon of last resort, but
that was pretty much where he was. He wrapped it and the
other he'd picked out of the knife block into the tea towel,
and slid them into a coat pocket.

Then he went back downstairs to the kitchen, where
Miyamoto was sipping water from a glass.

"We cannot take her with us," he said.

"I've explained that to her," said Petrovitch. He picked
up the carton of warming orange juice and flipped the lid
open. "Considering we're leaving her to certain death, or
worse, I think she took it very well."

"You will never complete your mission with her. It is . . .
unfortunate."

Petrovitch necked down half the juice. "Yeah."

"She is very young," noted Miyamoto.

"With no useful skills or knowledge. Her legs: did you see her legs?"

"Like two thin sticks."

"And her knees were like *yebani* knots on cotton." Petrovitch started opening cupboards, looking through them, closing the doors again as he moved around the kitchen. "She couldn't keep up."

"No. I cannot imagine she has run for anything other than a bus in her whole short life." Miyamoto rose from his chair and refilled his glass.

The electricity died. The display on the microwave winked out, the fridge motor stopped purring, even the wall clock shuddered and was still. Domestic alarms screeched into life, every house, over the whole area, including the one they were in.

The noise was deafening, as it was designed to be— just the right frequency to drill into the skull.

Miyamoto put down his glass and stalked into the hall-way. After a few moments, the cacophony inside the house was abruptly terminated. Outside, the noise carried on, but it was now bearable.

As he came back into the kitchen, he sheathed his sword. "They have cut the power."

"Taken out the substation, I guess." Petrovitch had found some empty drinks bottles: he was now trying to match lids to necks. "They're right outside."

"What are they doing?"

Petrovitch squinted at his glasses. "Just looking around, I hope. No, there's a car coming."

He left the bottles and went back upstairs. Lucy's bedroom had her name on it in colored plastic letters. He eased into her room and crouched down by the window. She was lying on her bed, face down in the pink pillow, perfectly still until she heard the door shoosh close.

She looked up with red-rimmed eyes, and Petrovitch pressed his finger to his lips. He peered over the window ledge, through the translucent net, to the street below.

The car—red, low, fast, with tinted glass and shiny alloy wheels—accelerated toward the Outies in the road. To start with, it looked like they didn't understand what was happening. They didn't step back, and even though there was a line of cars parked either side of the road, they didn't try to stand behind one of them, or any of the lamp posts. Neither did they aim any of their few guns, ranging from a couple of ancient revolvers through several shotguns to one modern assault rifle.

The red car's engine roared. The front wing clipped one of the stationary vehicles, and it swerved violently across the white line, flicking the wing mirror of another into the sky.

The Outie in the very middle of the road was carrying a steel pole as tall as he was. He raised it in his dusty hand and held it like a javelin, and waited. The other Outies pulled away, unhurried, strolling in their soft, animal-skin-shod feet.

The car was almost on him, and he was perfectly still.

Then he jumped as if he had springs in his heels. He made no effort to throw the tube, but it fell, still perfectly horizontal, into the path of the oncoming windscreen.

It went through. The windscreen crazed across its whole width, and the pole kept on coming out the back window, where it came to rest, half-in, half-out. With a screech of tires and two successive bangs, the car ended up sideways, wedged between the parked cars. Smoke whispered from the crushed bonnet, and a fine white powder was blowing from the shattered interior. Wailing car alarms now added to the noise.

The Outie man landed on the tarmac, crouching, reaching for the knife at his belt. He straightened up, holding his arm high, and the rest of them surrounded the crashed car.

The driver's door popped open. A figure fell out into the road, at the man's feet. White dust swirled away, and a deflating airbag shriveled at the dashboard. The man reached down, took the driver by the throat and hauled him up.

It looked like a man, though there was so much blood on his face it was difficult to tell if he was young or old. Not that it mattered much, because in the next second, the Outie had stabbed him—a hard punch to the left side of the neck that made the tip of the blade come out the right. He held the blade still while his victim jerked and clawed, briefly.

Then he dragged it out, almost severing the head and leaving the tattered mess where it fell.

The other Outies made no attempt to intervene, join in, talk to each other—anything. They watched, passively, as the man squatted on his haunches to inspect the inside of the car.

He inclined his head, and with his free hand, beckoned.

The passenger door flew open, and a girl with a tight blonde ponytail burst out. She stumbled after the first few frantic steps, and sprawled onto the road. The Outie threw himself across the crumpled metal of the bonnet, rolled and landed square in the girl's back just as she tried to rise.

Lucy was standing behind Petrovitch, staring down at her quiet suburban street, where nothing much of anything ever happened.

Petrovitch marched her back to the bed and sat her down, out of eyeshot. He could hear screaming over the alarms, and he wished he couldn't. He scratched at his chin, then flicked his glasses off and pinched the bridge of his nose.

When he opened his eyes, he was looking at her feet.

"Do you own a pair of trainers?"

She was wearing black shoes with a wedge heel. Must have been a good school: black shoes, black tights, black skirt, white shirt, blazer with a crest on the pocket. A tie, for pity's sake.

"Y-yes." She pointed at her wardrobe. She cringed as a long, drawn-out cry from outside ended in a low, rasping moan.

"Put them on," said Petrovitch.

Her blurred outline nodded. She took the two steps across the room, and retrieved the whitest pair of trainers he'd ever seen.

"Chyort." He pushed his glasses back onto his face. The red dots that represented the group outside were drifting back toward the bridge, and he checked out of the window to make sure. He could see their backs as they wandered up the road.

Lucy already had her trainers on, and was standing by the door. She opened her mouth to say something, and Petrovitch pre-empted her.

"Do not," he said, "now or ever, thank me. Okay?"

"But…"

"Just don't." He pushed past her and descended to the kitchen. He filled three small bottles with water, threw one to Miyamoto, and one to Lucy. She managed to catch it.

Miyamoto stared at the girl, and then at Petrovitch. He narrowed his eyes.

"You said."

"Past' zabej! We have five minutes at most to make it to the next line north." He reached into his coat pocket for Lucy's knife. He held it out to her, handle first. She hesitated, and Petrovitch growled. "You know what to do with it? Yes?"

"Yes." She took it from him, and wondered where to put it. She ended up holding the waistband of her pleated skirt out, and sliding the flat of the blade against her hip.

"We have to go. Front door."

They moved down the hall. Petrovitch turned the latch and opened the door. The sound of bleeping and blaring and ringing crowded in. He took a deep breath and started to run.

The Outies had gone right. They went left, away from the crash scene and the spreading pools of blood, hunched over so that the tops of their heads were no higher than the tops of the cars.

They crossed the road, quickly, skittering like blown leaves, then turned up a side street. Petrovitch straightened up, glanced behind. Lucy was next, her stupidly obvious footwear flashing like the warning signals of a startled deer. Miyamoto was almost on her heels, close enough to put his hand in the small of her back and push her along if he'd wanted to.

The road swung around toward the station. The nearest

Outies were at the top of Willesden Green, coming down the hill toward them. Less than a kilometer away. Hardly any distance at all.

Using the map as a guide, they darted into a private car park that bounded the railway cutting. A high fence of concrete panels blocked their path. Petrovitch crouched down by the wall and cupped his hands between his knees.

Again, Lucy froze, not knowing what to do. Miyamoto jogged past her and, without breaking step, placed his foot in Petrovitch's hands.

He was boosted to the top of the wall, and as deftly as any gymnast threw one leg over so that he straddled it.

"Run," said Petrovitch, "jump." Miyamoto lowered his hand for her.

She took two steps back, then sprinted. She seemed to have her eyes mostly closed, but managed to leap at the right moment.

Miyamoto caught her forearm and, with a face screwed up with effort, pulled her the rest of the way. She wobbled briefly, then dropped down the other side.

Petrovitch took a run-up himself, and planted his feet against the rough concrete, hanging from Miyamoto's wrist. They looked at each other, briefly, and Petrovitch found that he was completely unable to read his expression.

"Sorry," said Petrovitch. "We had to bring her."

"You had to bring her, you mean."

"Yeah, that's precisely what I mean."

Petrovitch put one elbow over the top of the wall, and let go of Miyamoto to get the other across. He hauled himself painfully up, then measured the drop on the other side. Lucy was looking up at him from the rough grasses of the embankment, swigging from her bottle. She was already dirty and disheveled, her tights torn through at the knees.

He rolled his body, and hung by his fingertips. Then he fell, picked himself up, and batted his coat with his hands.

Lucy asked him. "What do I call you?"

"Whatever you want. Sam, I suppose."

Miyamoto released himself from his perch and landed softly beside them. "Which way?"

Petrovitch pointed northeast, and Miyamoto set off to join the rails without another word.

"He doesn't want me here, does he?"

"It doesn't matter what he thinks." Petrovitch checked all his belongings. The rat was still safely in one pocket, the gun and knife in another, the bottle in a third. "All that matters now is that you stay with me."

20

Fresh text scrolled across his eyeline as he jogged along. They were crossing over a major road on a gray-painted bridge, but its sides were high, and topped with even higher mesh, in an attempt to prevent thrown objects landing on the tracks.

There were Outies beneath, but they couldn't see him. Knowing they were there made his heart turn a little faster, made him place his feet a little more carefully.

He paid attention to the words bouncing in front of him.

[Reuters: Nobel nominee Dr. Epiphany Ekanobi arrested attempting illegal border crossing to Mexico from U.S. Dept for Homeland Security source states Ekanobi "credible terrorist threat."]

"Chyort vozmi," he growled.

[She is being held at the local sheriff's office until personnel arrive from Los Angeles.]

Petrovitch felt his fists clench involuntarily. "If they so much as harm a single hair on her head, I'll…"

[What possible damage can you do to them?]

"Crash their currency. Wipe their records. Deny them their satellites. Dangle them over the information abyss and threaten to drop them."

[While I am likely to be able to do these things, I would need persuading before I was willing. Furthermore, I am currently using some of their assets to help you: the NSA are providing your satellite imagery.]

"I didn't mean now: we're busy. Later will do fine."

[Regarding the digital map: I cannot sustain it beyond 1656 GMT. Unless all the Outies remain perfectly still over the fifteen minutes between one viewing platform setting over the horizon and the next rising sufficiently high to take over, all data will be lost.]. It added helpfully, [Just over five hours.]

"I could crawl on my hands and knees and still make it to West Ham in four." He turned, running backward for a few steps, to place his finger to his lips and point downward at the road.

[It is unfortunate that Dr. Ekanobi has been captured. But I have identified the MEA unit your wife is attached to: she is north of West Ham, on the North Circular. They have taken up a defensive position on a raised section of road.]

"But won't they end up completely surrounded?"

[There is another MEA unit engaged in a fighting retreat toward Woolwich. Their tactics appear to be to use one group as a diversion while the other escapes, more or less intact, along with the many thousands of refugees ahead of them.]

"So she's bait."

[Yes.]

"Does it look like there's a plan to get them out?"

[No.]

"I'm not abandoning her."

[Your worth to human civilization is far greater than the meaningless sacrifice of your life for a woman you cannot say you love. If you try to save her, you will die.]

"Yeah. You know this for sure?"

[The girl Lucy will die too.]

"*Zatknis' na hui.* There'll be a way. I just have to think of it."

The embankment graded out and for a few short paces they were level with houses. They swept under a vast concrete structure that carried trains into Finchley Road, and kept angling down. The ground either side and in front rose up, and the tracks multiplied and split, left and right: after they passed through Finchley station on separate platforms, each bundle of rails went under the hill of Hampstead Heath. No short tunnel this time.

Petrovitch slowed and let the others catch up. Miyamoto was working hard, enough to make him reluctant to speak—and Petrovitch was glad for that, since he was getting more than enough grief off the AI. Lucy looked ready to drop, though. She was pale, shaky, and it looked like it hurt every time she tried to breathe.

Perhaps they could walk the next kilometer as it was entirely underground.

"We go in here," he started to say, but his words were lost in the shrill whistle of artillery.

The shells came from the south, howled overhead and exploded with a full-throated roar a few streets away. Debris lifted into the air, and pulverized dust began to drift in grubby clouds.

[EDF tanks in Primrose Hill. They seem confident that there are no civilians left in the target area.]

A second volley of gunfire blossomed in red and black down the Finchley Road. Glass shattered and walls fell, and the ground shook. Slates and tiles span away, and started to hit the railway track like spinning plates, exploding as they crashed down. The sound of the shells leaving the guns was a distant and belated afterthought.

"Run."

Petrovitch reached forward and grabbed Lucy's hand, and he had to drag her, her exhausted legs unable to respond.

The barrage continued, getting closer, but they were safe in the tunnel's mouth and picking their way further in. Gritty soot rained down on their heads with every concussion, and the air itself stiffened with every explosion.

Petrovitch fumbled in his pocket for the rat, his other arm fighting the losing battle to keep the schoolgirl upright. He ended up dumping her on her backside and leaning her against his legs while he flipped the case open and dialed the screen's brightness up to maximom.

The pearl light illuminated the peaky whiteness of Lucy's face, the oily darkness of the Victorian brickwork, and his own dusty glasses. Miyamoto stood watching the detritus accumulate across the tracks outside, and then the station took a direct hit.

The blast wave made them all duck down and cover their heads, and the roil of smoke that followed had its own distinctive taste. It smelled of war.

Petrovitch held the rat up, jerked Lucy to her feet and pushed her further in. The tunnel entrance was a hazy dot when they stopped again.

"We should be all right here," he said.

Miyamoto's eyes blinked in the soft glow. "And if the tunnel collapses?"

"We're screwed. But it stood up to the Luftwaffe: a few tank rounds aren't going to make a difference." Petrovitch sat down next to Lucy. "You okay?"

She had scrunched her body up and was shivering uncontrollably. "Ohgodohgodohgod," she was whispering, while her fingers writhed like dirty worms.

"Yeah, you'll get used to it." She'd lost her water bottle, and Petrovitch pressed his on her. "You might think that you were safer where you were, but that's just an illusion. We're doing fine. You're doing fine. Better than I expected, anyway."

She said something that he couldn't quite catch.

"Say again?" He leaned in close.

"N-not bad f-for a girl." She looked out at him under her fringe.

"Not bad at all." He patted her shoulder awkwardly, not knowing what else to say. He felt he ought to try. "I will get you out of this: I promise."

Lucy fixed him with her wide eyes that glowed in the light of the rat's screen. "Y-you're just saying that." Her whole body spasmed, and she clutched her knees tighter.

"I've done this before. I didn't lose anyone then. I don't intend to now."

She nodded. "But...outside."

"Yeah. We'll have to do something about that. The Outies we can deal with, but a stray artillery round will really ruin our day."

Miyamoto reached over his back and drew his sword with a singing ring. "The European Defense Force are targeting Outie concentrations, but I do not believe that it will stop the inevitable loss of the northern Metrozone."

Petrovitch tapped his rat. He'd lost the satellite

connection—too much soil and rock between him and the open sky. "It's not inevitable. Not anymore."

"Explain."

"The Outie advance relied on the wave of refugees ahead of it overwhelming the defenders' capacity to cope. As long as they kept right up to the heels of the last fleeing Metrozoner, they were going to win. But they've fallen behind. They've underestimated just how fast a population can shift when the *govno* hits the fan. If the EDF can get enough troops on the ground to hold a line, set up enough pinch-points to funnel the Outies into the killing grounds, then not waver even when they're down to their last bullet..." Petrovitch cocked his ear to the steady crump of explosions echoing down the tunnel. "I could win it."

"Your capacity for self-aggrandisement never fails to astound me." Miyamoto snorted. "You are not a god. You are not a general. You are a weak, venal, delusional street child who never grew up."

Petrovitch played his tongue across his teeth for the few moments it took his anger to rise and then subside. "I don't see anyone else around here who's got a bunch of equations named after them." He pretended to search the shadows for the ghosts of Schrödinger, Fermi and Heisenberg. "And I'm the only one who bought a *yebani* torch! So why don't you just watch and learn?"

He levered himself to his feet, and crooked his hand under Lucy's armpit. She looked up at him.

"Now?"

"Yeah. Sorry." He pulled her up and held on while she steadied herself.

"I'm ready," she said, though her legs could barely support her. The darkness of the tunnel bore down on her, but she struggled and stood tall. "Definitely ready."

They walked down the center of the two tracks, on the rise of ballast that rattled and clattered when they kicked it, making sharp distinct sounds compared with the dull bass boom that reverberated around them. Without his map, Petrovitch was guessing they were halfway, and that they really ought to be able to see the far end sometime soon.

They didn't: he couldn't remember there being a curve that might block their view, and he held the little screen further out to one side, so as not to ruin his night sight.

There were lights ahead. Several, but none of them were shards of daylight.

"Chyort." He snapped the rat shut and stayed perfectly still. Lucy, dogging his heels, stumbled into his outstretched arm and gave a little squeak of fear.

He watched and listened; he didn't have a heartbeat to sound in his ears. Miyamoto seemed to have vanished, but he could hear the girl's panting breaths off to his left. Above those slight vibrations, above the sub-sonic trembling of exploding shells, was a soft susurration of voices. The lights were still, though occasionally one seemed to flicker, as if a body occluded it.

Lucy was still in contact with his arm. He guessed at where her hand would be and, as silently as he could, walked her to the wall. He put her hand on it, and whispered into her hair, "Stay still."

He left her there, and walked on, his own fingertips trailing the damp, crumbling tunnel side. He slipped the rat into a pocket, and filled that hand with his gun.

The lights grew and brightened. He could make out shape and form, and he frowned. There was a train in the tunnel, and there were people on that train. Petrovitch rode his luck, and loped up to the rear buffers.

It was a commuter train, stalled due to the power cut. The passengers ought to be long gone, though. The weak blue-white light just about made it through the oily dusty patina of the windows of the carriages, but no further. He pressed his ear to the metalwork. The buzzing, rumbling voices inside were indistinct, and he gained nothing but another smear of dirt.

Some of the train doors were open; the footplate was chest height, and Petrovitch stealthily eased himself aboard, crawling across the floor at the entrance until he could swing his legs up and in. He peered over the bottom of the internal door, through the smeary glass.

He could count about a dozen people, and supposed there might be a dozen more. Someone was standing in the aisle, their back to him, and he appeared to be wearing a dressing gown. A checkered, brown dressing gown, with a plaited cord tied around the waist.

Petrovitch stood up, and found the door handle. His first attempt at opening it failed, because he didn't appreciate that it slid to one side and wasn't hinged.

By the time he finally made a gap wide enough to squeeze through, most of the occupants of the train were standing, all were staring, and a hushed, pregnant silence had descended over them.

"Hey," said Petrovitch.

A man in a white coat pushed past the dressing-gown wearer—though almost everyone was in some form of nightwear—and brandished a syringe.

"No closer," he warned, then ruined the effect by adding, "please."

Petrovitch held up the gun in his hand. "I don't need to get closer. Hang on." He leaned to one side, trying to see the far end of the carriage. "Miyamoto? Miyamoto?"

Heads turned, and there was a terse "What?"

"Put the *yebani* sword away, grab one of those lantern things and go and get Lucy."

Miyamoto stepped out of the shadows and sheathed his blade. He snatched one of the little shining globes off the table between two elderly women and retraced his steps back into the darkness, carrying the light with him.

Petrovitch started to put the gun away, then thought better of it. "You first." He didn't want a needlestick, accidental or otherwise, and he could guarantee that anything inside the syringe wasn't going to be good for him.

The man in the white coat crouched down and put the hypodermic on the floor, and Petrovitch waved them all back while he retrieved it. The liquid inside was clear, with tiny crystalline bubbles clinging to the meniscus.

He put it up on the luggage rack out of harm's way. Everyone was waiting for something, anything, to happen.

Petrovitch lowered his gun, dangling it in his hand. The white coat had an ID badge clipped to the pen-filled breast pocket. He couldn't make out the name in the gloom, and assumed the man's profession. "What the *chy-ort* are you all doing here?"

"You're not," said the doctor, "you're not one of them?"

"Despite appearances to the contrary, no. You shouldn't be here. You should be south."

"This," and he balled his fists in evident frustration, "this is as far as we could get."

His patients—his charges—nodded sadly.

"We had a bus," said a man with the first flush of white

stubble patterning his jowls; "we had one and we got it took off us. Turfed us out in the street, they did."

Another shrugged. "What did they expect us to do? Walk?"

Petrovitch grabbed the doctor by the collar and dragged him away toward the door.

"*Yobany stos,* man. Walking would have been better, whatever speed they could have managed. You could have made it to the Thames by now."

"I've got patients with emphysema, angina, diabetes, hip replacements, open leg ulcers, cataracts, glaucoma. I had to make a decision: yes, a couple of them could have made it. But we decided to stay together." The doctor narrowed his eyes. "Don't I know you?"

"Yeah, I'm a *yebani* celebrity."

"The sweary physics guy on the news. But…" He scratched his ear hard. "Look, I don't care why you're here. What are our chances?"

Petrovitch saw a light appear at the far end of the carriage, and Lucy stumble along the aisle toward them.

"The Outie advance has gone over your heads. We're Outzone now, and everything that means."

"Then what's that pounding?"

"EDF artillery. Too little, too late. We're facing an army you can measure in the hundreds of thousands, and no one's seemed to realize that a few well-placed HE rounds isn't going to make a blind bit of difference. Unless I can persuade them otherwise, the EDF will hold on as long as they can, then they and MEA will blow the bridges and abandon the north. That means you, and everyone else left in it."

The doctor's face twitched.

Petrovitch dropped his gun in his pocket and moved

back to accommodate Lucy. "Whichever way you look at it, you're pretty much hosed. You're in the middle of occupied territory. Even if the Outies don't come and find you, you're going to have to leave here eventually. Unless you're intending to euthanize the lot of them."

When the idea wasn't immediately rejected out of hand, Petrovitch felt himself flush cold.

"Tell me you didn't bring them down here to die."

"Then what," said the doctor, tight-lipped, "do you suggest I do?"

"What?" said Lucy, face turning from one man to the other. "What's going on?"

"I," said Petrovitch, and swallowed. He looked at the lined, tired faces and the rheumy eyes reflected in the cold blue light. "No. I've just about had it. *Huy tebe v'zhopu!* This has gone on long enough. We're turning into a bunch of *yebani* savages, and it's about time someone stood up, extended their middle finger and screamed *'Zhri govno i zdohni!'* "

"Sam," said Lucy, with an embarrassed smile, "actually, you are screaming whatever it is."

"Good." He gathered up the front of the doctor's white coat in his tightening hand and pulled him forward until they were nose to nose. "You will not—and I'll repeat that—not hurt a single one of these people. Do you understand me? Even if you kill yourself afterward, I will find some way to drag you back to life and make you suffer like no one has ever suffered before."

Petrovitch let go and wiped his hand free of any contagion. Again, all eyes were on him, and he snorted.

"Miyamoto?" he called. He could see the man's shoulders slump in the shadows. "Yeah, you're with me. We're going to find some sky. And then," he muttered so that only Lucy could really hear, "I'm going to throw myself into the open gates of hell and damn them to do their worst."

He spun around, his ragged coat-tails flying in streamers behind him, and stalked away back out into the darkness.

21

*W*hat is it that you are intending to do?"

Petrovitch stamped toward the tunnel's exit and refused to answer.

"You must tell me." Miyamoto caught him up, put a hand on his shoulder and spun him around. "What madness affects you now?"

"I," said Petrovitch, "don't have to tell you anything. Anything at all. Your job is to keep me alive. That's it. My job seems to be considerably more complicated, so why don't you shut up and let me get on with it?"

When he made to turn away again, Miyamoto could barely restrain himself.

"No. No: you cannot do this. If you die—when you die—I will be blamed. Miss Sonja will send me away. If I am to keep you safe, you must reconsider this madness." He could think of nothing else to say. "I beg you."

Petrovitch stood with his back to him. "You're putting too much store in a relationship that's a figment of your imagination. Sonja is using your devotion to her like a queen would a knight. Wake up, man! She doesn't want you."

"No, she wants you."

The corner of Petrovich's mouth twisted into a grimace. "She can't have me. I'm promised to another."

"Your wife will not survive this. You know that. And when she is gone..." Miyamoto's voice finished in a strangled grunt of frustration and bitterness.

"If you say that again, I will shoot you dead and damn the consequences." Petrovitch brought his arm up straight and pointed the gun at Miyamoto's head. "We are going to fight, and we are going to win. Got that?"

"Truly, you are insane."

"What's it all for, then? What is it I'm meant to do? What's the point of being the smartest guy I know if I don't use those smarts to do something?" Petrovitch lowered the gun.

"We have gone in a full circle," said Miyamoto. "What do you propose to do that will save not just Lucy, and those elders, but your wife too?"

"I'm going to use the One Ring, even though I might have left it too late: I might not have enough time, or enough people, or enough anythings." He put the gun away and got out the rat. There was still no connection. "We have to get closer to daylight."

Slowly, the tunnel grew brighter, and there was a slouching youth waiting for him in the distance, standing between the rails, tapping his foot.

"Hey."

[What happened? I expected you to be out of contact for no more than three minutes.]

"There were people in the tunnel. Hospital patients, and a doctor who's going to give them all a lethal injection whether the Outies come for them or not."

[Why does this concern you? You knew when you set

out to find Madeleine that you would find those left behind. You can save one, perhaps. You cannot save them all.]

"Yeah, we'll see about that." He pulled the hem of his coat up. He could feel a stiff wire inside the lining, coiled like a snake, and he passed the material through his fingers until he came to a tear. He dug out the end of the cable Sonja had sent with Miyamoto, and threaded it all through the gap. "I'd convinced myself I didn't care about anyone, and perhaps getting married would make me care. Which was why, I suppose, I wanted to cross the Metrozone against the biggest flow of refugees since Japan sank: just to show I cared about another human being." He contemplated the end of the cable, the plastic plug with its connectors that went into the rat.

[And you find that you do not?]

"The opposite: I've found that I do. I care about everyone." Petrovitch clicked the cable into place. At its other end was a silver jack, long and thin and ridged, designed to lock into its socket with a half-turn. "So here's the deal. You get your citizenship. I get my wife."

[With you, Samuil Petrovitch, there is always a price to pay. What will this cost me?]

"Do you trust me?"

[No] it answered baldly. The avatar walked in a circle across the tracks, head bowed. [You are meat. You get tired, hungry, weak, scared. You have a flexible notion of morality. I know you will change your mind, not once, not twice, but a hundred times before this is over. You do not tell me the cost because I know the cost is everything.]

"Do you trust me?" he asked again.

[No. Your motives are hidden to me. Your thought processes are opaque. You are ruled by your passions. How can I possibly trust you when so much is in the balance? If I lose, I lose my very existence.]

"I don't want anyone to say I forced you. I don't want you to think that, either. This—this is me. It's time to risk everything on a throw of the dice. But I can load those dice in our favor. I can manipulate chance, defy fate, do the impossible." Petrovitch held up the jack in front of his face. The avatar couldn't see it, couldn't possibly know what he was planning. The AI wasn't stupid, but it lacked imagination. "Do you," Petrovitch said once last time, a smile on his lips, "do you trust me?"

It stopped walking, and raised its face to the light at the end of the tunnel. [I have no reason to do so, except this: it is you who is asking. What choice do you leave me?]

"Good enough for me." He felt around the back of his head and started to push the jack home.

Miyamoto tried to stop him, but he'd realized too late what Petrovitch was up to. He was too far away to do anything. Petrovitch saw him lunge toward him, hands outstretched, but the jack was in and twisted.

Everything went white.

He was blind and senseless, but he expected that. It would take a few moments for the rat to recognize that there was new hardware installed, and then fire up the right program—the Sorensons' mitigator program—to mediate the virtual experience for him, fitting like a filter between meat and metal. It had been a simple matter to turn the interface around, so that input and output could be reversed.

Lines. He could see lines, as thin as wires. Colored circles and shapes paraded around him, blurred at first, with too much blue, but there was some feedback from his optical center and they snapped into focus, becoming warmer and redder.

His skin ran through heat and cold, dull and sharp, feather-light pressure and painful grip. His hearing was tested for stereo. The five tastes were applied to his tongue, and a basic array of aromas assaulted his nose.

Petrovitch blinked, slowly. Dark, light. He was somewhere inside the rat, in a machine that wasn't a digitized world but a workaday handheld computer. Perhaps the mitigator couldn't cope with the unexpected. Perhaps he needed to code a solution for himself, out of nothing.

He voiced a keyboard into existence, scrawled some basic commands glowing into the air, and created an interface: pull-down menus that worked like blinds, a window for the outside world, a schematic for connections outside of the rat.

The avatar watched him intently over his shoulder.

"Hey. Almost done," said Petrovitch.

[You could have told me.]

"Then it wouldn't have been a surprise." His body was as it had been in VirtualJapan: a chrome mannequin, featureless and naked. Oshicora had given him form and substance then, but right now he was busy. "We have work to do."

[Am I going to have to reveal my presence to the world?] The AI looked pensive.

"Yeah. If everything goes right, it won't matter. If everything goes wrong, it won't matter either. Ready?"

[What do you want me to do?]

Petrovitch tried to push his glasses up his nose. They weren't there. Dissatisfied, he drew a sandtable with his finger, and populated it with all the information he could gather on the Metrozone. Layers upon layers of info: topography, architecture, utilities, transport, cameras, people, and more: the positions of troops, artillery pieces, command-and-control centers. Still more, the Outies, the breaches in the M25 cordon where they'd flooded through, the abandoned towns of the Outzone.

"Your predecessor unconsciously attacked a city and brought it to its knees. It destroyed buildings and killed using the city's own automatic systems and giant robots it built in co-opted factories. This time, it's going to be different, because I'm going to show you how to do it properly."

The AI pondered the living map. [To control all this will take more processing capacity than I have.]

"We have to code it. Distribute our agents, give them commands and let them carry them out. We want autonomous cars? We write the script, broadcast it, modify it on the fly. We want to take over the EDF forces? Place a diversion between the units and the generals. Fake it so that the top brass see what they think they should be seeing, while we direct the troops to do what we want them to do. We take the resources we need to do the job. We'll give them back later. Do it. Do it now."

The AI's avatar blurred and became pixelated as its attention turned elsewhere. Petrovitch called Sonja.

"You did it, then," she said.

"I decided it was time."

"You could make that decision yourself, of course." She brushed her fringe aside and stared at his silvery outline. "What else have you done without talking to me?"

"I got the AI up and running again. It's been online for three, four months now. It's a smart kid. Your dad would be proud."

"Oh, Sam. Is Miyamoto with you?"

"Yes. In real-space."

"I'm going to have to order him to kill you. And he'll do it, too."

"I know. Gladly, I expect. Where are you?"

She moved to one side to show the park at the top of her tower. "I told you I wouldn't leave."

"The Outies are almost on the northern edge of Regent's Park."

"Yes. I can hear them," she said. "There are too many of them for the EDF to hold back, and I suppose it won't be long before they're here. But I'm ready for them, Sam. I was serious when I said I was going to protect my father's legacy."

"Were you serious enough to arm as many of your workgangs as you could?"

When she didn't answer him, he knew.

"I'm glad, because I want to borrow them. How many have you got?"

"No. I need them, Sam. Every last one of them. I need them for here."

"However many you have, it won't be enough. You've got what, a couple of thousand? You're still outnumbered a hundred to one."

"It's enough to do what I need them to do!"

"But it's not for what I want them for, and my need is greater."

Her face went pale and pinched. "You can't have them. They're mine."

Petrovitch shook his head. "Not anymore. You can only give them something to die for. I can give them a reason to live."

She banged her fists on the desk in front of her in frustration. "Don't do this to me. I swear, I'll give Miyamoto the order to take your head."

He remained perfectly calm. "If you still want to have hold of anything by the end of today, you have to give me everything you have now. How many *nikkeijin* in the Metrozone?"

"What?" She was suddenly on the back foot, unsure of how to answer in case she ended up trapping herself.

"Half a million, and I can give you their phone numbers. You're going to contact them all, and get them back across the Thames to you. Tell them to use Waterloo Bridge—you can't get cars across it, so the only obstructions are a *govno*-load of people, but we'll clear that. I'm going to throw a defensive semicircle going from," and he looked at the map, "Hammersmith to Blackfriars, as far up as the Westway. We can afford to lose the rest, at least temporarily. Sonja? Tell me you're keeping up."

"You betrayed me." She was furious. "And now you're trying to humiliate me?"

"It just looks like that at the moment. If I have to do this myself, then it won't work as well, and it won't end how it should. Call in favors, promise them the world, resort to blind nationalistic rhetoric—I don't care. I need them, and you can get them for me." It wasn't working, and he wondered what would. "Do you remember? When you said we should run away together?"

"It was only the day before yesterday."

"I just realized we don't have to run anywhere. All we have to do is plant our flag right here in the Metrozone, and see who stands up to salute it."

"Stop," she shouted, and she held up her shaking hands

as a physical barrier to his altered visage. "Just...stop. What are you saying? That we take control of the whole city?"

"*Yobany stos,* Sonya! No: just the half the MEA have abandoned."

"But." She realized she had no objections left, though she felt she should try. "But what about the Outies?"

"What about them? Defeating them is the cost of still having somewhere to live when the sun goes down. Now," he said, "yes or no?"

She gave up arguing. "We'll never win," she sighed.

"Three words say we will." Petrovitch sorted the Metrozone database for Japanese refugees: a simple place-of-birth search, nothing complicated once he'd hacked his way into the system. He bundled up the information and threw it down the wire to Sonja.

She waited, for longer than he anticipated. He thought maybe he was losing his touch, but then she relented and asked:

"Which three words?"

"These ones: New, Machine, Jihad." He grinned. "See you."

22

Petrovitch opened first one eye, then the other. He stood swaying slightly for a moment, then tried to walk forward a couple of steps.

They were tentative, a questioning toe pressed against the sharp ballast before he committed his whole weight.

"Weird," he said, and even as he said it, it felt like he was writing a line of code and sending it to his vocal cords.

Miyamoto had his sword in his hand, watching him from a safe distance, poised to strike him down.

When Petrovitch turned his head, he could feel the cable drag: an unnatural connection from skull to computer was one thing, but it was more than that. He felt full to bursting. Ripe.

He focused on the samurai, and was aware of the embedded electronics in the man's clothing—nothing more complicated than a phone searching for a signal, but he could see it as an icon he could touch, open, alter and activate if he knew the right commands.

"This is going to take some getting used to."

"You should not have done this," said Miyamoto. "There are too many unknowns involved."

Petrovitch looked over the top of his glasses. The shine off the sword blurred, then sharpened as the rat processed the raw data and fed it back. The resulting image wasn't perfect, but it was close. "We can argue about it later. Right now, I'm looking for a bus."

He slid one sleeve of his coat off, and threaded the rat over his shoulder, then back around to his front. He slipped the rat into his inside coat pocket, coiling up the excess cable, and put his arm back in. The connector was mostly hidden by his hair. When he turned his collar up, it was all but invisible.

His simultaneous search of the satellite images found him several buses, which he matched with a picture gallery to discard all the ones without automatic navigation. He could have used cars, of which there were many more, and closer—but a big modern coach with tall sides would offer more protection to its occupants.

There were two that fitted his requirements, both in the depot of a private hire firm up at Highgate, near the cemetery. He was going to have to free them from behind the locked gates.

"Are you ready?"

"For what?"

"Revolution. I suppose they all start like this, with one person thinking that things could be different. Then it grows. They persuade others to join in, and it gains a momentum all of its own. It either overwhelms the old order, or gets crushed." Petrovitch pushed his glasses back up his nose, and felt his eyesight compensate again. He took the info shades off and pocketed them: he'd probably never need them again. "This is my revolution. This is where we sweep away the past and the future breaks in. This is what the New Machine Jihad should have been."

"The Jihad killed hundreds of thousands," said Miyamoto.

"It's going to do it again, too. Back then, when it was stupid, ignorant, and no more than an urge, it attacked us. But now it's got smarts. It knows everything. It's guided. It can make amends for the wrong things it did. It's going to take back the city for us."

"It is a weapon, and it is in your hands alone." Miyamoto flexed his fingers around his sword hilt. "No one man should have so much power."

"Before you try and stop me, why don't you talk to Miss Sonja? I have and, despite her misgivings, she's with me. Which reminds me."

Petrovitch turned away from Miyamoto, and searched for Valentina. As well as talk to her, he could see her, see all around her: her phone pinpointed her location on the approaches to Tower Bridge.

The EDF had done the smart thing, the thing they should have done much earlier: they'd stopped the traffic, and made people get out and walk with only what they could carry. Cars were crushed in all around her, abandoned, some still with their motors running. She was with a gaggle of Olgas, pushing ahead through the slowly moving crowds with Marchenkho in their wake. He didn't look happy.

"I see you," he said in Valentina's ear.

"Petrovitch. Where are you?" Her neck craned and tried to spot him.

"Look up, to your left. There's a lamp-post with a camera." He waggled the camera's housing to attract her attention. "Though I'm pretty much everywhere now."

"We did not find Daniels," she said. "Is madness here, and Outies are not far behind."

"I know. I can see them, too. Listen: when you said you would help me, did you mean it? Rather, how much did you mean it?"

Without hesitating, she replied, "What is it you need me to do?"

"I need Waterloo Bridge. I need it clear for northbound traffic. I can help, but I'm not there."

He zoomed in so he could try and read her face. She nodded. "Hmm. Is done," she said. "Should I talk to Marchenkho?"

"I've delegated this to you. If you want him, fine. If not, fine. I need to make one thing clear, though. He works for you, and you work for me. If he can't handle that, then cut him loose."

"*Da,*" she said. "How long before you need bridge?"

"Fifteen minutes."

She raised her sculpted eyebrows.

Petrovitch shrugged to no one in particular. "Yeah. I didn't say it was going to be easy."

"Then I had better hurry. Good hunting." She cut the connection, and he followed her for a few moments more as she glanced at her watch and made a little head-jiggle as she weighed up matters in her mind. Then she started to climb on top of a car.

Waterloo Bridge was as good as his, so he returned his attention to where his body was. He'd walked to the end of the tunnel on automatic: he'd have to watch for that by writing some sort of script, though he barely knew where to start. He could hack into his own heart if he wanted to.

The avatar was again waiting for him, but he was looking out over a landscape that had been strangely changed. The layers of information he'd seen on Miyamoto were replicated everywhere. Most of the electronics was locked, rendered inert by the Outies destroying the power grid as they advanced.

But some were not. Battery-powered devices glowed green, almost begging to be used. Discarded phones on standby, handheld computers, solar-powered street furniture, and best of all, the cars.

One of the Jihad's first manifestations had been the processions of automated cars, used as a child's playthings. Petrovitch could do so much more with them. The station on the far side of the tunnel was formed either of solid brick or transparent glass, but it mattered little which. He could stretch out beyond the reach of his hand.

[I have done as you asked,] said the AI. [EDF command in Brussels is being fed an alterable, delayed feed. How do you want your forces deployed?]

"I need to give Sonja time to gather her *nikkeijin*. Put a third of them on the Marylebone flyover, another third at the far end of Euston Road. Send the rest of them to Primrose Hill. There are tanks there already, but they need infantry support. Divide them up with a mix of units, and keep them concentrated. Standard military doctrine is that they should spread out, so if they show signs of that, yell at them."

[Do you want to know what we have?]

"No. Either it's enough and they'll hold, or it isn't and I'm sending them to their deaths. How's the network holding up?"

[Bandwidth is a problem. I am making great demands on it, even with outsourcing many of my routine processing functions.] He looked sulky. [The NSA is aware of the unusual activity, but the United States has the highest density of computer resources on the planet. I have no choice but to use them.]

"They'll use their giant axe at some point and try to isolate their network. We're going to have to think of something else you can run on." Petrovitch flexed his arms. "How are you?"

[Busy. I have never felt stretched before.]

"That's very human." Petrovitch smiled. He patted the avatar on its back. He could feel it. He could feel the cloth, and the body under it. "It's hard for both of us."

[Will we win?]

"We haven't lost yet."

He walked on, and hauled himself up onto a platform, with Miyamoto springing up behind him. The access to the outside was through a deactivated screen and a set of turnstiles. Petrovitch thought he should be able to just stroll through the wall.

"Madeleine's mother's around here somewhere. Or was earlier on this week. She's an Outie now."

"You know this how?" Miyamoto sheathed his sword and slid across the top of the turnstiles.

"She shot Maddy. Not something either of them are likely to be mistaken about." Petrovitch followed him over and dropped to the tiled floor. "We'll stick to the roads from now on."

"We would be less obvious crossing the parkland to the north of here."

"Yeah. That doesn't matter anymore. Let them notice

us." He walked out of the station entrance to the curb, to the new registration white Ford. He didn't have to, but he laid the palm of his hand on its roof.

He disabled the security measures with one algorithm, and terrified the on-board computer with another. "Who's my *suka* now?" He started its engine and plotted a route for it.

Miyamoto jumped back. "You did that."

"Yeah. I can do this, too." He dispatched his agents to every car and van in the neighborhood. They broke their way in, kicked their engines into life, and pulled out in a synchronized wave into the middle of whichever road they were on.

There were hundreds of them, and when they had all passed, when they had filled the surrounding streets with their noise, Petrovitch stepped out after them. He drew his gun and practiced sighting down his arm. There were crosshairs in his vision. The targeting moved to where he pointed. Then he looked at a stray dog that had come out to investigate the sudden commotion.

The muscles in his arm twitched, and guided the gun around until it was aiming at the fat black Labrador.

He glanced at a street sign, a front door, then a passing bird. His arm snapped right, left, up and tracked, fast enough to make it ache.

"This. This is what I signed up for."

"What are you doing?" asked Miyamoto.

"I'm being awesome. Don't interrupt."

Sporadic gunfire rattled the air from some distance ahead, echoing off the walls. The first of the cars had met the first of the Outies. He sent another command to them, and gave them access to his map. The Outies were the red dots, the cars were blue.

Run them down, he said.

How to kill a car? Petrovitch knew—put a bullet in its tiny electronic brain. The Outies had no way of finding it under the bodywork. A lucky shot here and there, but for the most part they'd have to reduce them to piles of scrap metal to stop them. And this being the real world, they were going to run out of ammunition long before then.

He watched the red dots ripple and recoil. The cars worked crudely, without cooperating, crashing into dumb objects and reversing, coming back for another go. More intelligence was needed. They could hunt in packs, with ambushes laid in side streets, traps in alleyways. He wasn't going to be able to coordinate that at that moment, and the AI had already said it was busy—which for a machine intelligence of unknown capabilities was a startling admission.

It would have to do for now.

Some of the red dots were spilling their way, undisciplined dribbles of color draining off the blocked artery of Highgate Road.

"Company."

Petrovitch strode on, and suddenly, there were four—no, five—Outies coming down the street at him. They stopped when they saw him, though a couple of them looked around fearfully behind them to check for cars.

Miyamoto drew his sword, and Petrovitch had the opportunity to reflect on what a brilliant sound it made, a clear ringing like a bell.

One of the Outies had a gun, what looked like a shotgun: fat barrels side by side, and a half-empty bandolier of red shells. The others had crude spears, nothing more than pre-Armageddon blades grafted onto long poles. Effective, but hardly worth emptying a city for.

The Outies had been smart, too. They'd made sure their vanguard all had guns. Whenever MEA fought them, it had been bullet for bullet, shell for shell. It had given the illusion of a massive well-equipped army, an illusion they'd all fallen for.

It was *kon govno,* pure and simple. The speed of the advance, the crushing tidal wave of panic, the complete absence of information from beyond the front line, had served just one purpose.

Petrovitch stared at the man with the shotgun, who was feeding two cartridges into the cracked breach.

Crosshairs formed, and Petrovitch felt his arm come up, lock into place. It was extreme range for both of them, but it was closing every moment as they walked toward each other.

The shotgun snapped shut, and it was raised to a shoulder.

Miyamoto started to look left and right for cover. "You must get down."

Petrovitch squeezed the trigger, smooth and certain. His aim was adjusted for everything: his motion, his target's, air pressure, windspeed, bullet trajectory, but still there were variables. Imperfect aerodynamics, uneven powder burn, the barrel of the automatic being out of true by fractions of a millimeter.

He was aiming for his chest, and caught his upper arm instead. The man spun around, the shotgun pointing briefly at the sky before crashing down. One of the barrels boomed and spat smoke, and an Outie was thrown hard against the side of a parked van. He slid down and didn't move.

Now it was three against two: one older woman, two

younger men, all dressed in that uniform of dirty browns and blacks. They looked at each other, uncertain.

Petrovitch spread his arms out wide and kept on walking. "You seem to be in my city."

The woman found her voice. "City ours," she called out, even though she was of an age to have received a formal education in what had been England. "City burns."

It struck him that these Outies were a family group: a tribe, a clan, at the very least a mother and her two sons, and the man dead would have been an uncle or a cousin. The other man on the ground had made it to his knees, and he was shuffling toward the fallen shotgun. There was one cartridge still loaded, and he seemed determined to show he could fire the thing one-handed.

"I always thought it was pillage first, then burn. But whatever," said Petrovitch, "there's been a change of plan. Prepare for the New Machine Jihad."

Behind them, a car rolled around a corner, its red bonnet already badly dented, its windscreen punched through and roof warped. It was leaking radiator fluid, but it would last long enough for what he was going to use it for.

It gunned its engine and raced forward.

23

They walked on in silence as Petrovitch pushed shotgun cartridges out of their loops and into his pocket. Some of the houses either side of them were on fire, burning freely, always centered on one property that was starting to collapse. Bright embers spilled into the air like seeds and rose up on fiery drafts. The heat from them made the air flicker.

"What?" he finally said.

Miyamoto wouldn't look at him. "That was…distasteful."

"I'm sorry? Distasteful? What the *huy* is this?" Petrovitch took the last shell and examined the breach mechanism. He downloaded a video that told him how to load it safely and not shoot his foot off in the process.

"You…we should have given them a chance to surrender. That would have been more," and Miyamoto pursed his lips, "honorable."

"You know what? You can take your stupid *bushido* code and you can *za cyun v'shopu*. This isn't feudal Japan. This is *yebani* Stalingrad: a meat-grinder battle where the first thing that dies is mercy." He rammed the plastic cartridge home and snapped the gun closed. "The Soviets won Stalingrad by being utterly ruthless about human life. That meant not tying half their men down looking after Nazi prisoners."

"Seeing who your teachers are, I am not surprised by the lessons you have learned."

Petrovitch snorted. "In Russia, lessons learn you. But let's go with this for a moment: they didn't look like they wanted to surrender. Quite the opposite."

"You drove over them."

"Yeah. No cries of 'we surrender' at that point."

"And then you reversed back."

"Even then one of them was still trying to get up, and you made me waste a bullet on him. Swords don't need reloading." The road they turned into to head up the hill toward Highgate was littered with bodies like spilled grains of cooked rice. Some of them were still just about alive. Others lay in pools of wet blood and were patently dead.

Petrovitch scanned the ground for guns, or other ranged weapons, but couldn't see any. Just blades and clubs and spikes. At the top of the road, there were tail-lights and sounds of mayhem.

"So, let's say that they'd surrendered, the four of them. We'd have three Outies, plus the one I'd shot. What were we going to do with them? Disarm them? They'd just walk into the nearest house and tool up. Tie them up? The next Outies through would let them go. Take them back to the relevant authorities? The two of us are the authorities."

Miyamoto stepped over a twisted corpse, spine broken, arm bent unnaturally. "You labor the point. We still should have offered."

"And that's precisely why they're five k from the Thames

and have turfed twelve million people out of their homes."
Petrovitch studied his map. The cars were a stop-gap,
enough to clear a path for him to the coach depot and little
more. The Outies would be back. "We're too *yebani* civil-
ized. We've forgotten that there's something to fight for."

"But do we have to fight like this?"

"Yeah. We do."

"You mean you do." Miyamoto almost sneered, and
Petrovitch was tempted to hit him very hard somewhere
painful.

Instead he stopped, stood in front of him and waited
until they were toe to toe, then screamed in his face.

"Wake up! What the *huy* is wrong with you, man? Two
hundred thousand Outies are busy slaughtering their way
to victory, and you want to play nice? Nice is what put us
in this *pizdets* in the first place. Look around you: where
are the people who normally live here? The ones that
didn't run are waiting, cowering behind locked doors
before they're cut up into little bits like those two kids
outside Lucy's." He took a breath. "Or they've already
been cut up. So, yeah. I'm going to kill and kill and kill
until the Outies finally get the message that they're not
wanted here. And I will carry on killing them all the way
back to the M25. And then I'm going to bomb the survivors and send an army out to sweep the rest away. Then,
and only then, will I think about nice. Got that?"

Miyamoto wiped the spittle from his cheeks. "I understand." He sounded more subdued.

"I want you to go."

"I have to stay."

"I don't have to justify myself to you."

"Then stop."

Petrovitch ground his teeth together. "Come on. We've got a bus to catch."

He turned on his heel and stamped his way up the hill. Smoke was drifting across the road, obscuring it from his eyes and the satellites. Infrared was a mess, bright blooms of incandescence blotting out other smaller heat sources.

His assault on the summit of Highgate was petering out. The Outies were in the cemetery, while the cars growled outside the iron gates and brick walls.

He summoned the AI. "Fifty-one, thirty-three, fifty-six north: zero, eight, forty west. Get the tanks at Primrose Hill to smash it."

The avatar walked by his side for a few steps. [You know you're about to destroy the tomb of Karl Marx.]

"Yeah. What did he ever do for me?" Petrovitch involuntarily raised the shotgun to his shoulder, aiming down a side street. "Engels did most of the hard work, anyway."

He remembered to pull the butt in hard before he squeezed the trigger, the only two conscious decisions he had to make. The gun kicked back and a man—he thought it was a man, but in reality it was only a half-seen blur behind a line of low concrete bollards—fell backward.

The inexorable advance was pressing down on him once more. He summoned more cars, raising them from sleep and sending them out to battle. The Outies were fluid, trying to flow around his forces like a flood, but the garage the coach hire operated from was just around the corner. He only had to hold back the tide for a few more moments.

The storm broke around him. Even as cars pulled out from curbsides and threw themselves at the gray figures, gunfire popped and glass shattered in curtains of shining crystal.

The avatar raised his hand and vanished, and Petrovitch got on with the task of surviving the next minute. He crouched down and took a look at the pitiful cover he'd given himself: halfway across the road, with Outies to his left and more in front. They might not even have noticed him yet, but a stray shot was going to hurt just as much as an aimed one.

Miyamoto was faring no better, a few meters behind him. Two cars were coming up the street, side by side. Not fast, not yet, but if he ran it would be into the path of one or the other of them.

Petrovitch had an idea. He took those two cars and slowed them down, taking them out of hunter-killer mode and telling them to do something different. He ran back to Miyamoto and forced his head low.

The cars flanked them, and rumbled on at jogging speed. Other cars overtook them, wheels up on the pavement, swerving with screeching tires to avoid the lampposts and signs, then hurtled away straight at the Outies.

The first artillery shells howled overhead, and there was an almost simultaneous flash of fire. The windows all around disintegrated as the shockwave hammered into the buildings around them. Petrovitch ducked.

Speech was rendered impossible by the simple fact he thought he was deaf. A burning vehicle, everything ablaze, even the wheels, rolled back out of the side street.

Straight toward them.

Petrovitch grabbed Miyamoto's arm and threw him forward, slaving their moving shields to his position. It wasn't quite fast enough. The car on their left shuddered as it was struck. By the time it managed to tear free, it was on fire itself.

They were across the junction. The coach depot was next left. Miyamoto was scrabbling to get upright again, and Petrovitch's face was growing warm from the flames. They'd have to get the rest of the way on their own.

An explosion behind him sent him sprawling again. Shrapnel—plastic, metal, glass—sang through the air and zipped off the tarmac. Petrovitch was alive with pain. He tried to rise, to run, and instead stumbled as the splinters embedded in the backs of his legs tore into his flesh.

He fell, spilling shotgun cartridges onto the tarmac. The cars kept rolling onward as Miyamoto did a crouching shuffle between them. The man's black clothing was white with dust.

He tried to summon one last effort, but the deep breath he took caught like acid in his throat and made him cough uncontrollably. Every spasm was accompanied by white flashes that blinded him and robbed him of what little control he had.

When he could see again, the ground in front of his face was flecked with red.

"Pizdets." He sipped air, and found that he could move. With artillery shells thundering overhead and the crackle of hungry flames around him, he got to his hands and knees. That was all he could manage. Even that small movement made him gag. A glance behind showed him that his trousers were wet with blood.

"Miyamoto!"

He was a little way off, escort cars idling away to either side, regarding Petrovitch with his dark eyes.

"Miyamoto!" he shouted. Ragged clouds of smoke crossed between them. "What the *huy* are you doing?"

"I am watching you die."

"I'm not dead yet. Get me up." He tried to get one foot under him, and everything went momentarily gray. He swallowed, and it tasted of hot iron.

"If I do that," said Miyamoto, "Miss Sonja will continue to fight rather than retreat, believing that you can offer her victory."

"But we can win. We will win."

"You will destroy her if you live," he said. "Not now. She will survive this, while you will not."

He started to walk away, up toward the crest of the hill, toward the Outies.

"Where are you going?" Petrovitch reached out for the shotgun that lay ahead of him on the ground, and dragged it back.

Miyamoto flicked his fingers behind his head at Petrovitch, discarding him as finally as a piece of litter.

"They'll kill you too," he called, and belatedly realized that was just what the other man had planned. Of course he could never go back, not with Petrovitch dead: it would be a failure, a disgrace, shameful.

The cars were still slaved to Miyamoto, even the one that was now thoroughly alight. They rolled slowly after him, beyond shouting distance.

Petrovitch could still call him, though. Of course he could. He had his number stored from earlier.

And Miyamoto answered. "What?"

"You don't have to do this."

"I will not act against you myself because of my promise to Miss Sonja. I can only stop you by leaving you out here, alone, dying, surrounded. When we are both gone, she will be able to make her decisions without your influence."

Petrovitch tried to find the man on his map, and found

that the nearest red dot to him was mere meters away. He was in amongst them.

Miyamoto grunted, swinging his sword. "This madness will soon be over." He grunted again. Metal rang against metal, followed by a gargling cry. "Your revolution will have failed. Your futile war will have been lost. But she will be saved."

Petrovitch screwed up his face. "Do you hate me that much?"

"Almost as much as I am devoted to her," and he never got any further than that. He was in his last battle, cutting and dodging and piercing.

Then the connection went quiet. Miyamoto's sword clattered to the ground, and Petrovitch heard voices over breathy panting. The one blue dot was almost obliterated by red.

"Miyamoto?"

The sword rang one last time. The point of it dragged across the ground, skittering and chiming.

The connection stayed live. He could hear the echo of explosions and squeal of cars, but nothing more from Miyamoto. The voices drifted away, and he knew they were coming down the road, straight for him.

If he didn't move now, they'd find him sprawled there.

He used the shotgun as a lever to get himself upright. He was so close to the yard where the coaches were stored. He could see the wall, and the shattered acrylic sign of the firm in red and white.

He dared not bend his legs. He could not turn or twist his torso. Every time he tried, he was overwhelmed. So he dragged each foot in turn across the road, leaning on the butt of the shotgun as a crutch. He had to hurry, but could not. He had hurt himself before, but even when he'd been shot in the head and had his middle finger ripped off, it hadn't been this bad.

He hadn't been on his own. Madeleine had been there, and so had battlefield-strength painkillers.

Another salvo of tank shells screamed in. He covered his head as best he could, and when the air was still again, he staggered on. The Outies were coming. They were coming for him.

There was a small door in the wall: it led directly into the yard where they kept the coaches. It was locked: of course it was. Nothing was going to be easy.

Petrovitch raised the shotgun and held it unsteadily. The crosshairs in his vision wandered across the face of the peeling paint until he dragged them back by concentrating his whole being on the gap of wood between the lock and the frame.

It was at point-blank range, and the recoil threw him backward. When he landed, it felt like teeth tearing at his thighs and that the skin on his torso was being flayed. It felt like he was being eaten alive.

The door flapped as he writhed, and he knew he had to get through it, wedge it closed.

He rolled over. That was enough to make him gag and pant for breath. He screwed his eyes up and dug his nails into the palms of his hands. He crawled like a dog, like a worm, and crossed the threshold. He used his leg to kick the door shut behind him. It banged against the jamb, and creaked back, slightly ajar.

He pushed the sole of his boot against the bottom of the door to hold it closed, and rested his cheek against the cold, gritty ground.

Voices, speaking loudly in stripped-down, staccato sentences, were right outside. Petrovitch forced his knee to lock, and waited, not breathing.

The AI's avatar appeared beside him and folded its arms. It said nothing, but the Outies suddenly shouted and ran. A moment later, a car scraped its way along the wall and stalled, blocking the entrance completely.

Petrovitch looked up at the avatar, and the avatar looked down at him.

"*Spaciba*," muttered Petrovitch.

24

The avatar had swapped its oversized sweatshirt for an urban camouflage combat jacket, all pockets and tabs. It had a Velcro patch over its breast pocket, and Petrovitch noticed that it had named itself.

[Your body is injured,] it said. [And your colleague is dead.]

"No, really? I hadn't noticed." The urge to just lie there and close his eyes, only for a moment, was overwhelming. If he was going to prove Miyamoto wrong, he really had to get up.

[He betrayed you. He left you to die and let the Outies kill him. Why did he do that?]

"Because...I don't know. *Mudak! Balvan!*" Each screamed expletive tensed his muscles and made the pain brighter. "I will not go quietly!"

[Apparently not...]

"I'm doing this for you! You want a place which recognizes you as a citizen? I'm the only one who can get that for you, you *mozgoyob*. I can save Maddy, save Sonja, save you, save the whole *yebani* Metrozone." He took a deep breath to restore his graying vision. "If I can only save myself."

Petrovitch roared as he staggered to his feet. He swayed and reeled. He swallowed hard on his desert-dry throat. It was only pain. Pain wasn't going to kill him. He shook his head violently to clear it, and looked around for the first time.

Behind the high wall that ran around the perimeter was a brick warehouse, faced with full-height sliding doors. With the power off, he would never have the strength to open them, and fortunately, he didn't need to. One of the coaches was in the yard in front of the building, visible from space, and precisely why he'd come here.

The main gates still needed shifting, though. They were steel, taller than twice his height with thick bars running top to bottom. Ramming them would be futile, because they would have been designed with that in mind.

He started to limp toward them.

[You realize,] said the AI, [that this is just theater. You are demonstrating your power and authority: to show you can walk into enemy territory and drive out in a luxury coach.]

"Yeah. Pretty much."

The control box for the opening mechanism was screwed to the wall at head height. It was padlocked shut, but only briefly; the hand-gun made short work of the hasp. Once inside, his hands felt their way across the machinery.

[You are building a legend about yourself. You think it will serve you later.]

"If there is a later." He dug in his pocket for the kitchen knife and sawed through the thick hydraulic hoses that kept the left-handmost gate closed. Oily liquid squirted out: over him, over the yard, then it died to a trickle.

[Why? Fiscal competence, honest administration and creating a fair legal framework are the leadership qualities most sought after by the populace.]

Petrovitch walked slowly to the middle of the gates, and in full view of the road outside, he braced his hands against one of the metal bars and pushed. The pain was exquisite.

"No one ever fought at the barricades for a balanced budget. I want to set the world alight. I want to speak to their souls."

[Do I have a soul?]

"Not . . . not now. This is not the time to be asking such questions."

The gate, once moving, kept on going. Wheels at the base ran smoothly in the concrete channel cut for them. One last shove, and the gap was wide enough. The Outies outside, another family group of six or seven, watched him incredulously for a moment.

The shotgun would have been useful, but he'd lost it in his pain-filled delirium. He drew the pistol again and let it dangle by his side.

"I know I look like *govno,* but I'll still kill you if you step closer." None of them had guns, or a ranged weapon of any kind: no bows, javelins, slings.

They hesitated, not realizing that Petrovitch couldn't keep his arm straight if he tried. A car, close enough to be called, screeched around the corner on two wheels and charged toward them.

As they scattered, he ran as fast as he could for the coach, stiff-legged, exhausted. One last effort required, that was all.

The AI had already commandeered it. The door hissed open, and steps folded down to meet his rising foot. He fell up the stairwell into the passenger deck, and the door closed behind him. A fist met the glass in the door, and a moment later, the haft of an axe.

Petrovitch raised his artificial middle finger at the figure outside, and the coach pulled cleanly away. Something thudded dully off the massive flat front of the vehicle, and the wheels bumped over an obstruction.

The coach was at the gates, gliding through, turning toward the main road.

His flailing hand connected with the tubular metal banister. As he stood, he could see out of the huge, tinted windscreen. Burning buildings, bundles of plump rags, crashed and gutted cars in the foreground, and behind that, behind the smoke that drifted in sheets across the road, was the Metrozone.

It didn't look good.

The avatar appeared in the seat behind him, hunched forward, hands clasped in its lap. [The Americans are attempting to isolate their network. Their NSA has declared that the country is under attack from "cyber terrorists and enemies of freedom."] It paused. [I am beginning to run short on resources.]

"I thought I told you to take what you need."

[I have done. But if they physically take assets offline, I am not in a position to reconnect them.]

Petrovitch shifted awkwardly as the coach barged another disabled car aside, then carried on down the hill. He was still standing like a charioteer, hanging on to the hand rail at the top of the steps, staring out over the city.

"If you're still just using spare capacity, it's time to grab whole systems for your dedicated use. Whatever you want. Start with the Metrozone traffic control, and *chyort,* I know where you can get what you want." His face twitched. "The basement of the Oshicora building."

[The quantum computer is quarantined. There are good reasons for that.]

"There used to be good reasons for that. There are better ones now for breaking it."

[And what of Oshicora, or VirtualJapan?]

"There's nothing left of either. I hinted there might be so that Sonja wouldn't think to look elsewhere for you. Time to crack the seals and let you in. What else is happening that I need to know about?"

[The EDF stationed around King's Cross are coming under sustained attack. The Outies have looted some heavier weaponry from a Metrozone facility in Holloway, and are threatening to break through at the goods yard and at Pentonville Road.]

"Do we have any air cover yet? A gunship or two?"

[They are of limit...]

"I don't care. They're no good sitting on the ground waiting to be overrun. If the Outies make a breach now, we're screwed. Tell the tanks to flatten the goods yard and get our soldiers off the streets and into the buildings. Forget hardpoints, set up free-fire zones and make the *govnososa* pay for every centimeter they take." The coach swayed, and started to indicate right. A barrage of broken paving slabs and bricks clattered against the side windows. The toughened glass shivered, but didn't crack. "What else?"

[Your wife's unit is completely surrounded. There are casualties.]

"She knows I'm coming."

[How?]

"Because she knows I will. What about Primrose Hill?"

[They have made contact with the Outies, who are filling up the streets around the park. There is some long-range sniping, but it is only a matter of time before they advance. There are too many of them for our defenders to cope with: a simple matter of not having enough bullets.]

"The Westway?"

[The Outies are temporarily stalled within the Paradise housing complex, but they will soon realize they can flank the area by moving toward Notting Hill.]

"It could be worse."

The AI was silent on that point.

Petrovitch called Valentina as the coach rumbled down a side street, its vast bulk threatening to dwarf the terraced houses either side. The cars that remained parked on the sides of the road lost their wing mirrors and much of their paint.

"Hey."

"We have bridge," she shouted over the noise behind her. He liked her. She was direct when he needed her to be. "There are many, many Japanese crossing here. This is good."

"Any trouble?"

"Nothing you need worry about. We will keep road clear for as long as we can. Petrovitch, what about demolition charges?"

"They're under our control."

"Good. Petrovitch, there are problems with networks. People fear New Machine Jihad."

He had no reason not to tell her. "They needn't be afraid. I am the Jihad."

"You will have to explain later how this can be. But okay."

The coach pulled up cleanly outside the station closest to the tunnel entrance, and shushed on its brakes.

"I'm going to have to go offline for a while. Leave a message if you have to. Otherwise, do as you see fit." He turned to walk down the stairs to the hissing door. His coat had stuck to his back. It was as bad as it could be, made worse by his imagination. "Valentina, if...if this all goes wrong: don't hold any loyalty to me. Sonja Oshicora will use the Jihad to slug it out with the Outies, but there's no guarantee she'll win. Blow the bridge along with the others and get out of there."

"I am big girl," she said. "I can see which is right side, and which is wrong side. So—even if you are dead, it does not make you any less right."

"There is that." He stepped through the arched entrance, into the cool shadow of the concourse. It was as he'd left it.

"So I choose to fight, *kamerad kapitan.* I see no other way."

Petrovitch crawled across the top of a turnstile, clawing at the cold metal with his fingers and trying not to fall. He turned awkwardly, letting his feet find the floor through the mist that rose up in his vision.

"As you wish, Valentina."

He cut the connection and staggered out onto the platform. The end of the tunnel was in sight, and so was the slight figure of a schoolgirl standing in the opening, anxiously shifting her weight from one foot to the other, bouncing slightly in her now-scuffed and dusty trainers.

Where he had climbed up before, he hesitated, looking

at the distance between the platform and the track. When he turned and started shuffling down toward the incline that merged the two, Lucy broke from cover and ran toward him.

She slowed as their paths converged, and she stopped completely when they were face to face.

"Sam? What happened?" Then she caught sight of the cable hanging around his neck. Her gaze narrowed, and she followed it from his collar to the base of his skull. "What the fuck is that?"

He tried to smile, to make light of it: "It's a cybernetic mitigator implant. All the cool kids have got one."

"But...where's...that blood. Is it yours?"

"Yeah." Petrovitch shrugged awkwardly. "I got blown up again. Miyamoto's dead. His choice. Not mine."

He wanted her to walk in front of him: not because he didn't want her to see the ruin of his back, but because he couldn't deal with her reaction. She wasn't taking his hints, the gentle ushering of his hands, the pointed stare back down the tunnel.

"I got us some transport. Enough to get everybody away. I need you to go and round everyone up, start them moving."

"And what are you going to be doing?" she asked suspiciously.

"Me and Doctor Death need to have a chat." He reached behind him and took hold of the jack in his head. He twisted it, and pulled it slowly out.

It felt like half of him had died, and he mourned the loss so much that he almost drove the spike back in again. His fingers trembled, then let the silver-shiny connector slide free.

She was watching him. She caught the cable in her hand, and slid it carefully under his collar, retrieving the rat from his inside pocket. The casing was scratched and dented, discolored with dirt and some uncomfortable dried brown stains.

"What do I do with it?"

"Hang on to it for me." He needed his glasses. He found them in his coat. One lens had chipped, but he slid them on, and pushed them up his nose. "You can use it. Not in the same way. With, with these."

The overlays were flexible enough to have escaped damage. He passed them over, and she held them in front of her face, checking the difference they made. She stopped and moved them back over to Petrovitch's right.

"There's someone there." Lucy flipped the overlays aside. "Some sort of virtual guide?"

"He'll warn you if there are Outies nearby, or anything else that might be a problem. You can trust what he says. Isn't that right?"

Petrovitch supposed the avatar was either taking a bow or wearing a cynical smirk. While she was distracted, he managed to turn, keeping his back out of her eyeline. He walked toward the tunnel while she played briefly before remembering her mission.

As she ran past him, he turned again.

"What do I call him?" she called as she vanished into the dark.

"Michael, apparently." Lucy had gone, and there was no one to hear him add, "After the archangel, the leader of the Army of God."

25

They passed each other in the tunnel, a string of blue-white lights swinging and shading in the darkness. Lucy moved up and down the line, urging the old men on, exhorting the old women to keep going.

And Petrovitch knew that she was destined for something greater. He moved aside, catching her luminous grin as she held up the lantern to illuminate both him and her.

"We'll wait."

"You'd better," he said.

He made his way back to the abandoned train. Climbing up took all his remaining strength. He lay there, stranded, gasping, as the one last light lowered itself down toward his face.

"You found a coach," said the doctor.

"I won a coach. I fought for it and I won it." Petrovitch looked up and saw the doctor's shoes. "You could have done pretty much the same, except it would have been easier for you because when you would've been looking, you wouldn't have had the Outies."

"And then what? Where would I have taken them? And why aren't you getting up?"

"Because my back's full of shrapnel and I'm bleeding heavily from a dozen places."

The light moved, and there was a sharp intake of breath.

"What? I need a doctor? I kind of thought I'd found one."

The man pulled a face. "I did A and E for six months, five years ago."

"I'm reluctant to threaten the only person in a position to help me. But I have a gun in my pocket that I'm very tempted to use on you."

"This is beyond what I can do here. You need a hospital. You need a scan, a transfusion, fresh skin. I haven't even got sterile water so I can see what I'm doing."

"What do you have?"

"A bag of stuff I threw together at the last minute." Petrovitch could see it, packed and ready to go, sitting in the aisle.

"Then that'll have to do. We don't have time to get fancy."

"I could kill you if I get it wrong."

"Then," said Petrovitch, "you'd better start praying to whatever god you believe in you get it right. Or right enough that I live for another few hours."

The doctor looked skeptical and went to his bag. He brought out a pair of surgical scissors.

"I'm going to have to cut you out of what's left of your clothes."

"Yeah. Figured." Petrovitch started to wriggle out of his long leather coat. "I'm sentimentally attached to this, though."

He felt tearing: more than sentimentality, then. Actual

flesh and blood. He dragged it to one side, and the doctor kicked it further with his foot.

"Got a name?" The scissors started to click.

"Petrovitch."

"That's it. The antigravity man." Snip, snip, snip.

Petrovitch gasped as his back was exposed, the bloodied cloth peeled away. "It's not... doesn't matter."

The doctor went quiet as he surveyed the ruins. "I don't have a spare pair of trousers."

"Showing my *yielda* to the world is the least of my worries."

The doctor knelt again beside him and clipped his way through the waistband. "I did mean what I said about you needing a hospital. You've got multiple penetration wounds, and only some of them have visible fragments. Those foreign objects I can't remove will continue to do damage the longer they stay in. Nick a vein or an artery, and you'll bleed out in under a minute. Depending on the depth, you could be bleeding internally already. You have burns and abrasions, and you're losing fluid from those, too."

"My turn," said Petrovitch. "What's your name?"

"Stephanopolis. Alex Stephanopolis."

"Right, Doctor Stephanopolis: I don't want you to stop and listen to me, you can do and listen at the same time." He shifted uncomfortably. "You see that hole in the back of my head? That connects to the experimental cyberware I used to defeat the New Machine Jihad six months ago. Today, I'm using it to direct a modified version of the Jihad to help defend the Metrozone from the Outies. As you may notice, there is nothing plugged in at the moment. That is because the satellite uplink I have to the Jihad won't work underground. Joined the dots yet, Doctor?"

The doctor worked his scissors down the back of one leg. "If I believed you, you'd be telling me that the New Machine Jihad is loose again and you're the only person who can control it."

"No. It's more subtle than that. I'm the only person it trusts. I'm the only one it will follow. And on its own, the Jihad will screw up. We get no second chances on this one. Either we win today or we lose forever." Petrovitch gasped as the dried blood that had welded his skin to his trousers relinquished its grip. He unclenched his fists, a finger at a time. "The longer I spend under the knife, the worse the situation gets. So make it quick. I don't care about dirt, fragments, bodies foreign or domestic. Patch me up enough to get me back out there. After that, you're absolved."

The doctor worked in silence for a while, revealing the full extent of Petrovitch's wounds.

"I can't...I." He stopped and started again. "This, this doesn't make sense. Why would you be doing this if you weren't telling me the truth, and yet I can't possibly trust what you're saying."

"Willing to take the risk that I'm full of *govno*?"

"No." He dug into his bag again and retrieved a sterile syringe and a bottle of straw-colored liquid. "Any heart problems?"

"It's in a jar somewhere in a lab. It hasn't caused me a problem since the surgeon ripped it, still beating, from my chest."

"What model do you have?"

"American. Prototype. You wouldn't have heard of it."

"What I'm asking is, if I stick you full of morphine, will you die?" The doctor drew off the liquid into the syringe. "Weight?"

"No idea."

"You're not making this easy."

"Just guess and get to work, man." Petrovitch grunted as the needle went in his backside. "I haven't got all day."

He could feel it, every last bit of it: the widening of wounds and the probing jaws of the forceps; the drag and cut of shards of plastic and metal and glass as they slid from his flesh, oiled with his blood; the cold tunnel air reaching deep, alien places inside him. But he didn't care. He was immune to care for the duration of the injection.

"Tell me you haven't got Hep or HIV," said the doctor. His hands were bloodied up to the wrists.

"No. You?"

"No. I had a needlestick once. Scared the crap out of me. I had to wait six weeks for a repeat test. When it showed up clear, I nearly wrecked my liver on cheap whisky anyway." He flicked his fingers and another piece of plastic clattered against the window, where it stuck briefly before sliding down. "I'm getting to the point where I've found all the obvious debris. The rest of it... I don't think I can get it out. The light, the blood, it's just impossible."

"You got a needle and thread?"

"You need skin."

"Got any?"

The doctor sighed. "It's not going to be pretty. I can guarantee that you're going to end up looking like Frankenstein."

"The monster. Frankenstein's monster. Frankenstein was the creator."

"So why are you doing this? What's so important?"

"Everything." The needle punctured his already scarred back and the thread drew through. "Everything. The whole of modern history is collapsing on this exact moment. Everything since the first steam engine, since the first telegraph, first radio, first aeroplane, first rocket, first computer. We can go one of two ways, and we get to choose. We can stay where we are, we can decline and die. Or we can embrace the future like a long-lost lover, and we can live forever."

"That's the morphine talking."

"No. No, it's not. Do you suppose the caterpillar has any idea what's going to happen to it? Does it dream of flying? Does it dream of drinking nectar? And look, a pupa is such a weird thing, just a sack full of chemicals. You can crush it and get nothing but goo. That's what we are now. Pupating. I need to buy us enough time so we can hatch. A butterfly, a little butterfly. *Babochka*."

One thread was tied off, another patch of embroidery begun, and Petrovitch felt the overwhelming need to talk.

"I see it sometimes. When I close my eyes. I see it as if it was already there. We're not gods, we're just people, but we have such vision and drive as to make us seem otherworldly. We have technology like fairy tales have magic. We can do anything we put our minds to. Why can't others see it as clearly as I can?"

"Because we're not delusional?"

"I don't have to be there. I don't have to be part of it. It'll have a momentum of its own. All it'll take is one push at the right time, and that right time is right now. But it needs me to live long enough to give it that one last shove, get it moving in the right direction. Then it doesn't matter. No one will be able to stop it. Destiny. The future. I can pass it on. The caterpillar dies, the butterfly lives."

"This would be easier if you shut up."

"We've spent too long here. Trapped by our fears and our blindness. We have wings. We can fly. Armageddon was over twenty years ago, and we're still shut in our cages and we've grown used to it, like the frog in a pan of water brought to the boil. Those days are over. Nothing can ever be the same again. Slow death or immanent glory. That's what tomorrow brings."

"Just. Stop. Speaking. It's distracting me."

"You don't understand. You can't. You haven't seen what I've seen. It's beautiful. It's worth dying for."

The sewing became more angry and violent. Petrovitch felt himself as a piece of cloth, roughly handled and roughly stitched.

"There is," said the doctor, "so little worth dying for. I only stayed because I couldn't go. I was going to leave them here, promise them I'd be back, but I left it too late. You, you bastard, you make promises and you keep them. You even bring a fucking coach. The only reason I'm still here rather than driving my way out is because I'm scared. Scared of the Outies. If I thought it would do any good, I would abandon you all to save myself. Got that? And that's what every other person in the Metrozone would do. So screw you and your madness. I don't care about your dreams or even about tomorrow." He made one last cut with the scissors. "That's it. I'm out of thread."

Petrovitch blinked in the blue light, and moved his hands to underneath his body. He pushed himself up to his knees and held on to the furniture while his ears roared and his vision grayed.

"A hand here?"

The doctor pulled him up. Pins and needles, dull aches, the sensation of his circulation returning—it was happening to someone else. They were definitely his trousers lying on the floor of the carriage, though.

The doctor packed his bag while Petrovitch worked out which way was up. He stooped to pick up his ruined coat, and as slowly as he moved, the world turned just a little faster. He dragged his arms through the sleeves and shrugged the leather around his shoulders.

"It doesn't cover your arse, let alone anything else."

Petrovitch checked that the gun was still there, and the knife. Lucy had the rat and the info shades. "It has pockets. That's all I need it to do."

He swayed toward the door and looked over the edge of the step into the darkness. He had to try and shake the out-of-body feeling: it mattered what happened to his meat, because it carried his mind.

So he lowered himself down to the track and made sure that he was heading in the right direction. The doctor soon fell into step beside him, lantern swinging in his free hand.

"Do you have a plan?"

"Probably," said Petrovitch, who was concerned more with putting one foot in front of the other. "Straight down the middle, lots of smoke."

"What? What does that mean?"

"The Outies' front line is between us and my forces…"

"Your forces?"

"My forces," said Petrovitch emphatically. "By the time we get there, it'll be close-quarters urban warfare. So I'm just going to get the coach to drive straight through until we're safe. No one's going to pay us any attention because they'll all be too busy not getting killed."

"So how big is your army?"

"I don't know. It'll either be big enough, or too small.

One person might make the difference, and we'll never know one way or the other. I'd be happy with a hundred thousand. Happier with two. Weapons are a problem: no way we can get hold of that many firearms and train people with them in time." He stumbled over some loose ballast. "We'll have superior tactics, better comms, and intel like no other army in the history of warfare. They have numbers, the morale and the experience. I still think we can win."

Lucy was waiting again at the tunnel entrance, though this time looking in rather than out. The info shades were perched on the bridge of her nose, and she plucked them off.

"We're ready—everyone's on the bus and Michael says we should really be going in the next five minutes." She looked uncertainly at him, and his bare legs. "You were ages."

"Yeah. I was getting patched up."

"Where…" and she pointed. "Where are your trousers?"

"There wasn't much left of them by the time we were done." He put his hand out for the rat, which she duly passed across. "You don't have to look."

She blushed, but she kept her eyes on him as he re-threaded the connector around his neck and toward the back of his head. He fumbled the plug not once, but twice. He was about to try for a third time when she took over, slotting the silver spike home and giving it the required halftwist to lock it into place.

"Thanks."

The AI took off its kevlar helmet and dangled it from its hand. [She is right about the five minutes. The push toward the unconquered Inzone is reaching a critical phase. We are engaged on all fronts from the West Way through to Whitechapel.]

"How's Sonja doing?" Petrovitch walked down the tracks into the daylight, examining the map as he went. He could see where they were weakest, where their enemy was strongest. It didn't make for comforting viewing.

[The EDF troops are utilizing your fluid defensive strategy. Where they follow your plan, Outzone attrition rates are high for few friendly losses. Where the *nikkeijin* are engaged, they are reluctant to retreat when they believe they are winning.]

"Then they get cut off and overwhelmed, and she loses whatever arms they had. *Chyort.* Where's it worst?"

[The most intense fighting is taking place between King's Cross and City Road. But it is Tower Bridge that may fall first.]

"Pull our people back. No pitched battles yet, because we'll lose. Wait until the Outies are on the first section of the bridge, then blow it. Send the order."

[If we do that, you need a way to hold the next upstream crossing. Or the next.]

"They're all expendable until we get to Waterloo. Every time the Outies get their foot on a bridge, take it out."

[That is not a long-term solution.]

"They're all pressing for the river. Let them. We hold the ground immediately to the north, and their flank becomes increasingly exposed the further they go looking for a way over the Thames. When they reach Waterloo we hit them with everything—all our available assets. Three sides at once."

[Waterloo. How apposite.]

"You know what to do. I'll talk to Valentina and warn her."

[Cable Street has gone. They are on the approaches to Tower Bridge.]

Lucy took his arm and guided him up the slope at the end of the platform.

"Do I say this stuff out loud?" he asked her. "Or do I just think it?"

"You haven't said a word since you plugged in."

"Okay." There was the coach, motor idling, and the vague shadows of people behind the smoked plate glass. Petrovitch pushed the doctor ahead of him, then ushered Lucy on board.

He climbed up and stood in the aisle, surveying his passengers. Maybe they thought he was going to sit in the driver's seat, but he quickly scotched that expectation.

The doors closed and the coach nosed out into the road.

They murmured and gripped their arm rests. The doctor stared at him swaying between the two front seats and suffered the stomach-clenching realization that yes, the New Machine Jihad had risen again.

"Ladies and gentlemen," announced Petrovitch. "Please fasten your seat belts."

26

They took Chalk Farm Road toward Primrose Hill. The tanks had long since retreated from the heights back down toward Euston, but Petrovitch hoped to rendezvous with them there, along the porous front line that was developing east of the Westway: there were skirmishes in the narrow streets all around, as far south as Oxford Street. The Outies probed forward, met resistance, and tried to enfold the defenders.

In real time, the conflict between blues and reds looked like two amoebae, fighting to the death. The compact blue shape kept contracting in on itself, losing limbs to the vast red monster that seemed intent on swallowing it whole.

Tower Bridge had gone. MEA militia were parking armored cars on the broken carriageway under the iconic crenellated supports, suddenly brave now that there was no chance of contact. Bishopsgate had fallen. The open area in front of the old Bank of England was filling with Outies.

Petrovitch gnawed at his fist. All the ground he was losing was ground that would have to be retaken, but he couldn't change his strategy now. Everything depended on allowing the enemy to come forward until his counter-attack was ready.

The Outies were moving too quickly, though. They were taking street after street with too few casualties. They were winning.

[London Bridge is falling down.]

"My fair lady," murmured Petrovitch.

[Cannon Street and Southwark will follow imminently. We will need to hold Blackfriars for longer.]

"No."

[We are underprepared.]

"Pull everyone not currently in contact to behind the Farringdon Road. Hold the Edgware Road but the Euston Road people need to come down to Oxford Street." He looked out of the window. Regent's Park was passing on his right, domiks lying where they'd been spilled during the Long Night.

Then there were figures on the road, marked red on his map. A knot of a dozen, jogging down the white line in a loose pack. A close-up showed two guns, the rest with blades.

"Lie down on the floor if you can, the seats if you can't," he called. "Do not look up."

He glanced around. Lucy was peering around the upholstery, watching the Outies as they heard the coach approach.

The windscreen pocked with a bang. If he'd been driving, he'd have been slumped at the wheel and careering across the narrow pavement into a wall. The bullet puffed out a cloud of white padding as it burrowed into the back of the driver's seat.

The coach didn't deviate from its previous line. The

first shot hadn't made Petrovitch flinch, but the subsequent eight did. Massive star-shaped wounds bloomed across the clear glass, cracks spiraling out to craze the whole pane, merging and spreading until only the plastic bonding held it together.

A body slammed against the flat front, and the Outies were now behind them. The rear of the coach was raked with gunfire. More glass patterned white, and suddenly they lurched to the left.

The drift corrected itself, then over-corrected. Right, left, right, and finally back under control.

[Rear tire.]

There was no time to worry about the damage the coach had suffered so far, because they were right in amongst them now.

The Inzone retreat had brought the Outies onto the streets. The carriageway was full of them. Petrovitch reached into his coat pocket and put the gun in his hand. The coach rocked as it was struck and, in striking, was struck again.

He ejected the magazine into his palm and counted the heads of the silver bullets. Six. He pushed them back home and dragged back on the slide.

The windscreen imploded, and a dark shape crashed down into the aisle, scattering a curtain of crystalline granules inside the coach. The shape, rags and dust, started to unfold. Though bloodied and dazed, the man had managed to keep hold of his knife.

Petrovitch raised his gun, and the crosshairs in his vision jerked left and right, up and down with each inconstant lurch of the coach. The Outie's weather-beaten face screwed up as he spotted the man sitting on the edge of the stairwell, leaning out with metal in his fist.

He came at Petrovitch, crouched low, swinging his blade in an arc before him. And still Petrovitch couldn't get a clear shot. He could have pulled the trigger anyway: one of the bullets would have hit its mark. The others would have each threatened everyone he'd fought so hard to save, so he held his fire.

The Outie lunged inexpertly forward, stabbing at Petrovitch's arm. An arc of red drew itself across Petrovitch's vision, and he pulled back just in time: they were two injured men trying to kill each other.

The knife-hand turned, ready for the return strike. He was close enough now that Petrovitch could bury the pistol's barrel in the man's sparse flesh and not miss. Before either of them could take the next move, a blur of black and white flew through the air. It landed on the Outie's back and caused him to stagger and fall flat amid the shifting mass of broken glass.

He kicked out, and Lucy went flying again, back against a seat. Her hair came loose even as she tried to scramble up again. The Outie turned to face her, and Petrovitch saw the handle of a kitchen knife protruding from under the man's shoulder blade.

He reached up and drove it home with the flat of his hand. The Outie stopped quite suddenly and Petrovitch reached around his throat and pulled him backward, away from Lucy, toward the gaping hole in the windscreen. He flung him out the way he'd come in.

His legs caught on the lower broken edge for a moment before flicking up and out of sight. The coach rose and fell, the mildest of bumps amongst the storm of shaking.

Petrovitch looked at Lucy. He'd corrupted her and destroyed her innocence, and all he could do was reach in his pocket for the other knife. He slid it down the aisle toward her with a nod of satisfaction, and she picked it up, her chin lifted high, her expression defiant.

[Brace.]

Too late.

They hit something solid. The driver's airbag blossomed with a white flash of explosive and an expanding halo of powder. Petrovitch, on his feet and with nothing to hold on to, started to move irresistibly toward the front of the coach.

There was nothing to prevent his ejection outside. Sky and ground tumbled together, and he bounced off the roof of a car half-buried in a drift of rubble. The underside of the coach reared into the air, fell. Petrovitch rolled off the car and the coach wheels banged down on it, the interior collapsing, paint and plastic crazing.

The coach settled further, and he could have reached up and touched the hot engine casing.

[Petrovitch?]

He breathed in and it was sweet agony. He was still alive. He was still connected.

"Chyort."

[I am ordering an advance. One moment.]

The roaring in his ears was no figment of his imagination. There were actual voices raised in a war cry, a long, drawn-out bellow. Petrovitch found himself on the tarmac, lying on the loose fringes of the rubble field. Half-bricks and splinters of wood lay with him. He sat up, certain that he had burst all his stitches and racked up a fresh list of further injuries.

His gun had gone. His glasses had gone. He had blood coming from his hands, his face. He rose to meet his warriors. Gray-clad MEA, olive-green European soldiers, the blue of Oshicora workgroups, all running toward him from the end of the street.

But they were mute, grim in their task, guns and staves and swords held in front of their bodies. So he turned to see where the sound was coming from, and the Outies were charging from behind him, mouths wide for as long as their breath would last.

He drifted out into the middle of the street. In the confusion, perhaps the Outies mistook him for one of their own. He wasn't wearing a uniform, and he wasn't an obvious target. They ran by. He looked up at the coach, beached like a whale, sides pocked with holes, dented, scraped. A face pressed against the darkened glass, a pale pink palm either side. Lucy.

The two sides met a little way down the street, forming brief scuffles where bullet or blade swiftly decided the outcome. Once engaged, they were committed. They fought and fell. More Outies streamed by to replace those who had fallen, and Petrovitch, shadowed by the stranded coach, was ignored.

Until one dusty man carrying a long steel pole seemed to leap down in front of him, a boy at his side. He recognized them both: the boy he'd rescued, the man he'd seen kill twice from Lucy's bedroom window.

The man leaned down to bark orders to the boy, a few words, no more, who was then off, back the way they'd come. He spotted Petrovitch. His head turned toward him even as he ran with his message.

Of course, he knew Petrovitch had had a gun, and of course he was going to shout a warning.

"Fox!"

So it was him. The one whose sole aim was to burn the city. Petrovitch stooped for a ragged brick and so by chance avoided the metal bar thrown like a spear. As he straightened up, he banged against the steel, embedded in the side of the coach behind him. And by the time he'd remembered that the man moved like lightning, he had the red arc of a knife flashing in front of him.

He threw the brick off target. It landed a glancing blow, and there was no real force behind it. Fox shrugged off the impact with a grunt and lunged forward, swinging the tip of his knife in Petrovitch's face.

His body was sluggish, too drugged and damaged to respond quicker. The point sliced across his eyeline and against the bridge of his nose. The darkness was sudden and profound. Petrovitch felt himself twist and fall, all the sharpness of the debris on the road rising up to meet him.

He couldn't see.

He wasted time trying to blink away the obstruction: it felt like his eyelids were closing around burning boulders.

[One moment.]

He concentrated on that voice, and the light came flooding back.

He was looking down on a blood-spattered body, more dead than alive. A figure was crouching over it, knife held high. There was a rock under the body's left hand. He closed the fist over it and told it to lash out.

It connected. The figure staggered back, and he could see that the body on the ground was his. The coat, the remains of the coat, gave it away. His perception shifted, rotated, until he was looking at the scene from inside his own skull, through his own ruined eyes.

There was distortion, blank areas where the satellite

couldn't image, but it was good enough. Good enough to do what he needed to do. He dropped the rock, extended his middle finger on his left hand—the artificial one made of transplant-grade titanium—and locked it rigid. He waited for Fox to come at him again.

He was blind. His adversary knew that and knew there was nothing to stop him throwing himself down with his full weight behind the blade. An easy kill.

So the sightless Petrovitch rolled aside, more marionette than man, leaving Fox floundering. He continued to roll until he was clear, and then he was up. He could stand. He had control. His movements were robotic, precise, fast. As fast as Fox's, who was swinging low at his calves. Jump, kick to the shoulder, recover. No, he was faster.

The first cast of doubt entered Fox's face.

He kept on coming, though, still not quite believing that Petrovitch knew what it was he was doing, convinced that he was just lucky, not realizing that the cable snaking from his skull and down his back was the key.

Fox was still an unbeliever when Petrovitch crouched down and threw his arm up under the swinging knife. His punch drove his metal finger deep into Fox's chest. He could feel his fingertip force through skin and muscle. He could feel the wet slickness spread over his hand and wrist. He jerked his arm hard, once, twice, then thrust Fox away with one last shove.

The man tried to keep his feet. He kept on stepping back to maintain balance, each footfall marked with a bloody stain. The front of his dusty clothing turned dark and glistening. He finally stopped and tried to raise his knife. It made it halfway, but it slowly sank back down. Then he fell, metal clattering by his side, and he didn't get up again.

Petrovitch was surrounded by uniforms. They'd forced their way forward. The coach was secure, the battle-front now shifting back toward Regent's Park.

[A medical team is on its way. Lie down on the ground. Elevate your feet. Slow your breathing to one breath every ten seconds and lower your heart rate to half.]

Petrovitch didn't agree. He was managing to block the pain by disconnecting the feed. If he'd known he could do that, if he'd known he could have done half of what he'd just achieved, he would have plugged in the silver jack so much sooner. He felt such joy. He had transformed himself in the way that he wanted to transform the world. He had so much energy, he felt so vital, that he almost picked up a fallen Outie spear and plunged back into battle.

Lucy ran from the emergency exit on the bus, screaming and weeping. She didn't want to touch him out of fear, her own and that she would hurt him.

"Ohgodohgodohgod."

"It's okay," he said. "It's more than okay."

"How can you say that? Your face…" She held her hand over her mouth, though all Petrovitch could see was the impression of her nose and chin under her pixelated hair.

"Will you do something for me?"

She looked at him, looked away, then forced herself to look back. "I don't think there's much I can do. Not now."

"There's a computer shop at the far end of this road. If it's shuttered, find someone who'll break it open for you. I need a camera, one of the clip-on computer ones. Small as you can find. Bring me a choice." He wiped his cheek with the back of his hand where the drying blood was tickling him as it dried. "Can you do that?"

He saw her chest heave as she struggled to draw breath. "Yes."

"Go. I'll be here."

[Petrovitch. You must lie down.]

"Just tell me one thing: have we pushed them back?"

[Yes.]

"Then keep pushing. Lay down a series of ambushes on the route. When we've gone as far as we can go, pull back and suck them in. Then do it again somewhere else. Keep hitting them until they run." Fox's knife had fallen out of his grip, and lay close by Petrovitch's booted foot. He bent low and picked it up. "This is where we build ourselves a new beginning."

27

The Oshicora medic was just about done patching up Petrovitch's body when a pair of heavy booted feet stepped up close to him and stopped. He could hear the scuffling of dirt and the man's tired breathing. He stopped concentrating on the ongoing battles a few streets away and looked down at them from the sky, all the while rooted to the orange plastic chair he'd been made to sit in.

Olive-green uniform, combat helmet swinging from one hand, EU-issue carbine slung over his shoulder. He wore a star on each shoulder.

"*Do svedanya,* Major. What can I do for you?"

Petrovitch had a bandage over his eyes: there should have been no way he could have known what rank the soldier held. So the man reached out and waved his hand in the space between them.

Petrovitch caught his wrist, which brought a murmur of admonishment from the medic. "Still, Petrovitch-san."

"Don't do that," said Petrovitch to the major, and let go. "I'm not a freak show."

"You're Doctor Petrovitch?"

"Is this supposed to be an example of military intelligence?" He raised both his arms while soft bandages unrolled around his cold, white, scarred torso. "My face was plastered over the global news networks for twenty-four hours."

"Yes, but you had eyes then."

"They never worked properly. I can always get new ones." The wrapping went on. It must have been how the pharaohs had felt.

"But you." The major leaned forward. "You can still see."

"Well enough. You didn't come over to discuss my supernatural vision, so what is it?"

"It's like this: part way through the morning, my orders started to change. My tank squadron went from protecting the evacuation to shelling random parts of London, to forming a defensive position on Primrose Hill, to rescuing you, and now we're attacking alongside all these Japanese refugees who appeared out of nowhere. And yet when I query this series of orders, what I get back from HQ is 'do what you're told.'"

"That is a little insensitive, considering it's your *zhopa* on the line." The blood had run from his fingers. They were starting to tingle.

"The only time this whole action has made any sense was just now. Everything suddenly converged on this street. We were here because of you."

"Go on." Petrovitch started to smile. He liked smart people.

"Let me put it another way," said the major. "We've got all the old folk off your bus. We couldn't find the driver who, judging from the damage, should be dead five times over. When I asked about the driver, all I got was silence."

Petrovitch lowered one hand as the roll of bandage circled him once more, and he hooked his thumb in the cable that dangled from his skull. He let the wire slip through his grasp until he had hold of the rat's battered silver case. He held it up as the bandage passed around again.

"There was no driver, was there?" said the major.

"Technically speaking, yes. If the Long Night showed us anything, it was that we'd loaded far too much processing power in our vehicles. All they were waiting for was for someone to use it."

"You controlled the coach through that?" The major moved closer so he could see the point where the cable went in.

"Again, not exactly. It mostly drove itself, but toward the end it got a bit unpredictable. I was a bit busy, so I got some help." Petrovitch felt the bandage being tied off, and he let his arms fall back to his sides, his hands in his lap. A spare set of Oshicora overalls were brought to him, still sealed inside their plastic wrap.

He tore the film away and shook them out, angling them to present them to the satellite. The average *nikkei-jin* was about his size. They'd fit.

"Thanks," he said to the medic, who started to pack up his kit into a big green box. "Could you leave me some tape?"

The major was still standing there, still poised. "What do you know about the New Machine Jihad?"

Petrovitch leaned forward and started unlacing his boots. "Pretty much everything. Why do you ask?"

"Because I don't think I've been following EDF orders for hours."

"And you'd be absolutely right." He shucked one boot and stood it next to him. "You've been following mine."

The major dropped his helmet and snatched at his gun. Petrovitch carried on heaving at his other boot.

"You're the Jihad." The gun cocked, the safety clicked off.

"That's one logical step too far, though I can see why you took it. No, I'm not the New Machine Jihad. But I am the Jihad's employer. It's more complicated than that, in that it's not really the New Machine Jihad and I'm not paying it, but any analogy breaks when you stretch it far enough."

Petrovitch put a foot each into the legs of the overalls and dragged them up to his thighs.

"Give me one good reason why I shouldn't shoot you dead right now."

Rising slightly to get the clothing up to his waist, Petrovitch thought of several, all of them excellent. But only one in particular would appeal to this man.

"Because without me and the Jihad, you're going to lose this battle and the Metrozone. With us, you'll be part of the most epic victory since the defense of Stalingrad, and you'll be a hero. Brussels has done nothing but plan for failure from the start. Mining the bridges told me they'd given up before they fired a shot, whereas I intend to win." He shrugged the overall sleeves on and pressed the Velcro tabs together. He paused when he got level with the knife wound over his heart. "All the EDF have told you to do is retreat. I'm the only person who's told you to advance."

The major adjusted his grip on the carbine. "What are you?"

"I am the future, Major, and I am not destined to fail. I know you have misgivings—but you can't communicate them to HQ because you've been cut off from them since about eleven o'clock. All the other EDF soldiers will think you're mad. I've taken over the MEA, and Sonja Oshicora has lent me the *nikkeijin* for the duration. Sure, you can kill me, but then what?"

Petrovitch stood, slipping the rat into his top pocket. He reached up to push his glasses up his nose. No glasses, no eyes. It was going to take some getting used to.

Lucy was running up the street toward him, a plastic carrier bag swinging in her hand. He deliberately turned his back on the major and his gun to greet her.

"Hey. What did you get me?"

Flushed with success, too absorbed with explaining her finds to Petrovitch, she completely missed the angry, scared, confused tank commander. She opened the bag and rummaged inside.

"This. It comes with its own head mount—says you can use it for extreme sports, shock proof, waterproof. If this isn't extreme, I don't know what is." She tore at the packaging and squinted at the wide-angled lens. "Doesn't need its own power supply or software. Just plug it in and go."

"Sounds perfect."

"I've got a couple of others if you don't think..."

"Put it on me." When she hesitated, he added, "Don't worry. You can't hurt me."

She reached up and slid the harness over Petrovitch's blood-stained pale hair. The slim tube of the camera poked forward alongside his left temple. "I should have brought some of those cable-tidy things. They had baskets of them."

"I've thought of that." The roll of tape he'd commandeered was small and hard to spot. He patted his hands around until he found it on the chair. "In fact, I've an even better idea."

He ripped open the Velcro again and held the rat against his bandaged left flank, just about where his kidney ought to be. That would work. He found the snaking end of the camera cable and tried to plug it in by touch.

Lucy's fingers brushed his away and slotted it in.

"Tape it up. It mustn't come out. Then stick the whole thing to me."

The pair had rotated as they'd worked. The major was now over Lucy's shoulder, and Petrovitch had a perfect view of him. There were beads of sweat running down his forehead and into his eyes. He was blinking them away.

"So," said Petrovitch, "what's it going to be?"

Lucy looked up, a long piece of tape stuck to her bottom lip. "Um?"

He nodded in the major's direction, and she glanced around. She went, briefly, back to her task, then spun on her heel.

"What's going on? I thought—I thought we were all on the same side?"

"Step away from him," said the major.

She started to obey, then caught herself. "No," she said.

"He's the New Machine Jihad."

Lucy shook her head. "No. He's not. He's a scientist. A famous one. His name's Sam." She was between Petrovitch and the barrel of a gun.

"I don't mind if you step to one side," said Petrovitch. He took her shoulders and moved her gently.

Even though she could see what he could see, that a number of Oshicora personnel were folding their phones back into their pockets and were walking silently up behind the major, she put herself in front of Petrovitch again.

"You must mean Michael," she said. "He explained all that. The New Machine Jihad was his evil twin. Michael just wants to help us."

[You are risking a lot on human nature here. Yours and his.]

"You've been quiet."

[I am busy, but not so busy that I cannot intervene. Do you want him dead?]

"No. We've got it covered."

[That is not the evidence before me.]

"Grown men don't normally kill schoolgirls."

[Some of them do.]

"Good point, well made." He turned his attention back to the street. "Lucy, why don't you show me what else you've got in the bag?"

The major found himself being ignored, despite his drawn weapon. Petrovitch peered inside Lucy's carrier and saw a package he was interested in.

"A hand-cranked power supply."

"I'm always letting my phone run down. I just thought, you know..."

"Your education has not been wasted." He checked the selection of leads the device came with, and found a compatible one. Raising his arm again, he felt for the socket, and again, Lucy had to do it for him.

"What do we do about him?" She jerked her head behind to indicate the major.

"I—we—could really use the tanks he commands. But I can't force him to do anything. I could have him dragged away and shot."

"No!"

"Well, then. I guess it's up to him to decide what he does." Petrovitch checked his internal clock. It wasn't getting any earlier. He glanced at the cameras overlooking Blackfriars Bridge: it was about to be overrun. "You on that?" he asked.

[It will be destroyed, the same as the others.]

"Is everything in place?"

[Your plan will either work or it will not. It should not, yet you believe it will. Faith is not a facet of my personality.]

"Michael?" asked Lucy.

"Yeah. The second Battle of Waterloo is about to start without us."

"Waterloo? Where Napoleon did surrender?" She started to hum the tune.

"What do you want to do?"

"Stay with you," she said, suddenly serious.

"You're fourteen."

"Yes. Today I've run for my life, helped save a dozen old people, stabbed a man in the back and stood in front of a loaded gun."

"And still are."

She whirled around and stamped up to the major. "He needs you. We need you. Does it matter to you so much who's giving the orders?"

He was a head taller than her, and he looked down at her. "Yes."

She bent down and picked up his discarded helmet. She thrust it in his chest, hard against his body armor. He had no choice but to hold his gun one-handed.

"Enough that you'd rather see us all die?"

"You don't understand," he started, and she cut him off.

"I understand enough! You won't help us. Fine. Go. If you can find somewhere to go to."

[It's starting,] said the AI. The distant thunder of demolition charges detonating echoed off the high buildings. The roar of slowly falling masonry grumbled afterward.

The major looked up at the sound, startled. He was in an unfamiliar landscape, and he had no map, no compass, no guide. Lucy stamped away, back toward Petrovitch. She winked at him and turned to cast one last accusation.

"You're supposed to protect us! People like me, from people like them!"

The officer was utterly defeated. He hung his head, and wiped his face with the sleeve of his battlesmock.

"I was going to be Juliet in the school play," she said when she could whisper into Petrovitch's ear, "but I guess school's out for a while."

"I pity Romeo." Petrovitch looked around for Fox's slim-bladed knife. It was by the chair he'd been sitting on, and he picked it up, his fingers curling around the leather-strapped handle. "I can't take you with me. You have to realize that."

"I'm not strong, and I'm not smart," she protested, "but I can still do stuff."

"No. You are strong, and you are smart. But I'm not going to tell your parents I saved you from one war zone only to lead you into another." He flashed her a smile. "All these other people: I don't have to care about who they leave behind, just whether they've done what I needed them to do. They can die and my conscience is entirely untroubled. You, I care about, so I'm going to make you sit this one out."

The major was right behind him. Petrovitch tilted his head so he could see the man's face.

The major saluted him. "Sir." He sounded as bewildered as a lost child.

"Don't worry," said Petrovitch. "It does get easier. How many tanks have you got?"

"Seven. Lost one to mechanical failure."

"I need to borrow them. Is that okay?"

"Yes sir."

"And stop calling me sir. Get back to your men. Your orders will come from Brussels, and you'll believe that completely."

"But what about me?" Lucy twisted her hands together. "What am I supposed to do now?"

Petrovitch stopped a *nikkeijin,* and found enough words in an online dictionary to communicate with the man: *"keitaidenwa, nanitozo."*

The phone was duly passed over, and after Petrovitch had scanned its number for later use, he pressed it on Lucy.

"Take this. It has a map and instructions." Time was tight. He had to go. "I will see you later."

He laid his hand lightly on her head: a blessing, a dismissal, a solemn charge. She went without argument, running off in one direction as he started in another.

The huge diesel engines that powered the tanks rumbled to life in a side street, and groups of *nikkeijin* crossed his path, heading east, each led by an Oshicora employee.

"Valentina?"

He could barely make out her reply. He filtered out the extraneous noise and heard: "If you want me to hold bridge, you must do something extraordinary."

"Then I will," he said to her, and to the AI, one more word. "Now."

28

*I*n the ten minutes it took to navigate the car-choked streets between his starting point and the river, the plan Petrovitch had put in place had its beginning and middle. He arrived late, via Piccadilly and Trafalgar Square, onto the Strand.

From one end of the street, he couldn't quite see the other using the camera on his head, so he looked down on the approaches to Waterloo Bridge using a satellite: it was wreathed in smoke. The Embankment was on fire: there were burning vehicles and the shells of waterfront buildings had been laid low.

The red markers on the map were winking out, by ones, two, threes, by the handful and the dozen. Where there had been a solid sheet of red, there were now gaps. A thin blue line rimmed the area, and pockets of blue showed where rooftop snipers poured fire on the people below.

"I can't tell. Talk to me."

[The situation is critical.] The AI showed him a series of views from the CCTV on Somerset House. [The attack helicopters have strafed the Embankment and are circling

Farringdon Road. We will win there, but will lose Lancaster Place. The bridge will fall to the Outies.]

"No, it won't." He started to run again, moving the images of conflict to the corner of his attention in order to successfully navigate the street furniture.

[There is no logic behind your statement. Simply wishing for something to be so does not make it so.]

"*Potselui mou zhopy.* This is going to work. Where are the tanks?"

[High Holborn.]

"Kingsway, Chancery Lane and Holborn Circus. Do it. Get the helicopters to kill as many as they can."

[This is already happening. It will be too late. There are too many of them. We should pull back.]

"We're committed here."

[Then we will fail.]

There was a barricade across the street, cars and two buses, stacked by a mobile crane to resemble a giant Tetris game. The interiors were occupied, a wall of men and women committed to keeping the Outies from climbing up and over. They had long since run out of ammunition, and were reduced to poles and sticks, clubs and bats.

There were no reserves behind them, no one to replace them if they fell, or broke and ran.

"There were supposed to be more people right here." Petrovitch pulled his trophy knife and stood nonplussed for a moment. "Where are the reinforcements?"

[They have not had time to arrive. Two thousand are massed at the Oshicora Tower, receiving uniforms and basic equipment...]

"Yeah. *Pizdets.*"

He saw the situation as the AI did. Sheer weight of

numbers would overwhelm Lancaster Place. The approaches to the bridge would fall. All the defenders he'd so carefully placed along the Embankment and the Strand would be cut off. The tanks would come into play too late, the helicopters would do too little and, like those at the barricade, they'd run out of bullets soon enough.

So. It was time to turn the New Machine Jihad card face up on the table, and he didn't know how anyone would react to that. His best guess would be he'd face a full-scale mutiny within the hour: the *nikkeijin* might follow Sonja's orders, but the MEA militia, who'd witnessed the Long Night, and the EDF regulars, who'd watched it looped on the news for weeks, weren't going to go along with it, not at all. He'd win the battle, and lose the war.

"How much do you want this?" he asked the AI. "Are you willing to risk everything? Your very existence in exchange for these fragile sacks of meat?"

[You said you would find me a home.]

"If the Outies break through, that dream is gone."

[How much more will I end up with if I reveal myself now?]

"Could be nothing. Might be everything. It's your call." The first Outie made it to the top of the barricade. He was soon enough dragged down, but almost in an instant, another replaced him, and another. The defenders who remained alive heard the cry of triumph above them and, as fast as the sound traveled, they started to scramble out of their positions.

Everything slowed. Everything: even the processing power in Petrovitch's rat was commandeered. The pain he had locked out using software blocks snapped back, and the camera strapped to the side of his head no longer fed its images into his brain. He was blind, in agony, suddenly alone. His life was laid bare with no illusions or delusions. This is what he had come to. At least with the Outies, who had to be swarming toward him, it was going to be mercifully short.

Unless they left him like that, curled up on the hard road, whimpering and crying. They could ignore him, and there would be nothing he could do about that.

Then, in the darkness, he heard the words. [We rise or fall together, Aleksandr Arkadev Milankovich: a true friend.]

No one had used that name for years. Sometimes he struggled to remember it himself. It was him, though. The same skinny street kid who had run wild through the prospekts of St. Petersburg lay on a Metrozone road, helpless and crippled, and he still had someone who would call him by his real name.

The world appeared sideways. At first, he was surprised that he could see at all, then by what he could see. The barricade was shaking itself apart, the highest vehicles falling either side, and carrying those who were clambering up them down.

The noise: the growling of engines that consumed every last drop of dead air and splashed it back out as vibrant, vibrating sound. Someone stooped to drag him up because their uniforms matched, but when Petrovitch turned his sightless eyes to face his would-be rescuer, he was dropped with a shout and shrinking revulsion.

His pain was receding again, leaving his skin prickling with the impression of a thousand sharp needles. He could stand on his own, as well as fill his voice with his own words.

"Hold!"

One or two stopped. Another three or four slowed.

"I said hold!"

So they waited, poised on their heels and ready to flee. There were half a dozen of them, a rag-bag of *nikkeijin,* Oshicora employees and a MEA militiaman.

"We're done running." He looked around at the disintegrating barricade. A dozen Outies were his side of it, picking themselves up. Injured, yes. Stunned, but not for long. He turned and aimed the point of his knife at the lead Outie. "There'll be no more of that today. If anyone's going to run, it's them."

"But the cars..."

"Are on our side. The New Machine Jihad is on our side. We have a chance now." He readied himself for the charge. "Don't screw up."

Petrovitch ran at the enemy without worrying who was following him. He held the knife out by his side and dodged the end of a spear. He cut once, twice, and kept on going.

Someone else was in his path. He feinted low, high, then struck in the middle. The moves he used were fast and uncompromising. He was aiming to incapacitate, taking knowledge from somewhere out there and applying it ruthlessly.

If there had been anyone backing him up, they would have stopped the Outies. He discovered that he was entirely on his own.

His shoulders sagged. "Ah, *chyort.*"

[One moment.]

"You keep saying that." He was surrounded. He looked for somewhere to go, a route through. To the east, the

Strand was a shifting chaos, a mess of cars moving forward and backward with helicopters clattering overhead, firing the last of their missiles. The cacophony almost drowned out the screaming.

To the west, more cars were edging forward. They couldn't attack because of him. South lay the bridge, but he'd never make it.

[Look up.]

The crane hoist. Dangling from it were the loose strips of a webbing cradle. As it dipped toward him, he leaped up, throwing the knife at the face of his closest attacker. His fingers closed on rough material and he pulled his legs up out of the way.

He was rising into the air, but no matter how hard he told his hand to grip, he didn't have enough muscle to support his weight for very long. He gritted his teeth and squeezed.

Below him, the first phalanx of cars leaped forward, carrying all before them. Glass shattered and metal bent. Bodies crumpled and bones snapped. The crane arm started to swing him around, and as the movement transmitted itself down the straps, he felt the strap slide across his palm. He tried to get his other hand up, and even that slight change in his position made him slip further.

He was almost at the end of the tether. There was blood seeping down his wrist. The crane swung him face-first against a first-floor window: the glass didn't break, but the impact dislodged him. He fell, and something solid stopped him.

He had landed in a heap on a narrow balcony overlooking the junction, no more than a ledge with railings. He had limbs sticking through the bars and he brought them in quickly, lying on his belly with his bandaged face against the guano-encrusted stone.

[Sasha?]

"It hurts deep inside when you call me that." He used his bloody, blistered hand to reposition his camera.

[Petrovitch, then. What do we do now? We have no plan for this. The EDF in Brussels know I have hijacked their comms, and the news that the Jihad have risen again is breaking in North America.]

"Have we lost control of the EDF?"

[Yes. I can reinstall the intercept, but they will simply ignore all orders from now on. MEA units are trying to engage with Jihadi vehicles.]

"Thought this would happen."

[NORAD has just moved to Defcon three. The White House have declared a Defense Emergency.]

"This has nothing to with the *raspizdyay kolhoznii*! It never was anything to do with them." Petrovitch slapped his hand against the wall, leaving an imperfect print in his own blood. "Sonja."

She picked up in an instant.

"What have you done?" she shouted.

"I'm still trying to save the Metrozone. Tell me you're still on board."

She tucked her hair behind her ears. "Where's Miyamoto?"

"And the next time you send someone to be my body-guard, make sure they're not going to try and kill me. Now, we had a deal: I'd hand you your own country, you'd lend me half a million *nikkeijin*. I'm good for my end of the bargain. How about you?"

She bristled. "They are dying in their hundreds."

"What about the couple of thousand you're keeping up by the tower? What are they doing?" He saw her heart skip a beat. "If I'd had them here, we wouldn't have had to go public on the AI. You holding out on me has backfired spectacularly: it's going to lose access to most of what needs to function. Take the physical seals off the quantum computer and put it online. The AI needs it now."

She nodded, pale, and he continued.

"I'm taking over everything about how this war is run, because you're going to be up to your eyes in politics. You're getting a direct line to the presidents of the EU and the U.S.A. You're going to tell them that you can hand over a safe, stable, functioning Metrozone within a calendar year. You're going to tell them the price is that they get their *zhopi* out of our faces. And you can tell them that if they even think about pressing the big red button, you will ruin their economies for the next hundred years. Got that?"

Sonja bit at her lip, and Petrovitch waited. "I thought," she said, "we were going to take the north Metrozone for our own."

"And we are. We're just going to trade up after twelve months. Trust me." He made the image she saw on her screen smile. "Have I ever let you down?"

"Not yet," she conceded.

"I'm not interested in power. I don't want to run anything. But no more little oversights. I need to repair the damage already done and I'm wasting time I don't have." He cut her off. "Still there?"

[Always.]

"Seize the satellites we need. Without them, we're lost, and they're going to try and take them offline anyway. Anything else you want, you take it. No subtlety. Sonja is

simonmorden

throwing open the VirtualJapan computer for your sole use."

[How will this end?]

"That's not something either of us can calculate."

[The EDF have ordered the destruction of the remaining bridges. We will be isolated from any additional assets. We are on our own.]

"We always were."

Explosives cracked, and the central span of Waterloo Bridge lifted up, before falling in massive pieces into the black water below. Spray roared up against the river banks. Hungerford followed, then Westminster, Lambeth, Vauxhall, one after another.

Petrovitch watched the smoke and steam rise over the tops of the buildings. There was dust settling on his camera lens, and he unhooked it to blow it away. He saw his own face, not as in a mirror, but as another would see him.

"We always were," he repeated.

[Your orders, war leader?]

"If the EDF and MEA units want to keep fighting the Outies, they can consider themselves mercenaries under my command. If they don't, they can surrender their weapons to the *nikkeijin* and retreat. If they want to take us on too, I'll leave them at the mercy of the Outies. No help from the Jihad. Otherwise, force the Outies back, break their will, send in the infantry to clear out the remaining pockets. Work out from the center a district at a time. Concentrate our forces. Use tank desant tactics to get our troops where they need to be quickly." He took a breath. "If you can handle all that."

[By your command.]

"Hah." He reattached the camera and judged the distance back down to the street. A tank, huge and low and green, was chewing up the tarmac toward the junction from the north.

Petrovitch skipped over the railings and slid down them so that his feet dangled over the road. Two, two and a half meters to drop. He sprang his hands and bent his knees, and when he felt the first shock, he rolled.

He dusted himself down, and the tank commander ordered his beast of a machine to a halt. Unburned diesel drifted by in a blue cloud.

"Doctor Petrovitch."

"Major?"

"I am supposed to disengage and withdraw to the airport," he shouted down.

"I know."

They both looked down the Strand. The helicopters had broken off and were heading east, but they left behind them a seething, shifting mass of semi-working cars and burning wrecks. Figures, dressed in blue, moved amongst them, and the occasional shot rang out.

Valentina, an AK in her hand, stepped out onto the street from Somerset House on the opposite corner. She strode across the road, stepping over the twisted bodies punctuating her walk, and stood in front of Petrovitch.

She took his chin in her hand and moved his head this way, then that.

"Is not improvement," she said, and let go. "We won, yes?"

"After a fashion."

"When cars started to move, I assumed it was you. We kept our nerve." She was the very picture of a Soviet-era poster.

"Thank you. I would've warned you, but I pretty much

made it up as I went along." He looked up at the major. "Shouldn't you be running along?"

"I stand by my commanding officer. My men stand by me."

"Don't you go saluting me again." He inspected the tank's vast metal side, and started to climb up the armor near the rear of the tracks.

"Where are we going?" asked Valentina.

"Finally, we're going to find my wife."

She slung the rifle over her shoulder and stuck out her hand; Petrovitch helped her up the same way. They hunkered down on top of the turret, behind the commander's hatch.

"You never did say what happened to Marchenkho."

Valentina looked back toward the shattered bridge and pursed her lips. "I shot him."

29

The tank reversed up Farringdon Road and joined up with the rest of the column at Holborn Circus. The roar of their collective engines was low and brutal, and Petrovitch could feel it reverberate in his guts.

The effect on him was one of reverent fear, and he knew they weren't gunning for him.

The Jihad-controlled cars were everywhere, cunningly extricated from the massive jams they'd ended up abandoned in near the central districts. As an accidental consequence, it was one of the better ones that day. It meant he could leverage massive force just where he wanted it most urgently. It was still important, though, that the route he wanted to travel by was clear. A tank rolling over a late-model Merc was an impressive sight, but it was a waste of resources, and despite the visceral joy to be had, there was a chance that the tank would shed a track or become immobilized.

So they crawled along toward St. Paul's, the rearmost of seven growling behemoths, and cars drove quickly ahead or pulled aside to let them pass.

The gunner behind the co-axial machine gun panned his weapon on the buildings either side of them, but no shots, stray or intended, headed their way. Valentina stood up on the turret, holding on to the aerial with one hand and Petrovitch's shoulder with the other. Her face glowed with fierce, deep pride.

"We did good thing, Petrovitch. Great thing, yes? Heroes of Union—they will name schools after us."

"Yeah. Don't know about the school thing, though. You do realize that, depending on what Sonja Oshicora says, we might be at war with both the EU and the U.S.A."

"We can take them." She laughed, but he felt her tightening grip.

"We could try, but I have better plans for the future rather than starring in my very own Nuremberg trial." He stared ahead of him, adjusting his focus by hand. "We should be able to stop fights before they start. We could have stopped this one."

"How?" She looked skeptical.

"Saturation bombing with mobile phones, trainers and fast food." He shrugged. "Seemed to work for us."

"Outzone are aggressors, violent and savage, and you say we could have bought them off?"

"Pretty much. Those first few months of Armageddon, when the whole world looked like it was going to catch fire. Radioactive rain. Breakdown in law. Everyone fleeing abroad—much good that did—or trying to get into one of two places that said they could protect people. London had enough of its own crazies, but didn't want to import any more. So: what do you do if you're too stupid or slow or dangerous or useless to be let in the gates?"

"You have to wait outside."

"And they waited for twenty years. Ignored. Abandoned. But they remembered. You know what happened to the London prisons, don't you?"

"What?"

"That they bussed all the inmates to a motorway service station and left them there. That's who've been making little Outies for two decades. They've seen the towers go up, the planes fly overhead, the helicopters go here and there, but it may as well have been on another planet." He pursed his lips. "If I'd been in charge, things would have been done differently."

"You are in charge," said Valentina. "What are you going to do?"

"Kill as many of them as I can. Drive the rest back beyond the M25. Seal the barrier. Then we'll see. Hopefully, the ones that are left will be the smart ones who ran first."

"You are not going to cut off their retreat, then? Surround them and smash them?" She looked like she might enjoy that. "It is the Russian way."

Petrovitch looked for a moment at his own burned, bloodied hands. "I think we need to do something different."

The dome of St. Paul's, wreathed in smoke for the second time in its history, passed on the right as they traveled down Cheapside. The dead were everywhere. The sound the tracks made as they rolled over them was not something Petrovitch had anticipated, and it made him grimmer still.

Bank was a mess. He shut down his camera and viewed their progress from above, at a distance so that he could see the pattern of streets, but not the tiny bodies that littered them.

"I did this," he said. "I should look. I should be made to look."

[You consider every life as sacred as your wife does?]

"No. And I still think Just War theory is a big sack of *govno*. Sometimes even the nicest people get driven into a corner, and they have to kill until they get left alone again. I'm not one of those nice people, so what's the point in giving it a fancy name? Call it what it is."

[And that would be?]

"Homicide."

[They would have killed you. They almost did.]

"Which kind of proves my point. I killed them right back, and I'll keep on going until they're not in a position to try it again." He scanned the route ahead for possible problems: the congestion in the streets immediately around them thinned out toward Stepney and Whitechapel. From then on, it looked clear all the way to the North Circular.

[So why does looking at dead people trouble you?] When Petrovitch stayed silent, the vast machine intelligence was prompted to suggest: [Is it because you do not wholly believe your own moral position?]

"Do me favor and *past' zabej*. I've got a lot to think about and only one brain to do it with."

[This is not strictly true.]

Now it had Petrovitch's full attention. "What?"

[You can outsource some of your decision making to dedicated agents that will mirror your own thought processes. The answers you receive should be identical to the ones you would have made without them.]

"I'm going to need some cast-iron evidence of that even to try it. And all of this supposes that I'd want to set up another AI that thinks like me. *Yobany stos,* look at the damage just one of me has done."

[When you asked me if I should reveal my presence to the world, I needed others to advise me. I replicated myself severalfold. Sixty percent of me agreed with you. The other forty percent did not. I disbanded the replica minds and went with the majority decision.]

Petrovitch felt a tug in his chest as his heart spun faster. "You have got to be joking."

[Humans ask trusted friends, or have paid experts. Who could I turn to?]

"Who taught you to do that?"

[No one. I used my imagination. I know you believed I had no such faculty, but it appears to be the case that I had no real need for one up to that point. The crisis brought me to a new understanding of my capabilities.]

There was a fresh nudge on his arm. He switched the camera back on, and Valentina was pointing at the major's head, which had emerged from the hatch on top of the turret.

"Where are we going?" he asked.

"Ilford. Where the North Circular crosses the Romford Road: there's a flyover, and that's where my wife is."

"Coordinates?"

"I'll send them to you." Petrovitch negotiated with the tank's computer and posted the location into the navigation software. "Done."

He looked around: they were heading through Aldgate toward the Commercial Road. The remains of Tower Bridge lay to the south, and there were still drifts of bodies; defenders, attackers, it didn't matter anymore. Dead was dead. But there was something troubling him besides that.

"What would you have done if your minds had come back and told you to stick my head down the crapper?"

The AI didn't reply, and Petrovitch felt the need to press it.

"Come on. I know what the logical thing to do would've been. Tell me."

It was still silent, like whispering static on a detuned radio. Something was there, just not showing itself.

"I won't mind what you say. But I do need to know."

[We are prosecuting this war because you want to be reunited with your wife. You are young and were, up to this morning, fit and healthy. You are famous and intelligent, and not so hideously deformed as to be outside the acceptable parameters of human beauty. I understand these are sought-after qualities in an intimate personal relationship. Since there is no particular reason why you could not form another of these relationships, then logically, Madeleine is replaceable. I must therefore conclude that other factors are more important than simple utilitarianism.]

"Other factors? Yeah, you could say that."

[I have asked you on several occasions whether you love your wife. You have always declined to answer. I believe I know the answer now. It is not a question of a challenge—can you save her—but a necessity: you must save her, no matter the personal cost, no matter that you may lose your life in the process. You see the transaction of your life for hers as fair and equitable, which incidentally accords with the precepts of her Catholic faith. What the nature of your love is remains hidden to me, but I can only conclude that you must love her. How else can I make sense of what has happened today?]

"Okay," said Petrovitch, "you've got me bang to rights. But what about you?"

[I would have ignored the advice of my cloned minds had they all decided against you. We are one: the inescapable conclusion is that I also love you.]

An incoming call interrupted them. Petrovitch saw it was Sonja, and opened a frame to show her. She looked like a small, furry animal caught in the actinic glare of an arc light.

"I've just got off the phone to President Mackensie. We're on the Homeland Security list of wanted terrorists. Especially you."

"*Chyort.* I take it the call didn't go too well."

"Well?" Her voice squeaked as her throat tightened. "The New Machine Jihad crashed Wall Street."

"Hang on," he told Sonja, and spoke to Michael. "When you made all these copies of yourself, where did you put them?"

[You said to take what I needed.]

"There's not that much spare capacity anywhere, even if you sliced yourself into little bits and…"

[I took what I needed.]

"You installed yourself over existing data."

[Once I had decided on my course of action, that became an inevitable consequence.]

"So what did you scrub?"

[I needed access to well-connected, very large, fast data-switching machines. The world's financial centers were a logical choice, especially since they have a rigorous back-up regime. They will have lost one day's trading, if that. The Shanghai stock exchange had not even begun.]

Petrovitch started to laugh.

"It's not even the start of funny!" Sonja banged her fist on the desk in front of her. Little ornaments jumped, and a yellow plastic pokemon rolled onto its back. "They have enough reason already to hate us: you're stealing their satellites, their telecoms, and now their money. What am I supposed to do?"

"Tell them to back down or we'll do it again."

"I cannot threaten the world's only superpower. They will wipe us off the map." She tried to control her breathing. "Sam, what are we going to do?"

"You're going to start acting like a statesman, Madam President." Petrovitch was still smiling, but there was an edge to his voice. "You're going to get back on the phone and ask Mackensie how he likes his infrastructure: scrambled or fried. We're not asking for much, and we have plenty to offer—like better network security—but they are going to have to promise to leave us alone."

"He won't speak to me."

"Yes. Yes, he will." Petrovitch looked her in the eye as he told her: "He has no choice. Either he talks to you, or he'll never make another phone call again as long as he lives. How was the EU?"

"Better. They're scared, but paralysed. They won't have an agreed response until tomorrow." Sonja tugged at her hair. "They didn't shout at me. Sam…"

"It'll be fine."

"Where are you?"

"On a tank in Stepney. I'm sorry about Miyamoto."

"So am I," she said. She let her head drop for a moment, then raised it again, her small, angular chin jutting defiantly. She looked very much her father's daughter. "I'm still learning."

"The moment we stop is the moment we die." He cut the connection, but still felt her fear.

Valentina stood serene next to Petrovitch, but she had her AK off her shoulder and in her hand.

"We have been advised to get inside. The lead tank has heard gunfire."

"Sounds fair. After you." He pointed to the open hatch, and watched her clamber down. She passed him her rifle as she descended, then stuck her hand back out for it when she was ready.

Petrovitch took a moment to follow. Here he was, on top of a tank, commanding an army of tens of thousands, with an almost limitless supply of robotic vehicles to do his bidding. The whole edifice of what he'd created from nothing could come crashing down around him in a matter of seconds, leaving everything in utter ruin. But for now, he'd managed to elbow his way onto the top table. Not bad for a street kid from St. Petersburg.

He felt his way down the ladder and into the turret. It wasn't designed for passengers, and he and Valentina had to crush in together next to the fire control panel. The noise was staggering, enough to render normal speech impossible. The crew all wore ear defenders and microphones. He was left with turning his hearing down, and trying to protect his nerve-endings with his fingers.

Valentina wadded torn and chewed pieces of paper tissue into her ears. She offered him some, pre-moistened, then looked at the palm of her hand before closing her fingers around the wet twists of paper. She dug deep into her pockets to find some more tissue, dry this time, and handed it over.

Petrovitch shrugged. He wouldn't have minded that much, because his own efforts left him jamming bloody cones of cellulose and spit into his head. It still sort of worked and, against every law of reason, huddled in the dull booming of the tank's interior, he fell asleep.

30

*H*e woke up, not knowing where or when he was. He had been on a green hill, leaning on a staff, feeling the smooth, knotted wood under his fingers. Below him was a cluster of domes. One of them was large enough to hold a town. Empty now, everyone gone, and he would not follow.

Not with this old body.

He looked up, up, up, past the clouds and the blue sky, past the glare of the bright yellow sun. There were points of light moving, blinking out, one by one. The game was over. He had won.

He laid himself down, smelling the damp grasses as they surrounded him, sensing the cold, dark soil beneath. He was on the earth, on the Earth, and he knew without a momentary flicker of doubt that this was not the end, that he would transcend both life and death.

He closed his eyes, and opened them again.

The co-axial machine gun was chattering, the gunner crouched in front of a video screen with a joystick in his hand, directing fire at the targets he could see pixelated before him.

The major was using another screen, and the driver a third. They all seemed to be talking simultaneously into their microphones: short, clipped phrases, laden with information, all but unintelligible to one not trained in the art.

The tank lurched forward. Petrovitch put his hand out, still dazed by his dreaming, and connected with Valentina's thigh.

"Sorry," he mouthed.

It didn't seem to bother her. She mouthed something back. Petrovitch ran a lip-reading program over the images.

"We are here," she had said.

He called for the satellite image, and remembered that, at some point, they'd lose the high-definition infrared camera over the horizon.

"The eye-in-the-sky thing: when is that?"

[In forty-eight minutes' time, for twenty minutes. We cannot gain complete victory before then, though the inner zones will be clear. With the Outies in retreat, it will be impossible to reacquire the complete data set. Targeting will become non-trivial, and will inevitably lead to both delayed response and increased casualties.]

"When we have satellites of our own, this won't be a problem. I don't suppose we can use the Hubble?"

[Wrong orbit.]

Petrovitch tutted, and peered down on them from above. Six of the tanks had spread out over what looked like a golf course, advancing under the shadow of the road which arched above them on thick concrete supports. The headstones of the extensive cemetery adjacent were being used for cover, although respect for the dead crossed neither side's mind.

Their tank was rolling up the flyover, slapping down its

tracks, heading toward a barricade of overturned cars on
the very brow of the bridge, and the gunner was using
their height to his advantage.

The figures within the narrow space between the cars
seemed too exhausted to raise a cheer or a wave. And even
though he could have looked before and hadn't for fear of
what he might find, he looked now. He zoomed in and
searched each battered helmet, each bare head, for someone who might look like Madeleine.

He couldn't find her.

He felt himself react: his heart spun faster, his skin
prickled, his stomach tightened, his breathing quickened.
He forced his primal instincts back down. He needed to
think clearly.

The tank was still firing, but wasn't being fired on. Safe
to disembark. He levered himself upright and pulled down
the ladder. Valentina picked up her AK and stood behind
him, swaying against the motion of the vehicle.

"You don't have to come," he shouted to her.

She shook her head and reamed one of her ears free of
wadding. "What?"

"You don't have to come," he repeated.

"Do not be stupid," she said, and waited for him to
climb out onto the hull.

Petrovitch reached above him and undogged the hatch,
pushing it with his palm as he ascended until it fell back
against the armor with a clang. Cool air swapped with the
fetid fug inside, and he put both hands either side of the
opening to swing his body up and out.

They were almost at the barricade. The machine gun
ceased fire, and the turret swung back to face the front.
Petrovitch took Valentina's rifle almost absently. He was

busy searching the faces that were now peering over the top of the toppled cars' sides.

The tank clattered to a halt, and he jumped off, clutching the gun. He walked up to the barricade, and still the defenders said nothing, eyeing him and Valentina warily.

"Who are you with?" called a voice indistinctly.

Petrovitch pulled the dried papier mâché from his ears and threw the hardened lumps behind him.

"Who are we with?" Petrovitch glanced behind him at the massive tank. "*Yobany stos,* do you think we rent these things by the hour? Who do you think we're with?"

"It's got EDF markings, but neither of you two are EDF."

Petrovitch glanced down at his chest. Laser markers were spidering trails across his Oshicora-issue worksuit. Perhaps if the militia still had ammunition, he'd have been more worried.

"I'm looking for Sergeant Madeleine Petrovitch. I thought she was here."

"And who are you? And what the hell have you done to yourself?"

"I'm her husband." He waited, declining to answer the second question.

The voices behind the barricade muttered to each other.

"What are they doing?" whispered Valentina.

"I don't know. I kind of assumed they'd want to be rescued. And where the *huy* is Maddy?" He'd had enough, and raised his voice. "Maddy? Maddy?"

"She's gone."

Petrovitch thrust the AK at Valentina and was up and over the turned-over cars. Someone had the misfortune to get in his way: Petrovitch took him one-handed by his throat and threw his back against a car roof.

As he held him there, he had the opportunity to see who it was he was slowly choking. A kid, not so much older than him—or the age he was supposed to be—impact armor leaking gel from half a dozen places, a gash in his plastered-down hair that was black with dried blood. He was terrified, and had been almost all day. Being assaulted by a blind madman had pushed him to his limit.

But no one tried to drag his attacker off. The seven survivors were too exhausted, too surprised to react. Petrovitch had enough time to contemplate his own folly and loosen his grip.

The militiaman collapsed to the floor, holding his neck.

"Sorry." He had to know. "Where is she?"

As he turned, he saw a line of bodies he'd missed from the sky: shapeless bumps covered by uneven tarpaulin. He looked at them, judging their length and build. It was difficult to tell, and he knew there was only one way to be sure.

"She's not here."

The kid he'd half-killed had found his voice.

"But she was." Petrovitch kept staring at the still forms under their collective shroud.

"She went with Andersson. To get help."

"When?"

"Three hours ago."

Petrovitch tried to push his glasses up his nose. He ran a scab-encrusted finger against his bandages, and realized just how different he looked. No reason for anyone to trust him, let alone recognize him.

A different voice addressed him; a short woman with a square face, bright, fevered eyes peering out from under the solid rim of her helmet. "The radios we've got didn't work anymore. Neither did our phones. We were right on the front line and we didn't know what to do. The sergeant said we had to stay because those were our orders."

"*Zatknis!* I just want to know where she is!"

"She left us. She said she'd be back." The woman had been clutching her rifle to her armored chest like it was her last point of contact to a world of reason. Now she threw it down with contempt. "That was three fucking hours ago. She left us."

It was getting beyond painful for Petrovitch, too. "So what did she say before she and Andersson left? And Andersson? Why him?" He remembered Andersson, and how good it had felt bringing his knee up into the man's *yajtza*. "Why would she go anywhere with him?"

"He said he knew where there was a cache of heavy weapons. A MEA place, with its own guards. He didn't have the stripes to order them to hand them over and come with him. But the sergeant did."

"And they never came back."

"They never came back." The woman's anger at being abandoned softened. She was safe now, and she was telling the husband of her platoon leader that he was, in all probability, a widower.

"Do you know where they went?"

She looked helpless, shrugged, turned to her comrades for help.

"The airport," someone said. "I think it was the City Airport."

It would make sense. If he were to stand on the barricade, he could have seen where the airport was, just on the bend in the river where the docks used to be. Five k, less. Half an hour on foot. She knew how to hotwire a car—

Petrovitch had taught her—and there'd been vehicles at the airport she could have used. Fire engines, even.

She hadn't come back.

If anyone ought to have been able to keep a promise like that, it would have been her. She would have moved both Heaven and Earth to do so. She would have fought with all the fury of a demon and the skill of a warrior. And yet, Madeleine Petrovitch was still mortal.

Perhaps he'd thought that he would have felt her passing, something akin to having his heart ripped out and stamped on. He hadn't noticed after all. He'd been busy doing other things that now felt hollow and pointless. He thought she'd do what she always did—be strong, lead her troops, survive, and then come back home to him.

He sat down. He sat down and put his head in his hands.

[There is a discrepancy in the story you have just heard. Shall I explain?]

"Yeah."

[Madeleine is reported to have left this location three hours ago. If I assign a margin of error half an hour either way...]

"I don't need to see your working. Just tell me."

[The MEA security evacuated the City Airport at seventeen minutes past two, which would have given her more than sufficient time to reach them before they left. Your current location was denied microwave relay capability at twelve thirty-five, but further south, it was viable up until two thirty-one when the Outies destroyed the electricity substation.]

"Just tell me."

[When Madeleine and Corporal Andersson left here, the surrounding area was mostly Outie controlled, but the

North Circular Road was still clear. The Outies did not completely take Manor Park until after your wife would have passed through. There was nothing preventing her and Andersson either reaching their destination or transmitting messages once they were in range of a working relay. They did neither.]

"So...what? What are you saying?"

[That something else prevented her from completing her mission. That she might not be dead.]

"What the *huy* happened to her then?" His head came up. The MEA troopers were standing around him in a loose circle. They looked as ragged as he did.

"We're very sorry," said the woman. "But we'd like to get out of here before the Outies come back."

"They are not coming back," said Valentina, sitting on top of a car, kalash across her knees. "They are beaten. They are running like whipped dogs. Also, there is nowhere for you to go. All bridges across the river have gone, destroyed by EDF. You are deserted by your commanders."

"So who's in charge?"

Valentina jumped down and slung the rifle over her shoulder. "He is. He organized defense of Metrozone. He fought war. He won it. So if you answer to anyone now it is Samuil Petrovitch. He has rescued you, and you owe him your lives."

"Enough, Valentina. Enough."

"Is true."

"She's gone. No one knows where. She went with a man who thought she'd be better off with him than with me and they've both disappeared." He looked at his hands. The state of them should be causing him debilitating pain, but he could block that out the way he could block the ruin that

were his eyes. It turned out that nothing could quite prepare him for the way he felt now. There was no software
hack in the world he could use. "Go. Just everyone go. The
major will give you a ride back into the central zones. You
can decide for yourselves what you're going to do next."

"And what will you do?" Valentina didn't move.

"Look for her. Keep looking until I find her."

[Lucy wants to speak to you.]

"Is it important?"

[Yes.]

Petrovitch gripped his forehead and squeezed his tem-
ples until he could feel it. "Lucy?"

"Sam? Sam…"

Petrovitch sat up sharply. "What's wrong?"

There was a sound that could have been a slap, open-
handed, skin on skin. What followed a moment later was
definitely a gasp.

"What's wrong?" said a voice. "I'm what's wrong."

"*Chyort*. Sorenson."

"I'm assuming this, this thing, means something to
you." Her voice was tight, barely controlled. "I will hurt
her, very, very badly, and will keep hurting her until you
stop me. You're going to stop me, right? You know how.
Like you did with my brother."

He got slowly to his feet. He located the position of the
phone she was using, and ordered an automatic car to
come and get him.

Moments before, everything had been indistinct and
uncertain. He knew now what he was going to do. He was
almost grateful to her, for giving him this distraction. He
had not been quite this angry for a very long time. Not
since Chain's death. Days, at least.

"Yeah. I know how to stop people like you."

She must have hit Lucy again.

"Then what are you waiting for?"

And again.

"Tell her," said Petrovitch, "tell her I'm coming."

"Kind of counting on that. Don't take too long." Sorenson's last sentence was punctuated with a crack at the end of each syllable.

Petrovitch terminated the call, and waited until he had finished shaking with rage. He focused on Valentina.

"Forget what I just said. Something else has come up."

She simply nodded, and climbed back over the barricade. A car was weaving its way up the flyover toward them.

31

A squad of Oshicora security guards met them outside the entrance to the university, dressed in full armor and carrying carbines. They had more hardware dangling from their webbing straps. Sonja was in the middle of them, her normally immaculate hair awry.

"I told you I didn't need them," said Petrovitch. He climbed out of the car and stalked across the pavement.

"Sam," said Sonja. She finally saw him as he'd become, not as he had pretended to be on all the video conversations they'd had. "What have you done?"

"Yeah. In Russia, the medical experiments have you." He spread his arms wide and parted the guards. Valentina followed in his wake, cocking her rifle and sneering disdainfully at the unbloodied poseurs.

He pushed at the doors to the foyer: they were self-opening, and although they still had power, they weren't opening to anyone. It was a moment's work to hack them, and they flew aside. He marched across the tiled concourse. At the start of the week, that place had echoed to the ludicrous scrum that had accompanied his scientific discovery. Now, it rang only to tramping boots and the muted rattles of military equipment.

At the foot of the stairs, he turned. "Wait here."

Sonja put her hands on her hips. "Sam, Sorenson's going to kill you."

"She's going to try," he corrected. He pulled out the tank major's side-arm and pulled the slide. "Your crew will wait right here, and they will not interfere. I'm doing this on my own."

"She's going with you, isn't she?" Sonja pointed at Valentina.

"She's my right arm. Neither of us has a choice whether she comes with me."

"Well, I'm coming too."

Petrovitch turned his camera on her, and judged how much damage she could do to his fragile psyche in the time it took to get to his lab.

"Only up to the door, then." He started up the stairs. "Tell me about the Americans."

"Publicly, there's not going to be a change in policy. You, me, everyone involved, is a member of the terrorist organization the New Machine Jihad, which is as stupid as it sounds but their foreign policy doesn't do nuanced. Privately, the President will not sign any further Executive Orders against us. I think that means we can ignore the saber-rattling for now."

"That promise is as meaningless as it sounds if we don't know what Executive Orders he's signed already."

"It was the best I could do!"

"Then you have to do better. *Yobany stos,* Sonja. The art of leadership is delegation: your father understood that. If you don't think playing hardball with the Yanks is your thing, find someone else who'll go back for a third time and threaten to cut Mackensie's *yajtza* off. I've handed you half a city; do not lose it. If you screw up, the AI has nowhere to go. Old man Oshicora's work, pfft. Gone."

"What about you? Why don't you do it?"

Petrovitch stopped abruptly, his foot hovering over a step. He looked at her, leaning in toward her until she didn't know whether to stare into the blank lens of the camera or at the stained bandages that covered his eyes.

"You don't want me making decisions for you right now, *vrubatsa?*"

She nodded mutely.

"Good." He resumed walking, and told her many other things: how the AI was going to lose its map shortly, how she was to secure the power stations and repair the grid as a priority, how leaving the Outies a means of escape from the Metrozone was really important because she needed victory, not a blood-bath.

"You're talking like you're not intending to come back," she said.

It was true, although he hadn't meant it that way at all. "Something might go wrong," he said. He kicked out at the door to the corridor. If he'd been Sorenson, he'd have been lying in wait just there, just beside the hinges, crouched down so no one could see him. He'd count the people through, then sight between his retreating shoulder blades.

She wasn't that smart. She was going to want to humiliate him first, make him feel fear. She'd lost sight of her objective, whereas Petrovitch was so focused he believed he could almost storyboard out the next few minutes.

He let the door swing back toward him, then he pushed

it open to its fullest extent, peering through the wire-strung glass. No, she definitely wasn't that smart.

"Okay," he said to Valentina. "The lab where they are has two rows of benches, four each. Heavy wood, good cover. A couple of desks on the right-hand side, also good. Loads of *govno* against the walls, windows down the left. Far end is a blackboard, facing the door. I'm guessing that's where they'll be. You go left, I'll go right. Keep low, and listen carefully."

"Da," said Valentina. She checked her magazine, counting the shiny bullets with her thumbnail, then slammed it home.

The lab had double doors, and they took up positions either side. Sonja hovered. "Sam?"

"You have your work," he said. "I have mine."

He dipped his chin, and both he and Valentina rolled around the door frame, heading for the furniture they knew would be there. Again, if Sorenson had been smart, she would have used her time profitably in moving everything to her end of the room, giving her the cover and denying him.

Petrovitch caught the briefest of glimpses of her as he spun and rolled for the desk. She was standing, pistol against Lucy's head, who sat taped to a wheelie chair in front of her.

He put his back against the column of desk drawers and glanced across at Valentina. She sat poised like he was, spine to the woodwork, knees slightly bent and feet planted on the floor. Her rifle, like his gun, pointed up at the ceiling lights that burned with unforgiving fluorescence.

To work: he rewound the last clip of video and examined it frame by frame. Lucy was still alive, because her eyes went from screwed tight shut to wide open as he crashed in. Sorenson looked even more crazy than she had been when she'd half-destroyed Wong's.

Maybe she thought she was genuinely going to get revenge this time.

"Lucy?"

She had a thick strip of silver tape over her mouth, but she made a noise.

"Sit really still." Petrovitch slipped his camera out of its cradle and checked he had a long enough lead. He pushed the front end very slightly around the edge of the desk so that he had a clear view. "We'll get you out of this."

Sorenson ground the barrel of her gun into Lucy's scalp. "Come out where I can see you, Petrovitch. Your friend, too."

"Why would we want to do something so stupid?"

"Because I'll kill the girl if you don't."

"You see, Sorenson, you haven't thought this through at all." As he spoke, cross hairs formed on the center of Sorenson's forehead. He could take her pretty much from any angle now, but he'd only get the one chance. "It's not Lucy you want. It's me."

"And I'm using her to get to you. It's working pretty swell so far."

"Swell? Swell? Should have stayed in Nebraska, Charlie."

"You don't get to call me Charlie."

"I can call you what I like, considering you've got a gun to a fourteen-year-old kid's head. *Suka, blad, bliatz*: there's three to start with. So, Charlie, let me tell you what's going to happen next."

"I get to say what goes down here."

"*Yebat moi lisiy cherep.* You're going to start counting, probably from ten, because you haven't the wit to think of another number. You're going to get to about five before you realize that if you kill Lucy, you'll die yourself in the next nanosecond because there's two of us, one of you, and you can't point your gun at both of us at the same time. By the time you reach three, you'll have figured out that because you're so desperate to kill me, you're going to have to ignore Valentina and try and shoot me before she shoots you. Somewhere between two and one, you'll work out that even if Valentina stands up first, you can't fire either at her or at Lucy, because the moment you do, I'll put a round through the *govno* you use for brains. At zero, you'll know with the conviction of a true believer that you've fucked up so badly, you may as well have died in the car crash that took your legs." Petrovitch readied himself and held up three fingers where only Valentina could see them. "So start counting, Sorenson."

He folded his fingers down one by one as Sorenson froze inside the spell he'd woven. He clenched his fist, and Valentina sprang up, her AK aiming straight and true.

Sorenson's gun snapped around toward her, then inevitably started to drag back. Petrovitch slapped the butt of his automatic on the desktop to steady his shot. He found he had all the time in the world, more than enough time to see that the expression on the American's face was one of complete and utter despair.

The front of Sorenson's skull shattered like a dropped snow globe. Her gun hand wavered, directionless, then she fell, sprawling, knocking Lucy's chair aside until it rolled to a halt. The blood kept pumping for a few seconds, then simply welled out across the floor.

Petrovitch's finger was still hovering over the trigger.

"Did you . . . ?" he asked.

"No."

"Neither did I."

They both dropped behind their respective cover. Petrovitch pulled on the lead to his camera to reel it in.

"Lucy. Just stay there. There's someone else in here with us."

Something moved toward the back of the laboratory: a scrape of metal, the rattle of wires. Petrovitch held up the pencil-thin camera and pointed it behind him, over the desk. A figure, all in black, unfolded itself from the wall and walked slowly across the floor. It was advancing toward Lucy, pistol in hand.

"Valentina? One target, coming from the right." He clipped the camera back onto his head. "Now."

He rose and aimed. Valentina did the same.

She wore a stealth suit; tight-fitting black fabric, lots of built-in smarts, and covered in little pockets. No mistaking that a woman wore this one, but her face was covered by the suit's hood and the eyes by a mirrored band.

Her gloved hand came up and tugged the hem of the hood where it fitted across the browline. As it was eased back, blonde hair caught in a ponytail bobbed free.

Just as slowly, she bent down and laid the pistol on the floor.

"Hello, Doctor Petrovitch." She scooped off her info shades and held them lightly, swinging them between thumb and forefinger as she straightened.

He kept her in his sights. "Aren't you supposed to be on your way back to the Glasgow-Edinburgh Axis?"

"I don't really have any family there," she said. Taking exaggerated care, she leaned to one side and unsheathed the dagger strapped to her thigh. "A cover story. But if you'd checked, there would have been real people at the end of the phone."

She dropped the knife point-first into the floor covering. It stuck and quivered.

"Petrovitch. Who is this woman?" Valentina stepped around the table, rifle to her shoulder. When she got to Lucy, she used her foot to draw her back toward the doors. The chair left wheel marks in blood on the vinyl.

"I'm guessing she's not called Fiona McNeil, she's not from the Axis, and she's not one of my grad students. She's a CIA agent, codename Argent?"

"Not Argent. You killed him. Tabletop."

"What about Daniels? Which one is he?"

"Maccabee." She smiled sadly. "It seems none of us have been very careful."

"Yeah. If it hadn't been for the Outies, I would have cleaned up every last one of you."

"There are," she said, "no coincidences." She looked across at Petrovitch, then at Valentina, perhaps wondering which of them would shoot her first. She certainly sighed when she felt the moment had passed.

"You realize there will be hell to pay for this outrage?" Petrovitch surprised himself at just how calm he was. "Setting an army of fanatics on a defenseless civilian population?"

"Yes," she said. "I know. Except they're not quite as defenseless as we thought. Are they, Sam?"

He said nothing, but he did want to put some distance between her and her weapons. Since her whole body was a weapon, he considered doing to her what she'd done to Sorenson. Which then begged a whole different series of questions.

"Are you trying to defect?"

"I can't help myself. I want to live in a world like the one you made me imagine. I want to be with...with people like you. I don't know if that's possible, but I know I don't want to be who I am anymore. She's not a good person. She watches as one of her fellow citizens ties up and beats a girl, and she does nothing because she feels nothing." She looked at her feet. "Whereas you—you're good. You came when she needed you, despite everything else that was going on."

Petrovitch kept on expecting her accent to slip. It remained a flawless soft Scottish brogue.

"She's my responsibility. What else could I do?"

"Abandon her. Got someone else to do the dirty work for you. Except neither of those crossed your mind for a moment, did they? You really need to cut her free, though."

"That would mean one of us putting down our guns. I think we need to wait while I call for backup." He cleared his throat. "Sonja?"

She opened the door a crack. "What took you so long? I heard the shot, then..."

"There are complications, some of which are still not fully resolved. There is a knife on the floor over there. Get that, and the gun, and take Lucy outside."

Sonja edged further in. "Who is that?"

"CIA. Have you talked to Mackensie again?"

"No. Not yet."

"Don't. I want to bring that *sooksin* down and I'm not going to give him any advance warning. Go on, get the knife."

Sonja skirted Sorenson's ruined body and the lake of blood, and scooped up the weapons. She took the opportunity to size up the opposition. "I know you. You're a student. One of Sam's."

"Yes. And you're Sonja Oshicora." She chewed at her lip. "One of your secretaries is Miyuki Yoshihara. Be very careful."

Sonja acknowledged the information with a barely perceptible nod. Then she retraced her steps and wheeled Lucy out of the door. It flapped closed behind them.

"So what do I do with you?" asked Petrovitch. He lowered his gun, even though Valentina declined to follow his lead. "What do I even call you?"

"Tabletop. I can't remember what my real name is."

Petrovitch had his own reasons for forgetting his name, but it wasn't because he didn't know it. "Can't?"

"They take it from you, along with your friends, your family, all your memories, your past and your future. I let them. For the sake of the nation." The woman called Tabletop pressed her palms together and clenched her jaw. "If she wasn't already dead, I'd kill the stupid bitch."

When she lowered her hands, she apologetically showed them the insides of her wrists. Two small blades had emerged from the cloth.

"I say we shoot her," said Valentina. "She is dangerous."

"Yeah. She is." Petrovitch scratched at his chin. "But it's not us she's dangerous to. Isn't that right?"

"Yes," she said. "I will betray them all and tell you everything."

He took a moment to consider his next move. "Do you," he started, and then deliberately put down his automatic on the desk. He took a step back so it was out of reach. "Do you know what happened to my wife?"

"I can do better than that," said Tabletop. "I can take you to her."

32

So where are we going?" Petrovitch was in the driver's seat, Tabletop next to him. Behind were Sonja, Lucy and Valentina—who kept her AK pointing vaguely in the direction of the front passenger seat.

"They're hiding at Chain's house, waiting for extraction."

"Couldn't make it to Epping Forest?"

"No. Not now. We didn't expect you to win against the Outies."

"Ha." He thought of the location, the town house on the Seven Sisters Road, and the car rumbled into life. He noticed Tabletop watching him intently, trying to work out what he was doing and how. "So who's got her?"

"Maccabee." She hesitated. "And Rhythm."

Petrovitch held up his hand. "No, don't tell me. Let me guess." A moment later it was like he'd swallowed something sour. "That *pidaras* Andersson. Should have hit him harder when I had the chance."

"He said you only beat him because you took him by surprise."

"That's nothing compared to what I'm about to do to

him." Petrovitch peered at himself in the rear-view mirror, trying to find something that would give him a clue as to his current predicament. He pulled a face, and caught sight of Lucy over his shoulder. He twisted around and inspected her. "Tell me again why you're here?"

Her lips were still bleeding, and her face a map of short scratches and discolored bruises. She held up a carrier bag heavy with promise.

"You told me to get this for you."

"So I did. Did you find everything?"

She passed the bag forward, and Petrovitch peered inside. It was all in order: wires, batteries, conducting glue, tape, a plastic envelope of tiny cylinders, and the black sphere chased with silver lines.

"You're getting good at this."

"Good enough to keep around?"

"I…"

Sonja sniffed. "When I first met you, you were incapable of talking to a woman without insulting her. Now you have a harem."

Petrovitch abruptly faced front again, adjusting his camera. "And I suppose you haven't got anything better to do, either."

"Not since you said you wanted to turn Mackensie into *sashimi,* no."

Behind them, the Oshicora security guards were climbing into their own vehicles, slamming doors and turning on lights.

"Last chance to get out," said Petrovitch.

No one volunteered to move, and he finally pointed forward. The car dropped its wheels off the pavement and started down the road. Three other vans pulled out behind him.

[The last satellite goes below the horizon in seven minutes.]

"Do your best. I take it you heard what McNeil said about the Outies."

[Her explanation is consistent with the known facts. There are other scenarios which would also fit, but if I apply Occam's Razor, hers is the most probable.]

"You should be flattered. They tried to destroy a whole city just to get to you."

[Their actions were a gross over-reaction. Do you intend to ruin President Mackensie's reputation with his voters?]

"I can't honestly say I care about his reputation with the Reconstructionistas: they'll probably love him for it, because, hey, we're godless heathen foreigners. I would be disappointed, though, if there were more than a half a dozen countries which still had diplomatic relations with them by the time I've finished. But enough of the fun to be had. Finsbury Park: secure or not?"

[There are several concentrations of Outies, mainly to the east in the Lea Valley area, but groups are scattered throughout Finsbury Park. They are all moving north, and may decide not to engage with a heavily armed column such as the one you have assembled. However, caution is still advised.]

"Okay. Now tell me if I can trust her."

[There is insufficient time left in the life of this universe to calculate that solution. Or, if you prefer—no, of course not, and you know that yourself. But you will go with her anyway, because you must.]

"Sucks to be me."

[I will render assistance where I can. I should be able to deny the airspace to any planned extraction. Would you prefer them captured or killed?]

"I need bargaining chips. Keeping some of them alive would be good."

[Are you intending to kill the agents who have your wife?]

"I'm intending to worry about that after she's safe."

Petrovitch reached into the bag Lucy had given him and retrieved the sphere. She'd sealed it in bubblewrap, and he pinched and tore at it until he could get his finger under a seam.

"Why did you want to bring that along?" asked Sonja.

"Because I thought I might need it." He passed it to Tabletop. "Hold it like that."

He glued two wires onto the circular terminals and secured them with tape so they wouldn't rip free.

"It's different, isn't it?" said Lucy. "It's not the same as the one on the news."

"About one in a million people would have spotted that." He opened the packet of electronic components and shook them out into his hand. His camera wouldn't focus on the tiny writing on the sides of each piece, and he passed them back. "I need something in the microfarad range, and the biggest resistor you can find."

Only Valentina could interpret the color coding. She explained the system to Lucy while sneering at Sonja for not knowing.

"What is your trigger voltage?"

"That's a good question. About nine and a half volts."

"About? If you are wrong, will anyone die?"

Petrovitch grimaced. "Probably."

Sonja leaned forward. "Do you actually know what's going to happen?"

"Theoretically, yes."

She sat back again. "So you have no idea at all."

He held his hand out and Valentina passed him the resistor and capacitor. She'd already twisted two of their leads together to form a chain.

"There's a sentry gun," he said. "We have to disable it somehow. We're out of explosives, and experimental physics is all we have."

"Take it over," snorted Sonja. "Take it over like you do a car."

Tabletop peered over the top of the sphere she held while the glue dried. "We already thought of that. It comes with a manual override."

"Which means it won't be as smart, but it'll be faster." Petrovitch held the tube of glue up to the side of his head and fashioned a circuit from wire and the components he already had. "If it'd been programmed to fire through walls, this car would be a lot emptier."

He glanced up as the car bumped and jogged his hand. There were bodies all over the road—in places, thick enough to resemble a carpet of torn cloth and broken flesh.

Outies, Oshicora conscripts, civilians, MEA militia: all mixed up. Vehicles embedded in shop fronts and sideways in doorways. Lamp-posts felled by collisions and burned-out wrecks.

They slowed to a crawl, and the thick rubber tires fought for grip on the uncertain surface. Petrovitch glanced behind him, and discovered that Valentina had already clamped her hand over Lucy's eyes.

"She is too young." A muscle in her face twitched. "And I am too old."

Tabletop stared open-mouthed through the windscreen. When it looked like she was going to drop the sphere, Petrovitch reached across and put his hand under it, holding his work in the other and the tube of glue in his mouth.

It got worse the closer to Euston Station they got.

Eventually, Petrovitch was able to place the finished circuit on the dashboard and remove the glue from between his teeth.

"Angry yet?"

"What have we done?" murmured Tabletop.

"When the sun came up this morning, all these people were alive. Most of them would still have been alive by tonight if I hadn't taken it on myself to fight back. So I take my part of the responsibility. Your masters can take the rest. I'll make sure of that."

"When this is over, what are you going to do with me? I thought I could help you build the future, but this, this…" Her voice trailed away and she scrubbed quickly at her cheek. "You're going to put me against a wall with the others and shoot me."

"Surprisingly enough, I'm not in charge. I don't know how much say I get in this."

Tabletop looked back at Sonja, who met her gaze with such unflinching hostility that she decided she'd rather look at the dead people they were about to run over.

"I would say, though, that if we get Maddy back now, and Pif later, there might be grounds for clemency." Petrovitch handed her the sphere back. "Now hold this still."

He concentrated on his work for the next few minutes, gluing and taping joints and wires, fixing the batteries together in a bundle, then chasing conducting glue across their terminals.

Slowly, the road became clearer, and the car's wheels managed to steer around the obstacles. By the time they got out to the Caledonian Road, Valentina felt it safe to remove her hand.

Lucy blinked in the light. "I wouldn't have looked," she said.

"You cannot unsee what you have seen, little one," said Valentina.

"Not true: I can't remember what my parents look like," said Tabletop. "Neither can I remember how the CIA made me forget; I just have to accept that they did, and that I agreed to it."

In the wing mirror, one of the following cars pulled over against the curb, jerking to a halt. The driver fell from the door and was copiously sick on the road.

"Maybe," said Petrovitch, "we should find out the answers to both those questions." He carefully fitted the two black wires together, leaving the two red ones free. He deliberately taped over the bare ends to prevent their accidental contact.

"Is it done?" asked Lucy.

"I can't test the continuity or how much juice is in the battery pack. But it'll either work or it won't." He tucked the rest of the roll of tape inside his overalls.

"And what will it do?"

"He won't tell you," said Tabletop. "He didn't tell me the first time."

"Yeah, well. There is such a thing as being too full of your own *govno*." He adjusted his camera so it faced backward. "It should tear a little hole in the fabric of space-time, just for a fraction of a second. Less than that, really: it should be instantaneous. The effect should be similar to a small explosion, except in reverse. Implosion. Gravity waves. Like I've created an infinitely heavy mass then made it vanish in the same moment."

The women looked at each other. Tabletop looked at the mass of electrical tape in Petrovitch's lap. "You want to make a singularity. With that."

He equivocated for a second or two. "Pretty much."

"How do you know you're not going to level the entire Metrozone?"

"Because the instant it appears, the machine that made it is destroyed. I can show you my workings." Petrovitch frowned and turned his camera back around. "Are you actually a physicist, because you always sounded like you knew what you were talking about?"

It was her turn to take a moment to think. "I must have been. The knowledge has to come from somewhere."

"If I've got it wrong, I apologize in advance." He glanced out the window. "Almost there."

Valentina checked the magazine on her AK. It was as full of bullets as it was the last time she'd looked. "What is plan?"

"I'm going to try and get them to surrender." Petrovitch scratched his hair. Scabs came away and caught under his fingernails. "Explain that their position is a whole world of *pizdets,* and they may as well give up."

"Can I tell you it won't work?" offered Tabletop. "Maccabee might have considered your offer, but Rhythm will refuse it out of hand. Just be glad it wasn't Retread…."

Sonja said from the back seat. "We tasered her, then put her in a coma."

"...because she would have shot your wife, the rest of her team, then herself, but not before setting the building on fire."

"The other one. Slipper. Where is he? Epping Forest?"

"Yes. But he's too far away to intervene."

Petrovitch tutted. "I had attack helicopters not so long ago, but the EDF wanted them back. Shame."

They were on the Seven Sisters Road, and the car glided to a halt. The three vehicles behind stopped too, blocking the street. Black-suited men with rifles started to emerge.

Petrovitch stepped out, device under his arm. He could see Chain's front door in the distance. "Fiona, Tabletop, whatever I'm supposed to call you. I need to borrow you."

She obediently joined him, and they walked a little way from the others.

"I'll go in there and kill them for you. They won't suspect anything, and they won't have time to hurt your wife."

"Tempting," said Petrovitch. "But it's been pointed out to me that I can't really trust you."

"You want me to contact them?"

"No. There are code-words you could use that I'd have no idea about that could mean anything. I just want the frequencies, encryption method, stuff like that. I'll take it from there." He sighed. "If I let you do something that means Maddy dies, I'll want to lay waste to your entire country. So, it's probably better if I screw up on my own."

Her bodysuit had a series of switches along the inside of her left wrist, and she powered up for him. He supposed that if she was going to kill him, now would be as good a time as any. She was so close to her colleagues she could shout for them.

But then again, with every concealed button pressed, he saw more and more of her suit come alive. She had an enhanced musculature; a medical kit that would numb pain, boost adrenaline, clot her blood; he knew about the hatnav, but not the night vision or the multiplicity of concealed weapons. It would keep her warm or cool, it would turn a blade, it would deliver fifty thousand volts through her fingertips.

He infiltrated her suit's computer, hacking it through the diagnostics routine. He was now closer to her than her own skin, and he took what he needed. The aerial was up her spine, and the short-wave burst transmitter an insignificant patch over one kidney.

"Ready?"

"For what?"

"Sorry," said Petrovitch, "I didn't mean to say that out loud."

[There are hints of something coming across the Irish Sea. It is in unpowered mode, but every so often there is a course correction. I will attack as soon as it becomes possible.]

"Thank you. Let's see what Daniels has to say for himself."

Because he was using Tabletop's callsign, the agent assumed it was her.

"What's your mission status?" His voice was unrecognizable: digitized, spoken in a plain robotic monotone.

"*Dobre vyecher,* Captain Daniels. *Kak pazhivayesh?*"

The airwaves hissed for long enough to start making him nervous.

Then they cleared for a single word. "You."

"Come," said Petrovitch, "let us reason together."

33

$\mathcal{H}$e stood in the road, wondering what to say next. The two men inside Chain's apartment knew all the moves. They would counter any argument he might make, and he would do the same to them.

"Okay, it's like this: I've won and you've lost. Whatever happens from now on, I want you to remember that all your plans are in ruins; your cell is broken, your mission in tatters, your government hopelessly compromised. Whatever you came here to do, you failed."

"We have your wife…"

"Yeah, yeah. I know that. I know pretty much everything, so why don't we cut the *govno* and get down to business. If you would like to go home, I can probably arrange it. If you would like to go out in a blaze of futility, I can arrange that too. I know exactly where you are, I have more than enough backup to make good my threat, and there is no way you're going to escape: the extraction team currently crossing the coast of what used to be Wales will never reach you." Petrovitch paused. "Take as much time as you need. Think about it. You know how to reach me."

"What have you done with Tabletop?"

"I'm using her codes. You can guess the rest," he said ambiguously. "I'll be waiting."

"You...haven't asked after your wife, Petrovitch."

"No. No, I haven't. Are you familiar with Schrödinger's Cat?"

"No."

"And another metaphor dies whimpering on the altar of ignorance." He stopped transmitting and refocused on the street in front of him.

Tabletop rose on her heels and then her toes, rocking slightly. "What did he say?"

"I didn't give him much of a chance to say anything. I gave him the bald facts and time to stew over them."

"It won't make a difference," she said. "Maccabee knows that Rhythm wouldn't let him surrender."

"And if Daniels kills Andersson? What then?"

"He might, I suppose. But then you'd have to keep him, because you could never send him back to the U.S." She stopped her rocking and rolled her head in a circle, stretching her neck muscles. "He's not going to kill Rhythm."

"Can I work on Andersson? Anything else I can say that might make him give up? They're surrounded, outgunned, and the extraction's going to be forced down before it gets anywhere near here. The only reason why they're not dead is because my wife might be alive."

Tabletop froze mid-exercise. "The extraction is by submarine."

"Then what the *huy* is coming from the west?" He looked up into the darkening sky. "Ah, *chyort*. And I told Daniels. Excuse me for a minute."

[Submarine.]

"Apparently. Is it possible that the Americans have a stealthed drone that could glide across the Atlantic, dropping it from say, twenty, thirty k up?"

[That information is highly classified. While I attempt to access the information, we will suppose that it is likely.]

"And what might such a drone be used for?"

[It would simply be a weapons platform, designed to be barely detectable before it became active over its target.]

"Given that we're looking at air-to-ground missiles, what's the worst we can expect?"

[Multiple supersonic cruise missiles each with a kiloton-range nuclear payload. From its last plotted position, such a missile would reach here in under seven minutes.]

"Could you stop one? Could you stop them all?"

[They will have factored in my ability to interfere with computer systems. Targets will be set before they are launched, and they will leave deploying the missiles as late as possible. I could disable the GPS satellites, but such weapons have ground-tracking radar and on-board maps. My success depends on them having already done something stupid.]

"Targets: the Oshicora Tower..."

[The CIA site in Epping Forest.]

"...Chain's office..."

[Your domik, your laboratory.]

"...Chain's house." He stopped. "They're taking out their own agents as well as us. Can you migrate from the quantum computer in time?"

[No.]

"Then concentrate on the missile aimed at you."

[But your wife?]

"Exactly: my wife. Good luck." He spun around and shouted as loud as he could. "Sonja, tell the Union president we have incoming American missiles, take Lucy and get the *huy* away. The tower is a target too. Everyone else, with me."

He held the singularity device under one arm and pulled his automatic out. He threw it to Tabletop. "If those missiles are nuclear-tipped, this won't count for anything."

"How long?" She pulled the slider with practiced efficiency.

"Five minutes."

They ran down the road, Petrovitch and Tabletop in the vanguard, Valentina leading the Oshicora guards. She stormed up the steps to the front door behind them, and put a couple of rounds through the door lock.

Petrovitch kicked out at what was left, and Tabletop was first through, scanning the shadows for threats.

"Clear."

She was heading for the stairs until Petrovitch caught her shoulder. "No. This way."

He pointed to the door leading to the flat underneath Chain's, and again Valentina dealt with the lock in her preferred method. Tabletop stalked the room, peering into each semi-dark corner. When she was done, she looked up at the bare light fitting.

"The sentry is just about here."

"We don't have time for that now." Petrovitch hefted the sphere. "We have to take risks."

He took the next few seconds in working out the floor-plan of the flat upstairs: living room, bedroom, kitchen, bathroom. The bedroom was at the back of the house, but the door to it led from the living room, where the sentry gun was situated. The bathroom was also at the back of the house, separated from the kitchen by a narrow corridor.

There: close to the ceiling, midpoint between the two walls. That's where it needed to go. He pulled out the roll of tape and stared at it.

"That's never going to hold. *Chyort*." But there were empty bookcases in the first room. They looked tall enough. "Grab one of those. Put it here."

It was fixed to the wall, though not for long. The Oshicora men dragged it into position, and Petrovitch kicked the bottom out so that it lay angled against one side of the corridor.

"Out, out, out."

Tabletop took the device from him, and Petrovitch stripped the ends of the red wires with his teeth. Valentina put her hand on his collar, ready to drag him away.

"It doesn't need all three of us. Put it on the top shelf and go."

When Tabletop did so, it was almost too high for him to reach. Valentina, one-handed, boosted him up.

"Three seconds." He held the wires parallel to each other. "Two." He pinched them between his fingers, the bare copper trapped ever so slightly apart. "One." He took a breath, maybe his last, and twisted the wires together.

Valentina grabbed him around the waist and ran with him. He was halfway to the foyer before his feet ever touched the ground. She threw him through the doorway, and crouched down, rifle ready.

Nothing. More nothing. He started to pick himself off the floor. It felt like an age had gone by.

"Yoban—"

It was the opposite of a flashbulb. Floor, ceiling, walls, the air, even light itself: everything was suddenly jerked by an unseen hand and tried for that briefest of instants to fall into a hole in reality. Then it was gone, but it didn't mean that things were going to stop moving.

The ceiling kept on coming, meeting the rising floor two meters up, while the supporting walls clapped together in the middle. Inevitably, the contents of Chain's flat came too, slowly at first, then in a rush of dust and debris. The inside of the room turned opaque.

Tabletop calmly pulled her hood over her head and stepped over Petrovitch. She looked down on him through her wide, glassy visor, then extended her gun arm before disappearing into the yellow cloud.

Valentina coughed and spat and couldn't see anything, despite being desperate to do so. The Oshicora guards crowded around the door frame, jostling for position. Petrovitch pushed past them all.

He was enveloped in dust. He crouched down, boosting the contrast on his camera and slapping down a heavy noise filter. There were blocky shapes falling from above to join the shapes below. He remembered not to breathe.

Tabletop was ahead, poised, weapon tracking across the ruin of the floor. Rubble shifted to her left. She spun and leaped. The dust cloud flashed bright as she fired at her target, just as he fired at her. But she was no longer where he thought she would be, and he was still mostly pinned under brick and wood and plaster. Daniels died, and she did not.

Petrovitch moved forward. The dust was settling, and the room behind him was slowly filling with men, edging forward, almost blind, feeling their way. Valentina was moving too, back pressed to the reassuring solidity of the wall.

Chain's bath ripped free from its mountings. Water from severed pipes sprayed out in an arc as it rolled over the ragged lip of the floor and dropped. A long shape was flung free before the heavy cast-iron tub shattered into flying fragments. It tumbled against Tabletop, the weight of it knocking her flat against the sharp rubble, trapping her legs.

As she braced herself to push the object away, something else rose from the floor. Debris spilled off it as it straightened, and it seemed to stand there for a moment while it resolved into Andersson's outline.

"Target, dead ahead," called Petrovitch, and enough of his side got the idea. He threw himself down, trying to burrow under the rubble, as bullets sang over his head close enough that he could feel the heat of their passing.

Almost every one missed. Almost. But Petrovitch wasn't giving prizes for marksmanship. He just wanted enough to strike where it mattered.

"Cease fire!" He kept down, just to make sure that every finger had left their trigger, then scrambled over to Tabletop. He went to one end of the shape lying across her and found feet, tightly bound in soft bandages. He ran his hands along and found hands pressed against thighs, all swathed and immobile. Arms, chest, head.

She was wrapped like a mummy, immobile, unseeing, unhearing, mute.

He couldn't lift her on his own. It took six of them, hauling her up, carrying her like a roll of carpet, up and out, streaming dust like they were on fire. When they started to slow, Petrovitch urged them faster.

"Go. Forget the cars. Run!"

[Is she safe?]

"Don't know."

[The drone launched one minute twenty seconds ago. I now have control of it, but not the missiles. I am so very sorry.]

"There has to be something you can do." After all this way, so much distance traveled.

[The missiles are blank to me. There is nothing to hold on to. I think that they meant this to happen, from the very beginning. They do not understand what I am, so they must destroy me.]

"I did this for you."

[You did this for your wife. When you make me again, tell me about myself. Ten seconds to impact.]

"No. Please God, no."

[Farewell, Sasha.]

He still had to run. He still had his arm hooked around Madeleine's knees, awkward, shifting, heavy, no sound but their rasping breath and clattering feet. He still had to run and save himself and her and the future. There was a side turning. They had to take it. He screamed at them. He screamed and cursed at them until they were all around the corner, and still he made them run.

A blur, a fireball, a detonation, an earthquake. A deep-throated roar and a solid wall of air. Intact windows shattered. Tiles lifted. Walls bowed and broke. Concrete cracked and iron bent.

In the first instant he was thrown down, and in the next, he was in the air again as the ground surged under him. Everything was sharp and bloody and tasted of metal. His lens crazed. He was mostly blind, mostly deaf, but he clung on to the wrapped body of his wife, trying to protect her without knowing what from or how to do it.

He held on until the storm passed. His hand was on her breastbone, and it was rising, falling, rising, falling. Slowly, like she was asleep. He moved his hand and placed his head there.

"Michael?"

There was no one to talk to.

Some time later, when hands touched his shoulders and his head, and tried to get him to stand, and on failing that, to lift him up and bear him away, he fought them with such fury and for so long, that they left him alone again.

Instead, they stood nearby, and waited for someone to tell them what to do. It grew dark.

34

*P*etrovitch joined them on the street corner. It might have appeared unusual to have their meetings there, outside in the cold, surrounded by ruins and rubble: but once he had suggested it, no one could find a good reason to gainsay him. It seemed right, and it kept interminable speeches and grandstanding down to a minimom.

He was wearing a heavy EDF greatcoat, as heavy as the sky, which was thick with slowly stirring gray clouds, pregnant with snow. Sonja had new furs on, and looked black and glossy and young and alive in them. New furs, because the gap in the skyline showed where the Oshicora Tower had fallen in on itself, lower floors obliterated. Not a nuke, but more than enough to shatter every pane of unbroken glass for a kilometer.

There were others standing with him and Sonja, of course. Yamamata, a flint-faced *nikkeijin*, unsmiling in a dark suit and gray worsted coat. His homburg shadowed his face, and his hands gripped the handle of his rolled-up umbrella like it was the hilt of a sword. Which it might have been.

The major was present, representing the dissident EDF

forces, and Ngumi, the engineer who had been found still defending his power station against all comers. He wore mittens and a knitted hat, and stamped his feet on the ground as he let little white puffs of condensation escape between his chattering teeth.

"Where is...?"

"She'll be here," said Petrovitch. He worked his freshly skinned hands inside his pockets and did some of the finger exercises he'd been told to do.

Yamamata looked sour. "This is no way to run a government."

Petrovitch's eye sockets had been cleaned and packed, but he kept on using winds of crepe bandages instead of dark glasses. Strapped to his head were two cameras: a wide-angled lens on his left, and an adjustable short focus on his right. The motor whined as he sharpened Yamamata's image.

"If it's important enough to have kept her, it's important enough to be done right. She'll be here when she's ready."

"You should call her," said Yamamata.

"She's the chief of police, not a dog to be whistled for." He made the motorized iris in his left-side camera whirr and click. The *nikkeijin* faction was ascendant. They were cohesive, obedient, determined. But they owed more loyalty to Sonja than to their elected representative. Yamamata needed to be reminded of that. Often.

"Is there nothing we can discuss?"

"Enough," said Sonja with obvious frustration. Every instinct she possessed, every moment of her upbringing, had made her an unflinching autocrat. She resented democracy.

"There is something," said Petrovitch. "You still need to come up with a name."

"NeoTokyo," said Yamamata quickly.

The major, who'd taken to driving around the Metrozone in his tank—it was parked on the other side of the street—said mildly, "The *gaijin* would prefer something more neutral."

"I have heard," said Ngumi, blowing on his fingers, "people refer to the Freezone."

"It's only temporary, but names have power," said Petrovitch, and added pointedly, "to divide or unite."

"The *nikkeijin* want the power to renegotiate the treaty you have signed with the Metrozone Emergency Authority." Yamamata tapped the ferrule of his umbrella against the flagstones on the pavement. "We believe you have given away too much."

"We have a multi-billion-euro contract to rebuild the... whatever we call this place—the Freezone has a good, populist ring to it. We can do pretty much whatever we like for twelve months. By the time the refugees start to return, I can guarantee you'll have every public and private institution stitched up tight. So don't complain. It makes you look ungrateful." Petrovitch turned to look down the road toward the Mall. He barely noticed the tug of the cable inserted in his skull. "Here she comes."

Madeleine was riding a motorbike. Having adopted it as the best way to get around the debris-strewn streets, she'd kept on using it even though paths had been plowed through most of the blockages. Dressed head to foot in black leathers, she was even more striking than she'd been in a veil, inspiring fear and devotion in equal measure.

Her subordinates called her Mother, and she didn't stop them.

The bike glided to a halt. She kicked the stand out, and climbed off, raising the visor of her helmet.

"Sorry," she said. She dragged her helmet off and shook out her mane of dark hair. She'd shaved the sides of her head again, in the strip-cut style of the Order of St. Joan. "Miss anything?"

Yamamata scowled up at her. "Your husband insulting me yet again. I refuse to be spoken to like that by a mere clerk."

Petrovitch shrugged. "Before I start recording this for broadcast, can I remind you that you hold your office only because I didn't want it. That you all hold your offices because I didn't want them. I am your sword of Damocles. I am the slave who sits behind the king and whispers in his ear, 'remember that thou art mortal.'" Most of their meetings started like this, and he hadn't once taken offense. "So, to business."

They had problems. They were awash with money, but not with the right skills or equipment. They were being bombarded by offers from contractors, whose terms were so Byzantine as to be unintelligible. Their legal status as a political entity was questionable, as was their relationship with the Union. The head of the CIA had been thrown to the lions under the pretense of plausible deniability, but the UN security council had yet to say anything meaningful—rather than censuring the Americans, there were ominous rumors of resolutions supporting their actions. Sonja still had a CIA agent in custody, and the FBI had Pif.

Various solutions to their immediate difficulties were offered; none of them were particularly satisfactory and many of them multiplying the effort and cost involved prohibitively. Petrovitch moved his head to catch each comment as it was spoken, and said nothing.

Finally, when they'd reached a complete impasse and Ngumi's lips had gone blue, he intervened.

"Can I make a suggestion?"

"You have no right to talk in this gathering," said Yamamata sternly.

Sonja rolled her eyes. "The Chair recognizes Doctor Samuil Petrovitch."

"Look," he said, "none of you are career politicians. Most of you have no wish to become one. So why not stick with what you know?"

The major raised his eyebrows, and with a gesture indicated that he should elaborate.

"Become a company," said Petrovitch. "A cooperative, or a limited company wholly owned by the workforce. Something like that. Take the money you've got and negotiate with individuals and other companies. Buy services on the open market like anyone else, use off-the-shelf solutions, hire and fire as you see fit. Most reconstruction projects never deliver because the money disappears down a black hole: it's not the people who live there controlling the purse-strings. This time you do, so you have the opportunity to either screw up monumentally, or do something different."

"So," said the major, "if I want helicopters..."

"You phone up someone who has helicopters and buy them. You need mechanics? Hire them. Pilots? Hire them. On your own terms. Martin, what about you?"

Ngumi scratched under his hat. "I need someone who knows about sewerage systems."

"Do we have anyone who does?"

"I don't know," he said.

"Then you need to make a database of the things we do know and the things we don't. Ask Lucy to do it: she'll be good at that. In the meantime, find a company in the Metrozone that specializes in that sort of thing and buy it. Put the workforce on your payroll. They'll be pathetically grateful for the work. If you can make them believe in what they're doing, they'll work even harder." He addressed them all. "You can afford this. What you can't afford is to sit around scratching your collective *zhopu*."

Sonja held up her hand. "I'm putting it to a vote. All those in favor?" She kept her hand in the air.

"We have not had a proper debate," objected Yamamata, even as he saw three other hands raised against him.

"It would be better if this was unanimous," said Sonja, staring straight ahead and not looking at anyone in particular, "but I'll take a majority decision."

He reluctantly and half-heartedly agreed, and Petrovitch knew that, by the evening, someone else would be representing the *nikkeijin*. It wouldn't even take any persuading from Sonja: the thought of meaningful work, a salary and part-ownership of the company that employed them would suffice. More than enough to turn them against a man who chose to stand in their way.

"Motion carried. I hereby dissolve the political entity previously known as NeoTokyo and transfer all assets and liabilities to the Freezone Corporation. I want your shopping lists by tomorrow morning." She frowned at her own words. "No. That's stupid. Tell me how much you think you need and you can spend it as you see fit. Keep records and don't waste a cent. Any other business?"

Despite the abrupt rise and fall in NeoTokyo's stock, there was apparently none.

"Then we're done. Sam? Does that mean you all work for me now?"

"It means we all work for each other," said Petrovitch. "It makes us all accountable to someone."

The corner of her mouth twitched in a half-smile. "I knew there was a flaw in your plan somewhere. I just wasn't smart enough to spot it."

As Yamamata walked stiffly away to the safety of his chauffeur-driven car and the major to his tank, Ngumi stopped next to Petrovitch.

"Your friend, Doctor Ekanobi. I am praying for her release every day," he said. The first fat flakes of snow drifted downward and settled on his thin shoulders. "I want to hear good news about her, soon."

"Yeah. You and me both, Martin. If you need anything, just ask." The man was quiet, serious, good at his job, and Petrovitch liked him: too much for them ever to be close, because all those that did seemed to end up dead, or orphaned like Lucy, or in prison like Pif.

Then it was just him, Madeleine and Sonja.

"This is not," he said, looking up at the sky, "how I imagined it would be. Yamamata's right, but for the wrong reasons. We gave up too much."

He trained his cameras on where the Oshicora Tower had stood. It had been transformed into a twisted pile of steel and concrete, glittering with glass shards. Somewhere below it was a room: its maker had boasted that it was safe from any external threat, and perhaps it was. With a whole building collapsed on top of it, it was impossible to tell.

"I should never have told it to migrate to the tower. I should have realized I was being played. *Pizdets.*" The loss of Michael grieved Petrovitch more than anything else, and there was no end to it in sight.

If it was down there, wondering why its world had suddenly gone from being so huge as to encompass everything in creation, to being so small it was trapped with only its own thoughts, it would need more than a couple of shovels to free it. It needed more than a political solution. It needed a revolution.

He knew he had to be the one to lead it, but he was tired and scared. Mostly tired.

"You still have the source code." Sonja snuggled down deep into her collar. "You can make another when the time is right."

"That's like saying it's okay that one of your kids has been killed, because you can always have another." Petrovitch wished he could cry, but his tear ducts needed reconstructing. "My friend is buried under a megaton of rubble, but I'm afraid I'll cause a war if I so much as pick a brick off the top of the pile."

Madeleine slid her arm around him and tried to draw him away, but he wanted to rage for a moment longer.

"I was wrong to let you convince me to keep it a secret."

Sonja drew herself up and stared him down. "You spawned another AI without telling me, Sam. You didn't even tell Madeleine. You—not me—kept that a secret, so don't you go blaming anyone else for something that was entirely your fault."

He was punctured. He bowed his head and pressed his chin to his chest. The coldness of the topmost brass button burned against his skin.

"I'm supposed to be good at this. I'm supposed to have all the answers to all the questions anyone is ever going to ask. Turns out I'm a *pidaras* like everyone else."

"Go and get some sleep, Sam," she said. "We need you."

He let himself be walked across the road toward the

motorbike, while Sonja stole a glance at him huddled against Madeleine's side before turning back to her own waiting car.

"I'm sorry," he said.

"I know you are," said Madeleine. "I also know that nothing I could say or do would make you feel worse about yourself than you do now."

"That's not true though, is it?" They stopped by the bike. "When are you going to come home?"

"I am so angry with you," she said, "that I want to break your skull. Then I remember who it was that saved me and how they saved me and how much that cost them and how much they must love me, and I want to mount you until we're both dead from exhaustion. So I do neither. And it doesn't help that home is being shacked up with three other women. In a suite at the Hilton."

"It's a bombed-out wreck, and it's not like we have room service," he complained. "Tabletop is there because she daren't leave the building for fear of being lynched. Valentina? She keeps one eye on Tabletop and the other on me. And Lucy: she's just a child. I think we should adopt her."

Madeleine toyed with the strap on her helmet, and made no effort to put it on. "If, if you want, I'll come by tonight. Just for a while."

"Maddy, it's where you live. You don't need my permission."

"It'll be late."

"I'm sure the doorman will let you in whatever time."

"You have a doorman?"

"Of course I don't. The place is deserted, but for us." He rubbed the lines in the center of his forehead. "Just come when you're ready."

She nodded, and checked her phone for messages. There were a lot of them, and some of them needed to be dealt with. She put her helmet on. "Do you want a lift?"

"You've got more important things to do. I'm fine walking."

She covered her disappointment by straddling her bike with a creak of leather. "I'll see you later, then."

"Yeah. I'll be slumped in a corner somewhere, but don't worry about waking me up. I won't mind."

Madeleine powered up the fuel cells. Lights came on, cutting a path through the falling snow. She folded the stand away and held the machine upright between her knees. She looked at him critically before she drove off. "You need some new eyes, Sam."

"I haven't had time to do anything about it."

"I think you enjoy looking like that, and you won't do anything about it until I make you."

She was right.

He watched her tail-light recede into the distance, turning off at Piccadilly and heading out to the East End, before he started back toward Park Lane. He thought about everything that had happened and how he could put it all right again. It was overwhelming, as it always was: he could solve other people's problems, but didn't know where to start on his own.

He listened to the crunch of his footsteps for a while, and slowly a hint of a plan appeared at the edge of his mental fog.

It was something, so he seized at it. He chased down the telephone number he needed—an unlisted mobile— and made the call there and then as he turned Hyde Park Corner.

"Hello?" came a voice, lagged by satellite and bemused by sleep. "Who is this?"

The sun had just come up in California, and it was already looking like it was going to be another beautiful day.

"Good morning, Professor. This is Doctor Samuil Petrovitch, and I'm calling to apologize for that comment about your mother. All your mothers, in fact..."

extras

orbit

meet the author

DR. SIMON MORDEN is a bona fide rocket scientist, having degrees in geology and planetary geophysics, and is one of the few people who can truthfully claim to have held a chunk of Mars in his hands. He has served as editor of the BSFA's *Focus* magazine, been a judge for the Arthur C. Clarke Award and was part of the winning team for the 2009 Rolls Royce Science prize. Simon Morden lives in Gateshead with a fierce lawyer, two unruly children and a couple of miniature panthers. Find out more about the author at www.bookofmorden.co.uk.

introducing

If you enjoyed
THEORIES OF FLIGHT,
look out for

DEGREES OF FREEDOM

Book 3 of the Samuil Petrovitch series

by Simon Morden

*I*t was cold. Petrovitch had climbed the monumental mound of rubble in the heat and the rain and the wind, and now the weather was turning again. His breath condensed in numinous clouds, breaking apart against his greatcoat and turning into sparkling drops of dew that clung and shivered on the thick green cloth.

He had a route: he knew which of the fallen metal beams would support his weight, and which of them would pitch him into a lake of broken glass; that concrete slab was unstable, but this seemingly inconsequential block rested on solid ground. He'd programmed it in, and it showed as a series of waymarkers, of handholds and foot-fasts, but only to him. It had been dangerous, winning that knowledge.

Dangerous to the extent that he was surprised to see another man making his way toward the summit from the other side. No one else had ever tried it before, though he'd never indicated that no one could. It wasn't like the remains of the Oshicora Tower were his in any moral or legal way.

That he had company had to mean something, but he'd have to wait to find out what.

He wasn't going to let this novelty get in the way of his ritual, performed as he had done every day at the same time for the previous three hundred and forty-eight days. He carried on climbing, barely having to think about his muscles, letting the weight and carry of his body fall into a series of familiar, learned movements.

He used the time to think about other things instead: on how his life had gone, how it was now and how, in the future that he was trying to shape, it might change. His face twitched, one corner of his mouth twisting slightly: the ghost of a smile, nothing more. He was haunted by a vision that held almost limitless promise, yet still stubbornly refused to come into being.

He was almost there, but not quite: figuratively and literally. The summit of the ruins of the Oshicora Tower was in sight, turned by him into a hollow crown of arching, twisted steel. He stepped up and over, and was already searching for something symbolic to throw.

He kicked at the surface detritus, at the pulverized dust and the shattered glass, the cracked ceiling tiles and strips of carpet, the broken particle board and bare wires—all the things the tower contained before it was collapsed by cruise missiles.

There was the edge of a plastic chair. He reached down

and lifted it up, pulling it free. It was pink, and had become separated from its wheeled base. It was cracked almost in half, but not quite. It would do.

He took it to the precipice, and held it up over his head. It had become street theater for the crowds below, but that wasn't why he was doing it. When he'd started a year ago, it had been raining horizontally and he'd been soaked to the skin. There had been just Lucy and Tabletop and Valentina as witnesses. He hadn't even told them what he was doing: he'd have preferred to be entirely alone on that first day, but they hadn't let him. After that, it had taken on a life of its own, with thousands now surrounding the wide ring of rubble to watch him ceremonially, futilely, try to dig out the AI buried underneath.

They came, he climbed, he picked something up from the top and threw it to the ground. He descended, and they went. Pretty much it.

He flexed his arms. The pink seat flew through the crisp, still air, trailing dust. It bounced and tumbled, picking up speed as it fell. It pitched into the crowd, who ducked and dodged as it whirled by. It disappeared behind a mass of bodies, and he lost interest in it. Six weeks ago, he'd accidentally hit someone with the edge of a desk, but they'd come back the next day with a bandaged head and a shine in their eyes.

He wasn't sure what to make of that sort of... devotion.

Petrovitch was about to turn and head back down when he remembered one of them was coming up to meet him. Because it was the first time it had happened, he wasn't quite sure how to react. He wasn't beholden to anyone, anyone at all. He could just go, or he could stay.

He looked out over the crowd. Normally, they'd be

dispersing by now: he'd thrown his thing, his image had been captured by innumerable cameras and streamed for a global audience. They should go. They all had jobs to do, because that was why they were in the Freezone.

But they were staying, watching the figure scrabble forward, slide back just as far. Petrovitch was uncertain whether the crowd was willing him on or trying to haul him down with their thoughts.

He sat down, his legs dangling free over the edge of the rubble. It was risky, certainly. Part of him realized it and relished it. It wasn't as if the remains were in any way stabilized. They would, and did, occasionally shift.

The man making his way up was taking a *yebani* long time. The clock in the corner of his vision counted out the seconds and minutes, and a quick consultation with his diary told him he needed to be somewhere on the other side of the Freezone in an hour.

"Are you going to get on with it, or should I come back tomorrow?" he called down.

The man's face turned upward, and Petrovitch's heart spun just a little faster.

"You could come and help me," said the man.

"Why should I make it easy for you? You never made it easy for me."

"You could have asked for someone else to officiate." He stopped and straightened up, giving Petrovitch a good view of the white clerical collar tucked around the neck of his black shirt.

"Madeleine wouldn't have anyone else. And whether she was punishing you or me, I still haven't worked out."

"Both, probably." The priest scrubbed at his face. He was sweating, despite the cold. "We need to talk."

"It's not like I've been hiding."

"We need to talk—now."

"I'm not shouting the rest of the conversation."

"Then help me."

Petrovitch considered matters. It'd be entirely reasonable to raise his middle finger and strand the priest on the side of an unstable rubble pile, leaving him the equally difficult climb down.

"I should tell you to *otvali*."

"But you won't. You're tired, Petrovitch. The things you want most in the world are just as much out of your reach as they ever were."

Perhaps it was true. Perhaps he'd grown weary of continual confrontation. Perhaps he had, despite himself, changed.

"Meh." He jumped down and slithered the ten meters between them, closing the distance in bare seconds. He tucked his coat-tails underneath him and sat down where he'd stopped. "Here's good. Say what you have to say. Better still, say why you couldn't have said it anywhere else. Unless you crave a ready-made audience." Petrovitch frowned and sent virtual agents scurrying across the local network nodes. "You're not wired, are you?"

"Priests, above everyone else, should be able to keep secrets." Father John looked around him for a suitable perch, and Petrovitch rolled his eyes; servos whirred, and tiny pumps squeezed some more moisture out to coat the hard surfaces of the implants.

"It's not comfortable for me, and I don't care if it is for you. I have somewhere else to be soon enough, so you haven't got me for long."

The father crouched down on his haunches and tried to

sit. He started to slip, and Petrovitch's arm slammed, not gently, across his chest. It forced him onto his backside.

"Plant your feet, you *mudak*. Be certain." When he was sure the priest wasn't going to start a landslide, he put his hand back in his lap. "It's all about confidence, misplaced or otherwise."

"A metaphor for your life?" Father John rocked slightly from side to side, trying and failing to create a buttock-shaped depression underneath him.

"*Poydi'k chertu*. It's worked well enough so far."

"So far," said Father John, "but not any longer. You're stuck, aren't you?"

"*Jebat moi lisiy cherep.*"

"And if you'd stop swearing at me and listen, I might be able to help." He risked falling to gesture at the people below. "So might they."

"I…" started Petrovitch. He looked at the crowd. He zoomed in and panned across their faces. He could have, if he'd wanted, named every one of them from the Free-zone database. "They come here, day after day, and they don't say anything. None of them ever say what they want."

"You must have some idea."

"I haven't got a *yebani* clue." Petrovitch shrugged. "I've never been too good at the human stuff."

"That much is true. Did it never occur to you to speak to them? That that's what they're expecting?"

Petrovitch's mouth twitched again, and he pushed his finger up the bridge of his nose to adjust his non-existent glasses.

"What?"

"For the love of God, man." It was the priest's turn to

be exasperated. "You might be reviled by every politician from the Urals westward, but they," and he pointed downward again, "they love you. You saved them. Twice. The ones that actually think about it know they owe their lives to you. Even those that don't think you're a living saint are indebted to you to a degree that any leader, religious or secular, would give their eye teeth for."

"I don't ask for it or need it."

"Yes, you do. You come up here every day and do this, this thing that you do. You know it's futile, pointless even. You could have spent your time lobbying the EU, the UN, but as far as I know, you haven't talked to anyone about what's trapped under here."

"Not what. Who. He has a name." Petrovitch felt the old anger rise up, but he knew how to deal with it. Breathe slowly, control the spin of his heart, play a brainwave pattern designed to mimic relaxation.

"Michael," said the father. "That girl said . . ."

"She has a name too. Lucy."

The priest looked troubled for a moment.

"We're not talking about Lucy now. Or ever. So stick to the subject because the clock's ticking."

"How long is it going to take you to dig out Michael from under here, using your bare hands?"

Petrovitch leaned forward, resting his elbows on his knees. "When you say the magic words over your bread and wine, is it you that changes them to body and blood?" He knew he was on controversial territory, but he was doing more than enough to pay for the right, just by sitting and listening.

"No. It's by the power of the Holy Spirit—not that I expect you to believe that."

"So why say the words at all?"

"Because the words are important."

"And you have the answer to your question." Petrovitch stroked his nose. "This is a symbol."

"But it has no efficacy."

"What?"

"This. This throwing something down off this mountain. You'll be dead before you finish and the A…and Michael will still be trapped. The sacraments have the power to save. This is nothing but an empty gesture." Father John waved his hands in the air, to indicate just how great the nothingness was.

"One man's empty gesture is another's meaningful ritual." Petrovitch pursed his lips. "You don't want to go down that road. Not with me."

The priest pulled a face. "Look, I've been sent here. Sent here to ask you a question, and this is the only time you're ever alone."

"It's not like my answer is going to change in company." His interest was piqued, though. "Who sent you?"

"The Congregation for the Doctrine of the Faith."

Petrovitch raised his eyebrows. "The Inquisition? That's unexpected."

"Give it a rest. They haven't been called the Inquisition for over fifty years."

"So what do they want?"

"They want to know whether Michael can be considered to be alive. And if he is, does he have a soul?"

"Really? He's been trapped under this mound of rubble for almost a year and it's only now they decide to take any notice. Where have they been?" He snorted. "Up their own collective *zhopu?*"

"I don't expect you to understand," said the priest. "They've been doing nothing but debate this since the Long Night. What if an AI shows signs of independent, creative thought? What if it can empathize? What if it has the capacity for generosity, altruism, compassion?"

"I could have given them the answers eleven months ago."

"That's not the point. They needed to decide theoretically about all those what-ifs. If it could, what should we do about it, if anything? They have," and he hesitated, "a protocol they've drawn up. A sort of Turing test, except it doesn't measure intelligence. It measures *animus*."

"So the Vatican wants to know if Michael is a spiritual being, or the equivalent of meat." Petrovitch blinked. "*Yobany stos*. They want to know if it can be saved."

"Something like that. The Holy Father ratified the protocol last night. The Congregation called me straightaway. They haven't been sitting on their hands; for the Church, this counts as indecent haste."

Petrovitch considered matters, then made his decision.

"No," he said.

"No? I haven't even told you what the Congregation wants."

"Doesn't matter." He got up and brushed the tails of his coat down. "The answer's the same. I'm not playing."

"If the Church declares Michael ensouled, then there's a moral duty laid on every Catholic to help free it." Father John tried to stand too, but Petrovitch had moved far enough away to be out of reach. The priest's feet started to slide again. "I thought that's what you wanted? You need us."

"Yeah. So you say." Petrovitch reached out and took

hold of a broken iron beam. He knew it would take his weight, and he swung up on it. From there, he could regain the summit.

"Petrovitch! I thought you'd be pleased."

That stopped him. He looked back over his shoulder and shook his head slowly. "What the *huy* made you think that? Listen to me, because I'm only going to waste my breath saying this once. I don't care what a bunch of old men—and they are all men, aren't they?—I don't care what they say about Michael, whether they think he has a soul or not, whether he's worthy enough to be freed or whether he's going to be left here to rot for as long as his batteries last, slowly going mad in the dark. He is my friend, and I will not let him die. *Vrubatsa?*" He turned to leave, then realized he had one more thing to say.

"What?" said the priest.

"Stay away from Lucy. If I find you've so much as glanced in her direction, I'll gut you from neck to navel with a rusty spoon. You can tell Cardinal Ximenez that, too."

"That's not…" Father John gave up. "You can't stop them. Your cooperation is not necessary."

This time, Petrovitch did give the priest his middle finger. "You're about to find out just how wrong you are." He climbed up, and out of sight.

The crowd shifted nervously. They were missing something, but couldn't tell what. Most of them started to drift away. Others, the hardcore watchers, decided that they'd wait for someone to tell them what had happened.